CW00732638

Kelechi Okafor is a Nigerian-
– whether that's crafting wc
or screenplays; from directing
thoughts on society one epis~~~ ~~ ~ ~~~~ ~~~~~~~~ ~~~~~~~~
interview guests on her award-winning former podcast *Say Your
Mind*. In February 2024, Kelechi launched her new subscrip-
tion-based channel on her website, known as Keleidoscope. No
matter what form Kelechi's creativity takes – her work remains
rooted in globally relevant conversations and events, framed
through a lens of understanding that is firmly anti-colonial,
anti-white-supremacy and anti-heteropatriarchy. Keleidoscope
serves both as a personal exploration, and as a way to build a
community that is challenged to think critically.

Known online as @Kelechnekoff, Kelechi is also affectionately known as 'just a Baby Girl' by her followers, listeners and
community. Her path has been guided by flames left by Octavia
Butler, Toni Morrison, bell hooks, Audre Lorde, Chika Unigwe
and so many more voices from the past and present.

Edge of Here is her debut story collection.

Praise for *Edge of Here*

'A skilful, absorbing novel that is so much about seeing and
being seen'   **The Spectator**

'A one-of-a-kind voice . . . People need to read this book'
                                               Afua Hirsch

'One of the best books I've read this year'   **Aja Barber**

'As surreal as a season of *Black Mirror*, yet as telling regarding life as we know it . . . A stunning debut'   **Yomi Sode**

'Finally, a new era of sci-fi is upon us. EoH takes you to an alternate & future universe that is strangely also very familiar and current. Simultaneously deep and casual, Kelechi has crafted quite a collection – for these times & times to come'

Dr Anne-Marie Imafidon

'Written with verve and heart, the stories are as incisive as they are thought provoking. In story after story, Okafor demonstrates an imagination that is not afraid to explore difficult questions. This is a book we need right now'   **Chika Unigwe**

'With *Edge of Here*, Kelechi Okafor has crafted an interconnected world that is prescient and truthful in the way only fiction can be. These speculative parables are an invitation to meditate on where we are and where we are headed, in a unique voice that is determined in its directness but ever hopeful in its tone'

Jendella Benson

'Kelechi's words offer laser like accuracy and her stories penetrate straight into the areas that are missed in our lives due to the busyness of the everyday and their distractions. A must read for the hopeful!'   **Lavinya Stennett**

'Kelechi's debut is nothing short of stunning. Her writing is both bold and delicate and her ability to weave in social issues into masterful and captivating storytelling is truly a gift we all should treasure'   **Tobi Oredein**

EDGE OF HERE

Stories from Near to Now

Kelechi Okafor

First published in Great Britain in 2023 by Trapeze,
This paperback edition published in 2024 by Trapeze,
an imprint of The Orion Publishing Group Ltd
Carmelite House, 50 Victoria Embankment,
London EC4Y 0DZ

An Hachette UK Company

1 3 5 7 9 10 8 6 4 2

Copyright © Kelechi Okafor 2023

The moral right of Kelechi Okafor to be identified as
the author of this work has been asserted in accordance
with the Copyright, Designs and Patents Act of 1988.

All rights reserved. No part of this publication may be
reproduced, stored in a retrieval system, or transmitted
in any form or by any means, electronic, mechanical,
photocopying, recording, or otherwise, without the
prior permission of both the copyright owner and the
above publisher of this book.

All the characters in this book are fictitious, and any resemblance
to actual persons, living or dead, is purely coincidental.

'The Watchers' by Kelechi Okafor was previously published by Trapeze in
Who's Loving You, ed. Sareeta Domingo, 2021.

A CIP catalogue record for this book is
available from the British Library.

ISBN (Mass Market Paperback) 978 1 3987 1301 7
ISBN (eBook) 978 1 3987 1302 4
ISBN (Audio) 978 1 3987 1303 1

Typeset by Goldust Design
Printed in Great Britain by Clays Ltd, Elcograf S.p.A.

www.orionbooks.co.uk

Dedicated to my Ẹgbẹ́ Ọ̀run.
Thank you for reminding me.

Contents

Introduction

I had never considered myself to be a writer. An actress and director, yes, but never a writer. When people would suggest it, I would scoff. 'But you have such a way with words?!' they'd say. Yes, a way with words when it comes to taking this wayward society down a peg or two.

There are so many ways to share our truths though. In one regard, using social media to get my points out there to the world at large – but this collection of stories helps me to not only get a message out into the world but invites you into my inner world. I have often felt misunderstood in my quest for a fairer and more beautiful world. These stories allow me to share with you my deepest hopes and dreams, represented through the protagonists. I was particular about writing stories that weren't wrought with trauma as it pertains to Black women.

This is a world where Black women love and are loved back. This is a world where Black women don't have all the answers, but they pay attention to life when it offers something up. In every woman there is the story and there is the Story. I didn't have to make this part up, because in every Black woman I encounter there is a story dancing in their eyes and on the edge of their smiles. All they need is the space to tell that story. Until they decide to, I hope these stories allow them to feel seen, even in the most subtle ways.

WHY 'EDGE OF HERE'?

Because this is the space I've grown up in. That liminal space that feels like no place. Where you are both the observer and the hyper-observed. All the stories are borne of a simple truth that I've turned up the proverbial volume on. What does it look like if a Black woman literally carries everybody else's grief? What would it feel like for non-Black people to experience the real pain of racial trauma? I could give more examples but I'm not trying to steal the cute moments of revelation as you read through the stories.

I've lived life at the edge of this current reality for a while and I know the versions of reality that I propose aren't too far away. Join me in exploring the stories at the edge, before it becomes the centre of here.

The Watchers

In the sliver of space between this world and the next, we the Watchers reside. Our purpose is simple: to guide the souls we are assigned in the task they chose when they were formless orbs of light.

There are many times we have looked on as you humans (or, as we know you, 'the Watched') have described an experience as a mere coincidence, instead of accepting that there is a particular path you are on. Those gentle nudges are our way of reminding you of that which you never wanted to forget.

We can only help so much, because ultimately whether Watcher or Watched, we are all an aspect of the divine and must be allowed to express that divinity in the way we choose. We slip between time and galaxies, simultaneously observing all that has been, all that is and all that will be. Time is only a suggestion and yet I have watched as so many of you enter a world only to obsess over this measure of your own making. The Watched return eventually and are reminded that what seemed like a lifetime barely amounted to a moment here.

Returning to this place that is really no place while being every place, is a chance to reflect on the lessons garnered on earth, and to plan which lessons still need exploration until the time comes when all the lessons have been mastered.

The Watched tell themselves that time is the best healer

but what they truly mean is that love is the best healer. Time cowers in the face of love's many manifestations. In this realm, the Watched decide on a theme of love they want to explore in various lifetimes. The soul remembers the task, but once the Watched enter into a human form, they go through the forgetting that is necessary at the beginning of each lifetime. The Watched are always aware that they will forget once they enter the earthly realm, so they chart reminders in their human lives just in case they are to ever lose their way. It sounds simple enough, until the Watched enter into a world where so many obstacles have been put in place, some by those higher than us and some by those who are not, to test their will and power to love against all odds.

Many of the Watched tire quickly when they feel that they have very little control over the life they chose – but then there are others, like Chinonso and Ndidi, who persevere lifetime after lifetime.

They meet in each human stint having no memory of the other meetings, only a vague yet visceral sense of having met before. I must make it known to you at this point, dear honorary Watcher, that this isn't a love story of the sort the Watched seem to spend an amusing amount of their lives chasing. This love is not propelled by flimsy romance. Instead it is spurred on by the unwavering desire to evolve into one's highest self while in human form. In other pairings between two beings of light – or twin flames, as they are commonly known – there is an alternation between who remembers something of the task both beings agreed to complete. The being who remembers will usually be the chaser, the one tasked with helping the other to acknowledge something greater than the human flesh they now inhabit. The other, being the runner, will avoid the intensity of the calling for a number of earthly reasons. Between these two, though, it seems that Chinonso has taken on the role of chaser for many lifetimes, which isn't to indicate Ndidi loves less, because in fact her devotion to being human helps them both to grow in their understanding of humanity . . .

CHINONSO AND NDIDI

Today I watch Ndidi teeter in the heels she debated over wearing, while cocooned in her sanitation pod and navigating it on a cobbled pavement by Albert Docks. The pods were interesting inventions and still needed a lot of work, but in a world where the fear of pandemics had taken hold, government-issued sanitation pods had become the norm when out in public. Made from self-sterilising thin plastic, the pods would enclose the individual, allowing for normal range of movement while limiting contact with others.

I catch the 'fucking hell' Ndidi mutters under her breath as her ankles momentarily wobble in the pod because of the uneven ground and maybe the weight of her expectations of the evening ahead. 'Who the fuck chooses a slavery museum for a first date?' I hear her think to herself. Chinonso is the 'who'.

Chinonso loads his phone screen onto his pod to see if an 'almost there!' text has been sent by Ndidi. Nothing. He would usually be annoyed by this lack of an update but on this occasion it makes him smile. He likes that this woman he is about to meet seems to care very little about explaining herself and just seems to dance to her own tune.

'Nonso?' is what he hears that causes him to turn around and look straight into the face of Ndidi.

'Ah! Didi, hey!'

A thick Liverpudlian accent cascades out of Ndidi's mouth as she smilingly says, 'I told you not to call me that, professor boy, it means nowt. You of all people should know that you don't fuck around with Igbo names – they have meanings, you know. I noticed in the app that you shortened your name, but I won't be joining you in such rebellious behaviour.'

I look on at them meeting for the first time again and notice as always the way time bends to allow a brief instant of knowing. They both feel it but laugh it off as first-date jitters.

'I'm very happy for you to still call me Nonso,' he teases. They both laugh, while taking each other in. They've sent so many messages to each other on the dating app that they mistake the pre-existing deep connection with one another for merely feeling comfortable from such long conversations. Swiping on a person's picture on a dating app had become mechanical for the two of them, so it is a relief they cherish to have found someone that feels different to all the other dates they have been on. A brief silence is Ndidi's prompt to say what has been on her mind.

'Not being rude or nothin', but a slavery museum for the first date? I know I agreed but fucking hell, it's intense, innit?'

Chinonso worries for a moment that he might sound weird for admitting how he had come to decide on the venue of their date, but decides to be brave, as something tells him that he will be safe here.

'I actually had a dream about you before—'

Ndidi interjects, 'Oh come off it! A dream! About me? Do you use that line on all the girls then?'

Chinonso continues, sensing that somewhere in her tone Ndidi believes him.

'Before seeing you on the app, I had a dream where you turned to say something to me and it was in front of one of the displays at this museum.'

Curious, Ndidi asks, 'What did I say? And was I dressed like this?'

With the courage fleeting now, Chinonso smirks. 'I'll let you know when you say it. As for what you were wearing, I can't remember. But the shoes looked more comfortable.'

Ndidi is surprised by her own laughter at the cheeky joke.

'The museum will close soon, so why don't we go in and I can show you the things I find most fascinating here, then dinner after?' Chinonso feigns confidence as he states this because it is unlike any other date he has been on. Usually, it would be a coffee and a chat or drinks mixed with a fun night and mundane texts thereafter.

Chinonso's decision to move to Liverpool from London so he could teach Postcolonial Studies seemed very random to everyone who knew him, but, as he explained to them all, once he had seen the job vacancy, a gut feeling led him to apply. As you, honorary Watcher, are beginning to learn, nothing is really by chance. From Chinonso's father in Nigeria being an avid Liverpool FC supporter, to the 'Visit Liverpool' billboards Chinonso kept noticing when he was out and about. Everything delicately placed and carefully planned so this moment could happen. This moment where they would both make the choice to pursue their task in this life or not. It would seem rather peculiar to someone unfamiliar with fate and free will as to how these seemingly opposing systems could coexist, but the truth is that they were and always will be one. Chinonso and Ndidi haven't always decided to exist in the same lifetime as each other. It has happened in a few lives where one of these flames has decided to rest and simply ruminate on every lived experience, or has chosen a different galaxy completely. What usually happens is that they spend these lives learning something unique to them about the nature of humans and love, while feeling a lifelong yearning for another soul that they can't quite place. That isn't to say that they aren't happy in these lifetimes, because they are, sometimes even happier than the lives where they do meet. The only defining factor is that desire for another, yet not knowing who exactly it is.

'She's cute!' Ndidi points at a projected painting.

'That is Queen Nzinga. She ruled in the seventeenth century and actively resisted the transatlantic slave trade,' Chinonso shares almost automatically.

In the aftermath of the virus, all museums were forced to store artefacts in airtight vaults, and present the public with holograms of these artefacts instead, but despite this, Chinonso still knew of these African histories so deeply and couldn't quite fathom why he was so attached to learning and feeling as much as he was.

'I would've been like her, I think,' Ndidi says as she looks at the painting intently. 'I would've told 'em, "You want to enslave somebody, do you? Well come and enslave this, you knobheads!" And I would've cut their balls off.'

It is maybe her matter-of-fact way of saying what she would've done that makes Chinonso laugh – the type of laughter that breaks one's heart open.

'That is extremely graphic! Should I be scared?' Chinonso

says as he wipes the tears of laughter from the corner of his eyes.

Ndidi chides, 'You're making people look at us weird because we're laughing in a slavery museum!' But secretly she is happy that her no-nonsense manner of talking seems to enamour Chinonso. She is used to men being rather wary of her fire and trying their best to dampen her spirits by encouraging her to be more 'ladylike'; hence the heels on the first date.

'This was the moment, by the way,' Chinonso mutters shyly. This was indeed the moment he had seen in his dream, almost like déjà vu. Ndidi saying she would've been like Queen Nzinga and not realising just how much she had shared that spirit in another life.

Our role as Watchers requires an extensive knowledge of our Watched, so I remember the time well when Ndidi and Chinonso met as the slave ships arrived more frequently on the shores of Bonny, Nigeria.

It was 1756 and Ndidi's father, Chief Damieibi, saw it fitting to ensure the Portuguese traders knew of his daughter's beauty. He would've been elated that she marry someone capable of strengthening the family's reputation in the kingdom. Chinonso's family were newly converted Christians who had departed from their indigenous religion of the Ijaw people.

Their meeting in this lifetime was in a bustling marketplace where Chinonso sold his woodcarvings of ancient deities, much to the disapproval of his mother who desperately wanted him to be more enthusiastic about their new Christian way of life.

Ndidi had been ordered by her father to show Pedro, one of the highly regarded new merchants, their beautiful town. Ndidi very much enjoyed the attention of this exotic looking man, but couldn't help being repulsed by the trading of people who looked like herself. She understood, though, that her family's reputation and affluence couldn't rely on hereditary chieftaincies alone.

'This is very fine wood. It reminds me of your skin.' Pedro smiled as he looked at Chinonso's sculptures. Glad to have some interest in his work but understanding very little of what Pedro was saying, Chinonso began to explain to Ndidi about the deity known as Egbesu, who oversaw warfare. Chinonso didn't get much further, though, as Ndidi's eyes caught his and time waned and twisted.

In that split second, I saw them both forget Pedro's presence as well as the noise of the marketplace.

It wasn't about beauty here, dear honorary Watcher. What they both felt was the burning of meeting a kindred soul whom they had been searching for without ever realising that they were doing so.

Pedro asked how much for the mini carved god, and before Chinonso could answer, Ndidi stated a price four times more than Chinonso would've asked for. In that gesture he decided that he loved her and would spend his life doing so, regardless of their different status within the kingdom. A trivial reason to decide to love someone, you might say, but these two souls never needed much of a reason to love. Watching the different moments when either of the two decide in each lifetime to love the other is always endearing to witness. It takes a brave soul to choose love, which is why so many of your kind prefer to believe that they merely fall into love as a shield from all the other sometimes painful choices that come along with it.

It was a surprise to Chinonso when, the next week, Ndidi appeared at his stall again as he was packing up for the day. Her father, Damieibi, would usually ensure that she was accompanied by a guard, but on this day she had fabricated a vague friend whom she needed to meet for ceremonial dance performance practice. Damieibi had chosen not to remarry after Ndidi's mother passed away when giving birth to Ndidi's younger brother, so he was perfectly oblivious to the fact that generally ceremonial dance practices only began three months prior to the event, not seven months before!

'Hello, woodcarver.'

'Hello, chief's daughter.'

They both smiled at the feigned formality and began walking alongside each other without a destination in mind.

'I hope you haven't spent all the money I negotiated for you last week. Maybe you will buy me an orange from this seller.' Ndidi was teasing but was touched at Chinonso's instant indignation at being in any way irresponsible with money.

'I would love to buy you an orange but I gave the money to my parents. They still see it as dirty spirit money, but even dirty spirit money can pay for our home, so they accepted.' Chinonso was quite unsure as to why he was explaining all of this to somebody he had only said a few words to the week before, but of course, we know that his soul understood Ndidi's soul and would always remember her.

'It is funny, isn't it? Since they brought us this god of theirs, who is meant to give us so much when we die, we keep having less and less while we are alive.' Ndidi surprised herself with this observation as she wouldn't have dared to say anything similar if her father were nearby.

'I'm surprised you feel that way as you seemed rather enthu-siastic when you were showing the foreigner around last time.'

'So I shouldn't have shown him around and my father should

lose business, and I should end up having to join you in selling pieces of wood in the marketplace?' Ndidi was curter in her response than she had hoped to be, but looking over at Chinonso as they walked to nowhere in particular, she was comforted by the fact that he didn't seem offended by her comment. Chinonso indeed wasn't offended because he was too engrossed in this new feeling that he was experiencing due to her presence, which he could only describe to himself as a sweet pain.

I hovered by them as they chose a bench to sit on where the roadside met some woodland. Ndidi looked up at the majesty of the trees and recognised deep within herself that, without saying much, they had both decided to be like this together always.

Ndidi continued to meet Chinonso as he closed his stall every week even after the annual town ceremony had passed and thus the ceremonial dance practice should've ceased. Damieibi had gotten wind of Ndidi's meetings through one of his guards, and saw no real harm in them since Chinonso and Ndidi only ever seemed to sit on a rickety bench and talk until sunset.

Unfortunately, he had failed to remember that love doesn't require grand outings and such in order to grow. It is the very reason he had chosen to not take another wife after Ndidi's mother: when he was a boisterous aspiring businessman carrying yam around for his father, his wife had believed in him always. His love for her continued for his entire life and he wouldn't have had it any other way.

Pedro had taken a strong liking to Ndidi and had attempted a few times to talk to Damieibi about what a great business opportunity it would be for them both if he were to marry Ndidi. Of course, Ndidi's father saw this opportunity too, but couldn't ignore the ever so slight way Ndidi would recoil whenever Pedro made any gesture in her direction.

Damieibi had hardened himself over time to the selling of people because, as his father had told him, 'Yam is something we can only sell with the season. These devils will continue coming and taking our people. The sooner we have some control of the situation, the easier it will be to keep the devils at bay.' Somehow the ever-looming prospect of his own daughter marrying into such an industry softened the hardness he thought he had done well to build over the years. If these merchants were in fact devils, would that make Ndidi a sacrifice if he were to allow a marriage to go ahead? These were the thoughts that plagued Damieibi and they wouldn't cease until his last earthly breath.

As they sat on the rickety bench under the majestic trees as they had done many times before, not realising it would be the last time they would ever see each other in this lifetime, Ndidi told Chinonso of the plans her father and Pedro were making for marriage. I felt the pain in Chinonso's heart as he realised that he would need to do something lest he lose Ndidi forever.

'We can leave.'

'What?'

'We can leave here together. I can find a way to send my parents money that I make from my sculptures and I will take on other work to provide for us both. I know you will not have all the wonderful materials and jewellery you are used to now, but I will do my best to give you something.'

Ndidi wanted to think the idea was ridiculous and to believe that she couldn't live without the fine world her father had provided for her, but Chinonso's face gave her every reassurance that they would have more than enough, because they had each other.

'Maybe we don't have to run away. Maybe I can tell my father about us and he can find some extra employment for you.' The two flames hugged tightly and the celestial sparks that they could not see, but felt, danced around the two of them and ascended past me and into the heavens to mark their place in that lifetime.

And so it was that Ndidi told her father of the love she felt for Chinonso and her hope that her father might allow for them to be together. Ndidi's father was so taken aback by the courage of his daughter's request that he, too, felt bold enough to approach Pedro about calling off plans they had been making regarding Ndidi's hand in marriage.

One of the lessons we Watchers learn about humankind in every timeline is that their capacity for good far exceeds their capacity to do unkind things, yet, oftentimes it is the unkind things that people seem to focus on the most.

Pedro was a businessman first and foremost, and he considered the months of conversations he'd had with Ndidi's father as a negotiating of terms for an otherwise done deal.

He had arrived from Portugal pleasantly surprised at the beauty of this West African land and the intelligence of its people, but that did not mean he thought them equal to himself in the slightest. He was well aware of the intricate systems they had in place and the knowledge they possessed that far exceeded his own, but nothing could shift his perception that they were savage and that he had done well to engage with them amicably for this long. Pedro had already written ahead to King José to tell him of the pretty African girl he had secured to strengthen his trades deal with the locals.

I tell you all of this, honorary Watcher, so you understand that when Ndidi's father explained to Pedro that they could not go ahead with their deal because his daughter had already chosen a lover, he was met with rage.

It confirmed everything that Pedro had heard of these people, that they would be underhanded and sly in their business dealings. He had been told by other merchants that the best thing to do was to move with a firm and unrelenting hand, so the locals would understand where the power truly resided.

Pedro scoffed at the nonsensical love that was being positioned as an obstacle to his plans and so made it clear to Damieibi that if Ndidi did not accompany him on the ship and leave with him to the New World, he would take her woodcarving wretch of a lover instead. When Ndidi heard of this ultimatum and her father's insistence that he would find some way to fight back and call upon the other chiefs in Bonny, she knew she had to do something to save her father, Chinonso and her home. For Damieibi to enter into a battle with this merchant would mean many of the Bonny people suffering in the process.

Ndidi decided that she would leave with Pedro, and she prayed deep down that someday she would return to Bonny to finally be with Chinonso.

Damieibi felt great sorrow at having to accept his daughter's wish to go ahead with the marriage and to prepare to leave with Pedro within a couple of days. The great wedding ceremony he had imagined that would set him apart from all the other chiefs didn't go ahead, and he wouldn't have wanted it to, as the shame he felt at betraying his daughter was too much for him to bear.

Ndidi was beside herself that she could not find a way to let Chinonso know that she would have to leave at such short notice but somehow she believed that she would one day return. She did return, many years later when the town she had known had changed into something quite different and her father had passed away and the trading of humans was even more aggressive with mounting British influence.

Pedro had gotten his way, yet the unkindness I spoke of can only be apparent to you, dear honorary Watcher, when you learn that he ordered his men to go in search of Chinonso and to find a way to abduct him. To think that a lowly woodcarver could've posed a potential hindrance to Pedro getting what he wanted in marrying Ndidi was enough to rouse the spiteful snake coiled within his soul. Pedro's men found Chinonso in the nighttime, carving outside in his parent's small compound while the rest of the family sang praise and songs of worship inside. Chinonso was loaded onto the ship that would take all those men who were bought and stolen from their homes across the Atlantic Ocean to be sold off into the unknown.

As Ndidi stepped on the ship with her heart in pieces, waving goodbye to her father who was forever broken by the work of his own hands, she thought of Chinonso and his beautiful woodcarvings. Ndidi would only learn after departing Barbados, where Chinonso had been sold, that they had in fact been on the same ship for weeks, with Chinonso packed among many who had only just started the journey towards their misery and suffering.

Ndidi made no indication that she would seek revenge for what Pedro had done to Chinonso, but I would be with them both as Chinonso prayed to his deities and carved their images from bits of sugarcane shavings that he kept, and Ndidi prayed to the same deities for the strength to appear favourable to Pedro until the time was right to exact her vengeance. The deities looked upon them, as did I, and we all watched silently, knowing that the two were beings of light who would find a way to be together in another lifetime.

Years passed and Ndidi had become somewhat accustomed to the ways in Portugal, although many refused to grow accustomed to her. She tolerated Pedro's affection, which was only dressed-up ownership. Eventually, she knew the day would come when he would venture back to Bonny again for more 'stock'. Pedro had made quite an impression on the previous king of Portugal before his death because of Pedro's initiative at having returned home with the daughter of one of the main tradesmen, thus keeping business thriving. Pedro relied on his company men to travel to Africa in his place, but having received news of Chief Damieibi's passing, he had to return to Bonny to foster new relationships with the up-and-coming traders. For this reason alone, he allowed Ndidi to accompany him; not because it would mean so much to her to see her father's grave, but simply because it would ease communication with the locals.

Chinonso, meanwhile, thousands of miles away in Barbados, being treated as less than human on the best days, still held onto a capacity for love. Eventually he married Ebiere. Chinonso had chosen Ebiere because she was a kind and funny woman who originated from a town not too far from his own in Bonny. Although he cared for Ebiere very much, he would often think of Ndidi, praying that, wherever she was, she was being loved as much as he loved her.

Ndidi waited until the second night of her and Pedro's arrival in Bonny to add poison to Pedro's food. I looked on as Ndidi calmly placed the woodcarving of Egbesu, made by Chinonso all those years ago, over Pedro's body as his life-force left him and she thanked the deities for bringing her this far, back to her own land, to rebalance the unfairness of fate. Ndidi gathered her belongings and we left in the dead of night, never to return to Bonny.

This is the reason that now, in the Museum of Slavery, Ndidi could recognise the bravery of Queen Nzinga – because, in another life, she too had fought in her own way against the tyranny of those who wanted to own those they could not be.

'I have to say I've enjoyed walking around this museum with you, Nonso. You've mixed education with flirtation and I kinda dig it!'

Chinonso smiles broadly at the compliment. Time has passed by the two of them effortlessly in the museum and they both relish each other's company. They walk closer together, at times their pods brush past each other and, although the pods feel rather clinical, they both still feel the sparks that I see dance between them and ascend into the heavens, marking their place in this lifetime.

'Can I ask you something?'

Ndidi laughs. 'You had better not be bloody asking me why I'm single, I hate that damn question!'

'No! I wouldn't dare ask that – it's clear that it's because you've been kicking men in their balls.'

They both laugh and Chinonso continues despite his nervousness at the intensity of the imminent question.

'What do you think happens to love when people die?'

Surprisingly, Ndidi doesn't resort to a witty deflection like she usually would. 'I dunno, to be honest, I'm still waiting to really feel what love truly is, but my guess is that the love carries on. Kinda like a frequency, the energy just stays there for all of time. My grandma still says she feels my grandpa's love and he isn't here any more, so yeah, I guess the love stays because it doesn't need a body to do so.'

Chinonso is stunned by the answer. 'Maybe you should become a professor.'

'Oh feck off!'

They continue to chat cheerily as they leave the museum and both look out over the docks.

'Your turn: what do you think happens?'

Chinonso pauses before responding, 'I think it's similar to what you were saying, but I think the love keeps moving. It can't really stay in one place because it has to find you in every lifetime.'

'Wow, deep.'

Neither of them laugh this time, as an unexpected seriousness befalls the pair of them. It isn't surprising to me, you understand, because this moment like many others has happened before. What both Chinonso and Ndidi are experiencing is a soul decision. It is that space in a human's existence where they must make a choice while subconsciously remembering every time they have made a similar choice in other lives.

Whether Ndidi and Chinonso realise it or not, all the times they have loved and felt great pain as well as great joy it is being remembered by their higher knowing, and they are making the decision whether to pursue a love in this lifetime or not. They are not to know what will happen and what they will face. Chinonso always seems to choose to love Ndidi no matter where they find themselves. Maybe since Bonny, Ndidi has carried the weight of that life and fears a heartbreak and a loss that great happening again.

'Shall we get something to eat as planned, or have I bored you to the point of no hunger?' asks Chinonso, in a way that he hopes sounds casual enough to not appear too forward.

'Yeah sure, there's a Nigerian restaurant near Bold Street, I think?'

'With your strong accent I thought you might want something more European,' Chinonso teases.

'It's clear that you want me to show you just how African I am and that might require the sending of an AirSlap!'

People who pass by them see a cute couple happily navigating their pods down cobbled streets, but if only they could see what I see, dear honorary Watcher – two melding lights made from stars and lives gone before and yet to come.

The entire evening they tell each other stories of their childhoods and hint at their own hopes and dreams, while they share quick glances deep into each other's eyes almost as a way of reassuring themselves that the one felt what the other was feeling too.

'You know what made me laugh when I saw your profile on the app? It was your answer to what three things you would need to have with you in social isolation to stay sane.'

Ndidi laughs, remembering her answers. 'Malt drinks, a fridge and seasoning.'

'So would you season the malt drink? Because you didn't specify having any food.'

'Look, professor boy, you've got to read in between the lines.'

'You sound like a politician!'

Ndidi hadn't put too much thought into her answer, as the weird time of social isolation was something she would've preferred not to dwell on, especially since it had changed the trajectory of the entire world. One minute you could meet up and party with friends, the next minute the entire country was assigned sanitation pods, among other stringent new ways of living. During the early stages of the social isolation rules, Ndidi spent what seemed like endless time in her apartment attempting to get on with her graphic design commissions, but losing hours in her day creating images of beings made of all the elements in nature. Ndidi found the desire to create these images rather disconcerting, as she had never considered herself to be someone very in tune with nature, yet with all that time alone, she dreamt of places and faces and events which seemed far beyond what she had seen in her waking life. A persistent feeling of there being more to everything that she had ever known refused to leave her be and as soon as the government relaxed the rules on virus precautions, she pushed all the dreams and drawings somewhere far away inside herself. In Ndidi's mind, whatever could've been waiting there to be explored felt too soul-taxing, and she felt too weary even in her late twenties to follow this exploration through.

'Where did you go? Did I say something wrong?' Chinonso worries that he might've offended Ndidi by making fun of her dating profile. On other dates, he has found it rather odd how some women seem strangely embarrassed to have their profiles mentioned, as if they would rather pretend that's not how they had ended up on the date.

'No, not at all. I guess I just got a bit lost in my thoughts about how so many things have changed since that virus. Even the fact that you have to upload your monthly virus scans in order to be approved for dating capabilities on the app.'

They both smile wanly at each other, as they both wish to think of something lighter.

'There's an online Beyoncé concert next week. I had bought tickets for my sister, but she won't be able to go with me, so would you like to come along?' Ndidi feels uncharacteristically shy at making the first insinuation at another date. In the past she would've left it to the guy to initiate, but there is something about the fact that she doesn't want this date to end that reassures her of her choice.

'How is she not able to go with you – she could log in from anywhere? Only humans could find a way to flake on an event they can attend from anywhere in the world.'

'Hey! Is that a no or what?'

'Oh, sorry! No. I mean yes! I would love to go with you. It's actually a cool way to get past the "waiting fourteen days before we can meet up again" legislation. Only takes one no-pod fool to cause an infection uptick.'

'Exactly, professor boy. I'm smart, me!'

With their next date agreed, Ndidi insists on paying for the meal and they leave the restaurant. Outside they stand silently, not knowing quite how to end a date that they wish wouldn't end. Ndidi inputs her location into her pod to initiate the citywide curfew sequence, and looks over at Chinonso. 'So, guess that's it for tonight then. My oxygen supply in this thing needs charging anyway. Best get to practising your Beyoncé moves for next week.'

Chinonso playfully scoffs. 'I'm offended that you think I even have to practice! It has been really nice hanging with you, Di— I mean Ndidi.'

'It's been fun hanging out with you prof— I mean Nonso.'

Their pods head in opposite directions into the night, and that is where you leave them, dear honorary Watcher.

What happens next, you wonder? Well, both Chinonso and Ndidi will decide. I had warned that this would be unlike the romance stories you are accustomed to, where you are mostly gifted with an ending to ease your own anxieties about the fate of your experiences of love. We, the Watchers, look on from a space where endings don't actually exist. We see you without your constraints of time, thus we see you more clearly than you see yourselves. Rather than existing for answers, we are always hopeful that you might enjoy living in the questions. Breathe in and out of the unknown, because that is where the eternal wisdom you desire truly resides.

Chinonso and Ndidi have lived so many lives and yet somehow their story has only just begun. I will continue to leave the clues as they have requested and watch them find each other again and again, and each time their understanding of love growing so that when they meet once more in this sliver of space between this world and the next, they get that much closer to divinity.

The Ally-chip

'9.48 p.m. *Fuckkk*,' Emma Ikeji muttered under her breath. She could not wait for her shift to be over. Being a nurse in Accident & Emergency had a way of making her days fly by, but it was a weird sort of contraction of time because being so busy also somehow made the days feel long as hell. Emma looked at her phone. Ten minutes left of her break and still no message from Dre. She chastised herself internally for her neediness. *That's what you get for trying to change the vibe.*

The only task Emma wanted to preoccupy herself with for the next . . . nine minutes until she was due back in the ward, was to wrestle her mind away from these apprehensive thoughts about her sort-of-girlfriend, who had a definite-husband who was happily aware of their relationship.

Emma's eyes wandered up to the lopsided TV screen hanging on the worn-out green wall, permanently tuned, it seemed, to a depressing news channel.

'. . . *and the prime minister has said today that he plans to tackle the growing numbers of victims suffering from Ally-chip fatigue*,' the reporter on the screen was saying. '*The reaction to the ground-breaking emotional transplant technology sweeping the nation has yet to be fully understood* . . .'

Emma watched as right on cue a montage appeared showing Tòmíwá Fọlọ́runshọ́, the young Black woman who had invented the Ally-chip. Although Tòmíwá was now nineteen years old, the media kept using pictures of her fifteen-year-old self, the age she was when she invented the chip. A particular picture where she stood outside of a hut in a rural area in Nigeria was their absolute favourite to use. It all felt very deliberate to Emma, as if the underlying narrative was the world's benevolence in entrusting the augmentation of their brain functions to a little Black girl in Nigeria who lived in such a dwelling. In actuality, Tọ̀míwá was a robotics enthusiast from a well-off family. The hut in the picture was one of many on which her father installed solar panelling in order to help rural families have electricity – but that was something never mentioned on mainstream media.

Before she started dating Dre, Emma didn't bother too much with engaging in these issues, but Dre's consultancy on the rollout of the Ally-chip to willing recipients as part of her charitable foundation work had brought Tọ̀míwá's innovation to the forefront of Emma's mind. To keep up with Dre's discussions, as well as her own growing curiosity, she'd made sure to find out as much as she could about the Ally-chip. It was actually from a Black social commentator's page online that Emma had gained a more rounded understanding of Tọ̀míwá's talents and social standing.

From one of the few interviews with Tọ̀míwá that Emma found online, she'd discovered that Tọ̀míwá created the chip because she wanted to help her parents' relationship. She told *Punch Nigeria* – a popular publication there – that she feared her parents were about to break up, and her mother would often say her father just didn't understand what she was feeling. So, the industrious young woman got to work creating the famous, tiny chip. Its function was to intercept neural pathways in the amygdala, an area of the brain which dictates behaviour and emotions. For the chip to function, it needed to be programmed to either send or receive emotions, requiring both an Experience Donor, the person who the feelings belonged to, and an Experience Host, the person who would feel the emotion in their stead. The current version of the Ally-chip required the donor and host to be within four hundred metres of each other for the emotions to transfer effectively.

Tòmíwá's genius fascinated Emma. When asked whether her parents' relationship improved as a result of the chip, Tòmíwá said that her parents ended up not having the implantation surgery at all, and in fact her dad had married a second wife, which Emma found hilarious.

Tòmíwá told *Punch Nigeria* that although she had invented the chip, neither she nor her family had the capital and influence to bring it to the world. That was the work of billionaire and founder of major tech entity Plant8Con, William Bunker. Tòmíwá's boarding school was fortunate (or unfortunate) enough to have William as a patron, in his efforts to 'civilise Africa'. When William heard of Tòmíwá's invention from the school board, he'd decided that the true function of the chip should be to eradicate inequality. He had many schemes on the go, one being the trialling of pod-like capsules intended for people to walk around in, because he was convinced there was biotech warfare brewing.

None of this made sense to Emma, but the Ally-chip she could at least *sort of* understand. The thoughts of the chip's origins made Emma shudder and chuckle simultaneously as her attention was brought back to the screen. The montage had finished, and the news reporter had returned onscreen.

'*Earlier today the prime minister spoke with our political corres-*

pondent, Rónké. Abrahams, about what will be done for the victims of Ally-chip fatigue, and the worrying reports of cases on the rise . . .'

Emma wished that she wasn't bothered by the frequent use of the word 'victim' in the news reporter's comments. These were the things that she noticed and others seemed to be able to ignore. A victim would require a perpetrator, and in this case she was worried about who would be framed as the perpetrator.

The report switched over to an interview recorded earlier in the day and then appeared the bedraggled-looking man who was currently running the country. As he began to speak, Emma couldn't help but wonder, as she had many times before, how the leader of the country could encourage the public to trial a chip inserted into their brain with no intention of doing so himself. But people were unwavering in their support of him, no matter how many times he proved he was not in support of them. Now he had the nerve to complain about the very chip that not so long ago he'd been advocating for as some easy fix to addressing real issues.

Emma caught herself as her thoughts prepared to spiral into an internal rant about the state of the world. The drab green walls and the wonky television, along with the overly sterile smell of the break room weren't helping though.

'Let me be clear,' the prime minister continued. 'A pioneering group of people have done a brave thing by having these chips inserted, so that they can genuinely empathise with what the Blacks of this country are going through. However, we will not hesitate to hold Africa accountable for the fatigue and discomfort that these well-meaning people are now experiencing.'

And there it was. The perpetrator in this narrative had been announced.

Rónké interjected, 'Surely, Prime Minister, a whole continent cannot be held responsible for the innovation of one young woman in one country? But more importantly, you must be aware that the issues the white people who have had the chip inserted are facing are due to the sheer magnitude of racism in this country? And is that not, indeed, what they signed up to experience?'

Emma couldn't help nodding at the reporter's questions. The more she thought about the whole Ally-chip furore, the more she considered that people's attentions were being misdirected from the person they *should* be focusing on if they really wanted someone to blame, and that person was William Bunker. Unable to stop watching, Emma could see the prime minister was perplexed by the direct questions being asked. They made sense. The expression on his face was gone within a second though, and replaced by more bravado and a slimy smirk.

'Right,' he began. 'Well, I can see how this might be hard for you to understand. However, we are following the science on this, and it's possible that the Blacks are feeling these feelings more deeply so that it might be a more intense experience for their allies.'

'Or it could be that those feelings have always been this intense due to the persistent nature of racism?'

Suddenly the image of the prime minister and the reporter juddered as the camera began to shake, and shouting was heard off-screen. The camera haphazardly tilted upwards, and Emma saw the legs of the cameraman – who appeared to be hurrying towards the prime minister while still filming – launch into the air.

The image on the screen returned quickly to the reporter

in-studio. 'We want to apologise to our viewers who saw this live earlier. However, we decided to show the video again in its entirety in order to demonstrate the severity of the issue we're discussing. The cameraman who was filming was in fact an Ally-chip recipient, also known as an Experience Host, and he was overtaken by the emotions evoked during that conversation. We are told that his Experience Donor was in fact nearby during the interview and had felt rather distressed by the prime minister's comments. You can be assured that the cameraman is resting, and nobody, most especially the prime minister, was harmed during the altercation.'

Emma thought about the pointed mention of the ally and not the Experience Donor – the person who would actually have been affected by the horrendous comments made by the leader of the country. She smiled despite herself, remembering a phrase that Dre would always say when she saw Emma get worked up about something – *This world turn mad yunnuh!*

The world truly did have a weird way of turning. As she peered over Dre's shoulder late at night while she drafted comms ideas for the Ally-chip rollout over the past few months, it seemed to Emma that it was much more of a challenge to get Black people to donate their emotions than it was to get white people to want to experience them. Emma's curiosity would have her reading the feedback from Dre's focus groups and noting that Black people still very much cited medical racism as a reason not to have any unnecessary surgery. She knew first-hand as a nurse that their fears were justified. Often when the two women would lay in bed, her girlfriend's mind would still be racing. They'd talk in the dark about Dre's feelings of conflict at using her own cultural knowledge to convince fellow

Black people to do something that she wasn't entirely sure of herself. But Dre genuinely believed that it could be possible to make change as a result of the Ally-chip, even if the people she had to work with to bring about that change sometimes seemed very shady in their motivations.

Emma held her breath for a moment, and then a moment longer, until it felt as if her lungs were burning. She needed to feel invigorated – or at least convince herself of such – if she was going to remain the calm, authoritative person providing comfort to strangers for the rest of her shift. Emma expelled the air wrapped around one word as she thought about the news programme she had just watched: '*Dickhead.*'

There were only two minutes and forty-four seconds left of her break, and Emma wanted to relish every second. Once she was back on the ward, it would be another five hours of chaos before she could finally drag herself home and into her bed.

Suddenly, the Tannoy blared. '*Could nurse Emma Ikeji report to A&E triage, please?*'

Hearing her own name irritated her, because Emma knew that meant the premature ending of her break. Being summoned specifically by name was rare, so Emma let curiosity quell her irritation. She took a quick glance at her phone – still nothing from Dre – then popped it back into her locker and returned to work.

Emma hurried through the corridors and headed towards the entrance, already hearing sounds of anguish ripping through the A&E. Her rubber clogs squelched against the squeaky vinyl floor as another proclamation of distress came from a patient somewhere nearby.

'I am just so tired! So bloody exhausted! I need a break. It's like the pressure just won't ease off. I can't think!'

Those words sounded consistent with what was now casually known as Ally-chip fatigue. There had been so many cases presenting to A&E over the past three months that Emma had become well-versed with the symptoms – overwhelming tiredness, powerful headaches, and an indefinable depressive malaise. She was sought out frequently to assist doctors who were still grappling with the growing phenomenon, and this had meant more hours, less time with Dre, and no increase in pay.

A few nights back when they'd been out to dinner, Dre watched Emma yawn for the third time since they were shown to their seats and had asked if she might be taking on too much.

'Baby Love, as much as it is beautiful that you're doing extra hours to help with this wave of shenanigans around the Ally-chip rollout, I hate that it means you're so tired and there's less of you when we do things like this,' Dre had said. 'I guess my working on it means I'm a bit responsible, eh?'

She gave Emma a beseeching smile, and although she'd intended for her response to be acerbic but witty, it just came out as snappy. 'Well yes, and if there's less of me, it's only matching the less of you that I've had to contend with in our little situation.'

Emma knew that Dre hated their relationship being called a 'situation', and so the silent stand-off when their eyes met over the candle in the middle of their table was to be expected. Dre had broken the silence by taking Emma's hand into her own and whispering playfully across the table, 'Newsflash babe – polyamory is hard.'

Emma couldn't help but laugh. The honesty was refreshing, if at times rather uncomfortable. As they chatted and giggled over fresh pasta dishes in the dimly lit restaurant, Emma knew that she would keep wanting Dre and keep wanting this.

Emma's thoughts returned to the chaos in front of her at the A&E triage area. Lying on a stretcher was a sobbing woman in an emerald-coloured ballgown, looking like a traumatised Cinderella. Stood to the side of the woman was an older nurse who appeared to be doing her best to calm her.

As soon as Emma's eyes met the emerald-gowned woman's, she smiled in relief between sobs.

'Emma, right? Thank God! I am so glad you're here! I said your name to them on the off-chance, but I wasn't even sure if it was the right hospital.'

Emma froze. She didn't quite know what to make of this random woman knowing her name and more importantly, asking for her specifically. She tried to cast her mind back to a time she might've treated someone who looked similar, but it was clear this woman wouldn't usually be at this type of hospital unless it was an absolute emergency.

As the woman blabbered away, Emma tuned out her nasal voice and instead took in her appearance. Blonde, delicately highlighted hair that was meticulously preened into a messy up-do, and her eyes – although currently bloodshot from the Ally-chip fatigue – were an unsettling green-grey, made more noticeable by the colour of her dress, as well as her plumped cheeks and Botox. If the exquisite ballgown and dazzling emerald jewellery weren't giveaways as to the woman's wealth, Emma could tell by her lips that the woman was clearly born into money. They were the only area of her face untouched by medical intervention, and over the years Emma had observed to her amusement that really rich people didn't tend to plump their lips with fillers. It was as if the thinness of their lips said something of their class and breed, and they would rather die than have anybody forget that.

She tuned back in to hear the woman saying, '. . . taking me to this hospital from the gala, and as the ambulance men were seeing to me, Andrea said that her friend Emma had dealt with a lot of cases like mine. Ally-chip fatigue – that must be what I have, right? Anyway, she just couldn't stop singing your praises and saying I should ask for you when I got here. I see what she means about spotting you by how beautiful you are. Gosh, look at all that hair! I won't touch it, don't worry. I know better. Ha! This chip, for my sins. My head feels like it's in a vice!'

No sooner had the woman finished speaking than the next wave of sobs and screeching of tiredness suddenly exploded from her. It was clear she'd been attempting to feign good humour, as someone of her standing might regularly do, but apparently the excruciating pain from the exhaustion her brain was experiencing was all too much for her. It was all starting to make sense to Emma now. Andrea – Dre – did a lot of work consulting with philanthropic organisations like the one Emma imagined this woman must be involved with. 'Teaching rich white people how to use their money for good even if they never stop doing bad' was Dre's secret description of her job. She would often declare this while smoking a spliff out of Emma's apartment window during one of the few evenings in a week where they could meet up and just be. Emma pictured Dre's locs resting effortlessly on her shoulders, the light from taller buildings around them reflecting off the pale brown skin of her girlfriend's taut back. *So beautiful . . .*

It was during one of Dre's 'good money once bad' initiatives that the two women met. A baroness had jovially declared at a televised conference that she felt Black women were simply having too many babies and maybe required some form of libido medication, and so her publicists advised her that she needed to ingratiate herself with the Black community. As a result, Dre had been approached to organise a free wellness day for Black women sponsored by said baroness. Emma and Dre would laugh themselves to tears whenever Dre would tell the story of how she ensured that she booked the best of everything from the Black-owned business vendors, and had encouraged the panellists for the wellness talks to charge the highest end of their usual fee, since it would all be covered by the baroness' bank account. Emma was walking through the park on her way to work when she'd caught sight of the event. She wasn't in any particular rush as she wasn't due to start her shift for a while, so she'd slowed down and taken it all in. A park full of Black women in all forms, chatting and laughing, and others being guided through a yoga session.

'Are you joining us today?' a voice had asked from behind her, relaxed and low. Emma turned around to see who was speaking to her and there was Dre, gorgeous, full lips smiling inquisitively. For a moment, Emma felt short of breath from the surprise of how beautiful she found this woman to be.

'Oh no, I can't join. I'm heading to work, but it looks amazing. I wish I'd known earlier.'

Dre didn't miss a beat.

'Well, maybe we could swap details and I could let you know of any other events. I know the tech savvy peeps are swapping profiles and not phone numbers but I'm not all the way there yet.'

'Me neither.' Emma had laughed. For the two women the spark felt instantaneous, so when Emma realised over their first meet-up for a coffee that Dre was in a polyamorous marriage, it confused her. Yet the pull of their chemistry together made her want to explore even more. Their relationship felt easy and honest, even with the third person – Dre's husband, who Emma didn't know too much about – being in the mix.

Her mind would've kept wandering around the loop of her relationship with Dre, but the anguished screeches in the A&E department brought Emma back to the present.

Focus on the chaos.

'Are you going to take over from here or not?' The sharp enquiry came from the older white nurse who had initially been seeing to the sobbing patient, and now seemed clearly offended that her services weren't required in this situation.

Emma returned the nurse's tight-lipped smile with an equally sharp, 'Of course.'

As soon as Emma took the clipboard being held out to her, the older nurse cast her eye over the wealthy woman, then shot an unimpressed look at Emma, before finally turning and muttering as she shuffled away.

'Caterina Holmes?' Emma said.

Hearing her name jolted Caterina from another round of sobs, and she instantly went back into what Emma had suspected was rehearsed humour, fine-tuned over the years. 'Yes, that's right. As in the sugar company Hibson & Holmes. But don't worry, I used my white privilege well; I took some of my family's vast wealth from those shameful sugar plantations way back when and donated it to inner-city causes. That's part of what I've been doing through your brilliant friend, Andrea, as well as her work with these blasted Ally-chips, of course. No fault of hers though, and she was so kind to recommend I come and see you after I collapsed.'

Emma tried not to focus on Caterina's assumption that she and Dre were just friends, nor the irksome notion that plantations were a thing of the past, given Emma could clearly see that Caterina was extremely rich in the present. She was starting to feel the warm curdling sensation in her stomach that would usually indicate she was getting annoyed, but she wanted to persevere, not just so she could wrap up her shift, but if she made a great impression on this Caterina woman then she would surely feed back to Dre.

And what would that really change for our relationship? Emma caught herself thinking.

Something, she hoped. Dre hadn't ever complained about her husband, and as far as Emma knew, Dre's husband had never complained about her either. Yet Emma couldn't help but feel out of place in their whole dynamic. She felt conflicted for wanting Dre all to herself, but she understood (from what felt like hundreds of websites she has visited) that Ricardo was Dre's 'primary partner', and that if Emma wanted to keep things going with Dre she had to be fully onboard with that. Dre had joked that Ricardo hadn't considered that his wife might find a connection with another *woman*, and Emma secretly hoped that this would be the beginning of Ricardo's discontent with the marriage. But that was eight months ago, and from Dre's description of him, or the random times Emma would hear him in the background while they were on the phone, he seemed pretty relaxed with their growing bond.

As she and a porter wheeled Caterina through the corridors

to a side room, Emma wondered if she had agreed to look after Caterina as another reason to be able to contact Dre later, since there was no response to her previous text:

Emma: Dre, I want more than what this is . . .

Emma *did* want more. She was unsure of what 'more' would look like in a polyamorous set-up, but she was definitely sure that being with Dre made her see life in a more textured way. Emma wanted to see life in that way on more than just a couple of days a week. Caterina being wheeled into the hospital and asking for Emma on Dre's recommendation felt like fate, and she wouldn't let her girlfriend down. *Or maybe I'm clutching at straws, but I need to find something that could cement things with Dre . . .* Emma also had to admit that there was also something separately intriguing about Caterina on her own merit, if one could call it that.

The side room was much quieter, and instantly the patient looked more at ease. Once settled in, Caterina's wailing significantly subsided, but Emma knew this could sometimes be attributed to dehydration and shock. She began setting up an IV drip for hydration while talking to the woman to ensure she was still cognisant.

'Shall we get you out of that lovely gown?' Emma asked as she took Caterina's observations before putting in a canula and prepping to take bloods and set up an IV.

'I think I would rather keep it on for now. Who knows what would happen to it if it were just flung somewhere.'

'Of course,' she responded in a clipped manner. Emma couldn't believe that in the midst of the woman's suffering, she still had time to be . . . whatever she was being in that moment.

'Have you heard from my husband? He should be here by now.'

'I haven't been told about your husband being in contact. Did he travel to the hospital another way?' Emma noticed the change in Caterina's green-grey eyes as she asked the question.

'Interesting one that. He didn't actually accompany me to the award ceremony. He left me at the steps on our way in. We had a teeny bit of an argument in the car, and well . . . no, that is not quite truthful. The argument started long before that. But I would've thought he would've been informed by now, as my next of kin.'

'I am sure reception is trying to get a hold of him as we speak.'

Caterina's voice sharpened even further. 'Oh wow. You're sure now, are you?' she said sarcastically. 'Only a few moments ago you weren't even aware whether he had been contacted.' But she must've caught the sting of her words from the fleeting expression of annoyance that tightened Emma's jaw. 'Look, I'm sorry for being so catty with you. I am just so exhausted. It's this constant pounding as if my brain is trying to escape through my eyes. I can't wait for the doctor to get here so I can find out if I could get this thing removed.' Caterina must've perceived a judgement that hadn't even crossed Emma's mind, though, because her next few words seemed to tumble out as if propelled by guilt. 'Of course, I'm just thinking out loud on that front. I wouldn't want people to think I wasn't dedicated to playing my part in a better world, I'd just like to do it a bit more comfortably, you know? I mean there are other factors, but . . .'

An awkward silence settled, and Emma began to draw blood from Caterina's outstretched arm. The woman had clearly hoped that Emma would prompt her for what the other factors were, but since no prompt came, she continued anyway.

'If I'm honest, I am actually a bit glad my husband – his name is Chuks – isn't here. He's my Experience Donor. I am already tired as it is, I couldn't imagine feeling all his feelings as well as mine right now if he were closer by. That's why I'm in two minds really. As excruciating as this headache is, without the chip how would I know what he's feeling?'

Emma knew she would have to respond, lest the conversation become even more strained. But the only response she really wanted to give to the woman's rhetorical question was, 'I dunno, maybe just ask him how he's feeling?' But finally, she managed to muster something that she felt was a good enough contribution to their discordant chat.

'Chuks. That's a cool name. Is it short for something?'

Emma already knew that it was. Although she did not speak her mother's dialect, Igbo, she knew cousins and uncles who had all manners of variations of the name. Something grated her about the way Caterina had stressed Chuks' name to make clear he was a Black man. It made Emma want to see just how connected this woman was to the culture.

'Yes! It is actually. Its Chukwuemeka. I butchered it so much at the beginning of our relationship that he suggested I call him Chuks, like his friends do.'

Emma carefully withdrew the needle from Caterina's arm. 'I had a friend in school called Chukwuemeka,' she said, deciding to say Chuks' full name as she handed her patient a small plastic cup to pee into. She ensured she pronounced it correctly so Caterina could hear, although after all these years it was clearly a hopeless cause. 'I think he said the name means "God has done so much".'

Caterina made her way into the bathroom with Emma's

help, and her voice travelled through the gap in the en-suite's door as she provided her urine sample. 'Yes, I think Chuks said it meant something similar. It is so interesting, isn't it?' Caterina returned from the bathroom with the cup in her hand outstretched towards Emma.

'What is?' Emma asked as she accepted the cup and placed it on the tray with everything else drawn from Caterina.

'Well, just how, you know, Black people give their children these names with such hopeful meanings even though they've been through so much *suffering*. It is extremely brave.' Emma began to feel that warm prickle of annoyance building in her stomach again. She wasn't sure how much more she could endure of the conversation.

'I don't think it's a thing all Black people do, and I think it predates the suffering you mention, if that suffering is in reference to the slave trade and colonialism.'

Caterina smiled again, the smile making it to just under her bottom eyelid. 'Andrea was right about you. Whip smart. Did you study history as well? Or maybe it's a cultural thing to know so much? I read that the girl who designed this chip currently fused into my brain was only fifteen at the time that she invented it? That's amazing. You should be proud.'

Emma worried that she might not be able to endure the rest of her shift with this woman's ignorant comments and attitude. *But if Dre can tolerate her, I can, too,* Emma attempted to convince herself. If Caterina left the hospital singing her praises, then who knows? Maybe Emma would be able to quit her job as a nurse and work with Dre on helping Caterina and people like her spend their money on good works, and they could live happily ever after. *OK, too far.*

'You know who would be proud that we are having such deep discussions?' the woman asked, as if reading Emma's mind. 'Dre. Do you think you'll be speaking with her soon? I'd love to let her know how well you've been taking care of me.' Just then, Caterina winced as another jolt of pain apparently shot through her head. 'Oh! Once we fix my brain so it doesn't feel like it's melting out through my ears, I'll be sure to tell her how much of a star you've been so far. Hard work must be in your veins.'

For fuck's sake.

Although Emma felt her face getting warmer from sheer anger at Caterina's ignorance, she made a conscious effort not to let it show. This woman's attitude must be what people called 'well-meaning'.

Emma let her words travel out of her mouth with her sigh. 'OK, I'll just go and check with the receptionist as to whether she has managed to get hold of your husband, and I'll also speak to one of the doctors on shift to find out when someone is likely to come and see you and what will be done about your chip.'

Emma was relieved to be out of the room even for a few minutes. The peach-coloured walls in there had started to make her feel sickly the more she talked with Caterina. In the reception area, Agnes, an older Nigerian woman whom Emma had worked with for years, was filling out a spreadsheet.

'Caterina Holmes, the patient in room five – has her husband been contacted?'

'Yes oh. In fact, I was waiting for you to come outside so I could discuss with you. I told him of her condition and he said that I should contact her mother instead. How can somebody be so wicked?'

Emma couldn't bring herself to admit to this older woman that after spending the last thirty minutes with Caterina, she could understand why Chuks might not want to come to the hospital, but she knew that even objectively the situation was still sad. 'Auntie, I think you should call Caterina's mum, and I will check with the doctors, but for now we won't say anything about her husband.'

Agnes' face lit up. Growing up with a Nigerian mother who was also a nurse and similar in age to the receptionist, Emma knew that they loved nothing more than being shown respect with a familial mode of reference, not to mention having some gossip to get them through their shift. Emma smiled at her knowingly.

Once Emma had found one of the doctors on shift and explained her patient's situation, Dr Tate, the doctor she'd spoken to, could not have been any more useless. He said that Caterina would be better suited to Dr Mbatu, one of the doctors who would be starting her shift shortly, since he felt like he didn't understand enough about the Ally-chip's nuances and 'wouldn't want to take any risks'. Emma wasn't surprised that for some mysterious reason he thought that 'Dr Mbatu will be much better suited to working out the issues with the chip, since she's . . . you know . . .'

As Emma walked back to room five, her usual giddiness in the lead-up to the end of her shift wasn't present anywhere in her body, because she knew and had already accepted on some level that she wouldn't leave until somebody from Caterina's family could be with her. Emma still wanted her girl's client to think even more highly of Dre after interacting with her. This felt like Emma's first chance to do something deeply meaningful for Dre, knowing how much she cared about her work and redistributing ill-gotten wealth. Caterina's pockets were deep, and murky. This felt like it mattered, and so Emma had to stick it out, however reluctantly. *This is why they say catch flights not feelings, Emz*, she chided herself in playful exasperation.

Once she arrived back at Caterina's room, in as reassuring a voice as she could manage Emma explained that there was in fact no news to report back. Thankfully, her patient didn't seem upset by this update. She had splayed herself across the bed on her back and seemed to be staring up at the ceiling, humming along to the theme tune of an advert playing on the television on the wall across from the bed, with her mind clearly elsewhere. Hopefully the mild pain medication had been enough to appease her until the doctor could investigate further.

'Would you like some more water?' Emma asked. Caterina seemed to not have heard. 'Would you—'

'No, no I'm fine,' Caterina replied in a sing-song voice as if it were a continuation of the advert. 'You know, I'm not surprised that you haven't been able to get a hold of Chuks. When he gets angry, it's just the most frightening thing.'

Emma's safeguarding training came tumbling through her consciousness. Regardless of how overbearing she may have found Caterina, if she was in danger it was Emma's responsibility to note this. 'I am sorry to hear that. I don't mean to pry, but I just want to understand better and ensure I am doing everything I can for you. What exactly do you mean by "frightening"?'

Caterina laughed, as if she were laughing at both Emma and Chuks. 'Heavens no, nothing violent! He wouldn't say boo to a ghost *most* of the time. He's not angry in the way that I've known other—' The woman seemed to have caught herself just in time, but Emma could already guess what she would've ended her statement with. At this point, she steeled herself simply for the sake of doing her job and finding out if her patient was in danger.

'Please continue.'

Caterina searched Emma's eyes for some kind of obvious judgement before she tentatively went on, 'I guess what I am trying to say is that, I was attracted to him for the very reason that he was different to how Black people had been described to me all my life. I think that sparked my interest in wanting to help underprivileged people, because if he could be so caring and funny and charming, that means that so many more people could be the same if given the chance.'

Emma drew in a breath. 'Sorry, I'm just trying to understand. Did you meet him at an organisation where he needed help? You mentioned Black and then underprivileged. One doesn't always mean the other.' Emma tried to lighten her statement with a smile, but she could tell that wouldn't add cushioning to the heavy weight of her pushback at what Caterina had said.

The woman's smile crept back out to meet Emma's, this time falling into her surgically contoured cheeks. 'See, if Chuks were here, this is when I would have felt that prickly anger that sometimes rears its ugly head. I don't always get things right, I admit, but whenever we're around Black women like you—'

'Like me?'

'I just mean Black women with opinions. He starts feeling all of these things like *anger* and *shame*. I asked him once – and I will never forget it – why he would be so angry with Black women whenever we were around them. And do you know what that man said to me? He said the anger was actually towards *me*. After everything I've sacrificed for our relationship, he felt anger and shame towards *me*!'

Emma wondered how Dre was able to tolerate this sort of behaviour all of the time from people like Caterina in order to work with them. To constantly interact with someone who felt their acknowledgement of your existence deserved praise must surely be unbearable. Emma amused herself with the thought of being Caterina's Experience Donor just so she could have the woman feel how annoying her ignorance was for the person dealing with her. Maybe there would be some potentially fun parts to the Ally-chip after all, even if she couldn't see herself ever being part of the 'Chippies', as they'd nauseatingly named themselves on social media.

'I'm sure there are multiple layers to what he felt that might not all be about you.' Emma didn't know what else to say. She had never met him, but felt a shooting rage at this Chuks guy for explaining so little of his emotions to this woman. The lack of a nuanced explanation only left Caterina thinking that Black women had exposed her to her husband's judgement in some way. Nothing about Caterina seemed evil; she was just woefully white. The way that she saw the world was solely informed by the role and function she was meant to play in it. Being married to Chuks clearly hadn't changed that, because even in his Blackness he apparently still fit into her world, however uncomfortably.

The strained silence between the two women fell away at the sound of the doctor who was now on shift walking into the room – a tall Black woman with long braids. 'OK, Mrs Holmes, is it? I am Dr Mbatu and I will be looking after you.

My apologies you weren't seen sooner. As you can appreciate, the Ally-chip is a rather new addition to our area of knowledge and it is important that we are properly informed before making any decisions. How are you feeling?'

Caterina seemed more cheerful now that some of the pain she had subsided momentarily. As she began to reply to the doctor, Emma could already sense that something would be awry in whatever she said, and that the painkillers were not strong enough to be the cause of it. 'I am feeling alright for now. Thankful to have had Emma here to look after me. Isn't it wonderful that we have reached a stage in our evolution where being a patient at this hospital means I'm being cared for by smart Black women like you both? You must all be so proud.'

There it is, Emma thought while busying herself rechecking her notes and Caterina's observations. She made a point of avoiding Dr Mbatu's glance in her direction, because she just knew they had both heard the same thing.

Dr Mbatu smiled widely at Caterina, almost as if overcompensating for the awkwardness of her patient's comment. 'I will go and check on the lab results of your blood tests. Thank you, Nurse Emma, for sorting those. I'll also go ahead and arrange an MRI to ensure that there is nothing amiss with the chip on the amygdala, or any abnormal swelling.'

Caterina sighed. 'I am happy with that for now, although after collapsing this evening and feeling this mind-shattering pounding in my head, I would like to know my options for whether it's possible to just remove this blasted chip.'

Dr Mbatu nodded with understanding. 'It is usual in the patients we have seen experiencing Ally-chip fatigue for them to consider removal. What we advise is to have the chip removed at an authorised Plant8Con site, if our tests indicate that you'd be well enough to wait until you can get there. Once we run these tests, I will have more of a definitive answer for you.'

'OK. Thank you so much. I trust you.' Caterina giggled, before rubbing her head as an ache apparently presented itself again in her skull. 'All this drama over this chip! Honestly, they should've done more checks before putting it on the market. The girl was fifteen at the time, for heaven's sake. It is, of course, wonderful that she created such an amazing thing to help humanity, but I can't imagine she had all the tools she needed over there in Nigeria. They barely have electricity. It is sad that suffering such as mine is becoming more prevalent because of the chip. The pain of having it has shown me that sometimes I'm too caring for my own good.'

Emma stared more intently than ever at her tablet as she took down notes from Dr Mbatu's comments while the doctor quickly went over Caterina's vitals. She could appreciate that there was some pain and discomfort in having Ally-chip fatigue, but she felt literally nauseous having to witness Caterina becoming a martyr to herself by using her Black partner's pain as a proxy. The silence was now a glass orb in the room. It seemed Caterina was unaware that it was born of her ignorance, and that anything capable of shattering that silence would indeed leave them all scarred in one way or another.

'The girl's name is Tòmíwá Fọlọ́runshọ́,' Dr Mbatu said. 'A brilliant mind, and I can't wait to see what she does with all the electricity now available to her at Harvard.' Her tone was dry, but her extremely toothy smile never faltered.

Caterina didn't seem to notice it though. She suddenly beamed as she turned her attention to the television on the sickly peach wall. 'Heavens! It's me! Must be from earlier on this evening at the gala.'

Dr Mbatu and Emma both turned to see a superbly preened Caterina on television in her green gown. She was on stage at the Philanthropist's Award Gala, accepting her award for leading the awareness of Ally-chip integration over the past year. The camera panned to the standing ovation Caterina received. Emma held in a lovestruck squeal as she caught a glimpse of Dre in the crowd, looking breathtaking in a floor-length black gown, her locs wrapped up beautifully into a thick, intricate bun. It all made more sense now. Emma had known Dre was attending an event but somehow it hadn't dawned on Emma that part of the award ceremony was lauding the early adopters of the Ally-chip. There she was texting Dre about wanting a deeper relationship while not realising that her girlfriend was all dressed up for a work event with the likes of Caterina.

The camera shifted back to Caterina on stage, her face colonised by the massive smile that seemed out of place near such soulless eyes. Then, as Caterina began her speech, she seemed to sway, grabbing onto the lectern to steady herself while the concerned ceremony host inched ever closer, his eyes darting around for help from someone in the wings. Caterina suddenly let out a piercing screech and clutched onto her head as if trying to hold her brain in place. A moment later, she collapsed onto the stage floor.

Emma glanced over at Caterina here in the room, feeling somewhat sorry for her, and noticing that the smile had crept off her patient's face at some point.

The television screen switched to the newsroom. Rónké Abrahams now had relocated to the studio since her earlier interview with the prime minister, and was joined by a guest. The caption at the bottom of the screen read 'Dr Simon Crispy – Neurology expert'. A sombre-looking Rónké began by acknowledging yet again the distress for the viewers who might've watched the footage they'd just aired of Caterina and apologised. Emma noted this with interest. A white woman being shown in physical distress warranted an apology, but if people like herself were shown on the news or social media in peril – while they were being chased, searched or murdered – they got no such special treatment. She couldn't remember a time when she saw similar footage of white people.

'What can you tell us, Dr Crispy, about what happened to Caterina Holmes and others like her?'

'Well, this is definitely a case of Ally-chip fatigue. It is shocking that more people aren't rushing to have these chips removed. It's too dangerous to host these emotions at such a constant rate. Like everyone at that ceremony, I commend people like Caterina for having the chips inserted in the first place, and many well-meaning people have sacrificed their wellbeing in order to help others, but it is simply too exhausting and debilitating. And what's more, we do not yet know the long-term effects of experiencing such emotions.'

Rónké nodded in understanding, but the steeliness in her eyes gave her away. 'So I just want to understand, Dr Crispy, Ally-chip fatigue is the result of the host's brain being unable to repeatedly withstand something distressing happening to their Experience Donor. The chip only changes who is actually feeling the emotions generated by oppressive attitudes, but it does not change the words or actions that lead to them. So surely the way to tackle this would be to address the prevalence of the words and actions that cause the emotions to arise in the first place?'

Simon Crispy paused for a moment as if pondering Rónké's question. 'I am not an anthropologist so I cannot really speak to these actions and words or their prevalence. What I do know from my area of expertise is that if some people are predisposed to feeling heightened emotions, when kind-hearted people offer to feel those feelings for them it can be overwhelming for these very generous Hosts.'

Rónké's audible sighs indicated that her patience seemed to be wearing thin. Emma couldn't tell whether it was the tiredness of having to report for so many hours, or the asinine conversations she was employed to have. Or maybe both. 'The longest anyone has tolerated an Ally-chip is five months,' she said. 'But for argument's sake, perhaps we should consider that those who have to feel these very same emotions for all their lives don't just get to remove a chip and have that distress cease to exist.'

'So are you saying you would rather they keep the chip in their brain and suffer?'

Rónké expelled another animated sigh before carefully removing the earpiece that would allow communication with the producers of the news program. 'No. That is not what I am saying. I am saying that people like yourself and the leaders of this country talk about Ally-chip fatigue as if the Donors are to blame for the emotions that arise out of the way that society treats Black people. In the short time that this chip has been available to the public, awards and grants and groups have been set up to celebrate and support the hosting Allies, while the actual people who are subjected to this treatment are still in the same position as before.'

Simon's eyes glazed over and his lips pursed until they practically disappeared into his face. Emma had seen that look many times before. He was no longer listening. Instead he muttered, 'I feel sorry for whoever *your* Host is.'

Emma watched as Rónkẹ́ rose up from her seat, pulled her microphone pack from the back of her skirt and threw it down on the table. Simon leant back in a fear that was clearly disproportionate, and then the television screen suddenly went blank.

Dr Mbatu and Emma both looked at each other, the corners of their lips honouring a hint of a smile, their eyes dancing with understanding.

'It's rather disappointing that Onky feels that way,' Caterina said, mispronouncing obliviously. 'I'd always liked her as a reporter, but surely it's not helpful to rant like that? I can't help that people noticed my efforts and wanted to celebrate it! Things are terrible for Black people and for other groups too. Berating those of us trying to help is the reverse of what she should be doing.'

It was as if watching Rónkẹ́ speak up in the way she just had cemented Dr Mbatu and Emma's silent pact not to react to Caterina's woeful comments.

'There really is no time to waste in ensuring that all is well with you, Mrs Holmes,' the doctor said. 'I'll be back shortly once I've sorted your MRI, spoken with our consultant and have your results back from the lab.'

Emma was left in the room with Caterina once again.

Silence.

She was thinking about making a vague excuse to step out of the room, too, when Caterina croaked, 'I got us the Ally-chip as an anniversary present. I wanted my husband to know that

I wanted to truly be one with him and feel what he felt. We have been married for a few years, but we'd never really spoken about Blackness and things like that. I saw him for him and not his colour. I thought he felt the same way too.' As Caterina continued to speak, tears began streaming from her eyes onto the pillow. 'I didn't think it would be that hard to have the chip until we actually had the procedure done. Suddenly I could feel his discomfort around my parents – who are *lovely*. I could feel his shame and anger and sometimes his guilt in the few times we would interact with Black women. I could feel his fear and angst whenever we passed the police. When we were around my friends his quiet rage seemed to consume me, and sometimes it didn't even go away when it was just the two of us alone. There was no letting up. It's like he feels things all the time, and having the chip means I feel it too. I just want to make it stop – for me *and* for him.'

Emma nodded, not wanting to interrupt, and Caterina continued. 'We had an argument before the award gala. All because I suggested that young people shouldn't be Experience Hosts for the Ally-chip as it's just too much to feel all of those negative things all of the time. Chuks felt differently. He thinks the whole point of the Ally-chip is so people know what injustice feels like and how much of a role it plays in people's day-to-day lives, and that once they do, then the real changes could be made. So I asked whether he would let our children get the chip, since we are trying for a child. He said no, because they would have experiences to *donate*. I mean, yes, they'd be partly Black, but they'd also have my genes. They would grow up differently to how he did, and they aren't likely to carry those burdens. We'd be moving past all this Black and white stuff.' Caterina turned to lay on her side in the foetal position. 'He just went on and on about how little I understood about him, even with the chip. He had the audacity to say that I wouldn't be able to buy our child's way out of experiencing injustice. As if I would ever think that was possible?' She sighed. 'Two years ago he would've agreed with me on these issues, but now suddenly he's started to change, and make *me* out to be the enemy.'

Emma didn't know who she agreed with in the argument between Chuks and Caterina. She found them both to be exhausting in very specific ways. Caterina because she seemed to be performing her understanding of racial inequity, and Chuks because it sounded like he had run away from his own understanding for so long that he seemed only now to be muddling his way back. Having someone feel the more distressing emotions *for* him had perhaps provided clarity to consider other aspects of his life that he previously might not have paid attention to.

Emma had listened to some of her colleagues chat in the break room about whether they would be a Host or a Donor, and she had taken very little interest in the conversations. She wanted all her emotions and experiences to remain with *her*, and maybe it was unfairly critical to think so, but the donation of one's most visceral emotions, which were the result of a system made over centuries, seemed like some weird kink to her.

A chip that was meant to allow an understanding of the interpersonal context of racism had been turned into a global conversation about how benevolent white people were for having the chips inserted, and then how self-sacrificing they were to endure Ally-chip fatigue. She didn't want to be a part of it.

Before Emma could respond to Caterina's tearful thoughts, a woman barged into the room, short and petite with stern green eyes. She looked like an older version of Caterina.

'Darling! I rushed over as soon as I heard. This has gone too far! Your father and I could tolerate your choices up until this point, but it must stop! And where is your husband now? Probably off somewhere spending our money.' She turned to Emma. 'And why are you just standing there staring? Could you get the doctor in here immediately?'

Emma noticed that Caterina didn't correct her mother on the comment about Chuks and her family's wealth. It made Emma wonder how Caterina could consider this woman 'lovely'. Then again, *apples and trees,* she thought. She felt a relief knowing she had kept to the promise she had made to herself that she would stay with Caterina until a family member arrived. Now she was off the hook, she'd find someone else to take over. Her shift was well and truly at an end, and she'd done all she could for this patient. As Emma turned, about to leave the room, Dr Mbatu returned looking slightly perplexed.

'Well, Mrs Holmes,' the doctor began, then noticed that Caterina's mother was in the room. 'The lab has confirmed that you are pregnant, so we can't rush ahead with tests like we had initially talked about, or with the potential removal of the chip. Were you aware of this?'

Emma was slightly surprised, but she knew she had to leave the room quickly if she didn't want to get caught up in more hours of tension.

Caterina's mother stood straight up in a rage. 'That is quite enough. We will have Caterina transferred to a hospital far more suitable, since she seems stable enough for now.'

Caterina said nothing as she stared at the peach wall, neither woman acknowledging the mention of pregnancy.

'I'll just—' is all Emma could muster as an excuse to leave the room. She quickly backed out into the ward, turned in her rubber shoes and rushed to the main reception to write up her handover notes. She briefly chatted to the nurses who were curious about Caterina since they'd also seen the news on TV, making sure not to say much because she was desperate to go home and wash the unsaid words she had left lingering in the air unclaimed off her body.

'I'm here for Caterina Nwabueze – sorry, Holmes.'

Emma spun around in her desk chair to see a tall, slim-built man standing at reception. His brown skin seemed dull under the hospital lights. He had let his hair grow out without shaping its edges to frame his face. He wore tortoiseshell-rimmed glasses and a very concerned expression.

'Hi Chuks – my apologies, Mr Nwabueze. I've been Caterina's nurse this evening. We tried to call you earlier . . .' Emma wanted to get an idea of Chuks' state of mind before directing him to Caterina's room, suddenly realizing that the physically closer he got, the more Caterina would have to absorb his emotions via her Ally-chip. His wife was in too fragile a state to feel much more.

'Yes, sorry about that. I had to get myself together and thought it best for her mum to be with her instead. I . . .' Chuks searched Emma's face before he continued, as if wanting to ensure his thoughts would be safe with her. 'We had just argued, and I was feeling so many things. When I heard what had happened to her and I saw the news, I was of course worried, but my earlier feelings hadn't shifted, and I thought about the chip. How could

I let her feel that? I don't know what it's like for you here, but it's hard enough managing white people's reactions on a normal day, talk less of managing their feelings about your feelings.'

Emma was taken aback by how forthright Chuks was being. She had expected him to be closed off around her as a Black woman, based on what Caterina had described. She nodded. 'Yes. I know what you mean.' She drew in a breath. 'Your wife was in a lot of pain earlier.'

Chuks winced at the mention of Caterina's discomfort. Somehow in all the discord that Caterina had described, Emma had overlooked the couple still loving each other. Relationships weren't as easy as TV sitcoms made it out. Love alone wasn't enough. She loved Dre, yet it wasn't a magic wand that offered them a simpler relationship dynamic. Love could be the reason for the relationship but love clearly could not do the work of relating – people had to do that.

'I knew we shouldn't have gotten that stupid chip,' Chuks was saying. 'She managed to talk me into it, saying how great it would look for us as a couple setting an example of a racially equal marriage. It made me laugh at the time, because a racially equal marriage where her parents wouldn't allow her to use my surname in public was rather laughable.'

Emma was very tempted to point out the patriarchal motivations of surnames and marriage in general, but realised, as Dre would usually tell her when she was about to get on her soap box about something she had watched or read, *this is not the time, Baby Love*. She settled for a 'hmm'.

'It's like she was happy to wear every aspect of me except for my name,' Chuks continued, his voice shaky. 'My emotions became something for her to parade around and be praised for. It brought to mind some of Chinua Achebe's work that I started reading a couple of years ago; it felt like my emotions were being colonised in the way Nigeria was. I just needed my feelings to myself for bit and not have to explain or apologise for them. That's why I left. And then this happened.' He drew in a deep breath. 'But I am stable enough to see her now. Even with her mum present.'

Emma regarded him for a moment, but then thought about all that Caterina had said. It wasn't up to her to work out what happened between this husband and wife. She directed Chuks towards Caterina's room. She knew the news that was waiting for him and how challenging that would be to process, but it also was not her place to tell him anything beforehand, or worry about the repercussions of his emotions on hearing it – for him or Caterina.

Emma finished her notes and wanted nothing more than to get out of the hospital. Her mind drifted back to Dre, and whether Caterina's report on how well she was looked after would put Emma in a positive light for her girlfriend. Maybe, like so many things, she'd have to leave that up to fate.

Stepping outside into the September night's breeze felt good. Emma could make out three cameramen sat on the pavement; they had clearly identified Caterina's whereabouts and were desperate to get the candid shots of her when she would eventually leave the hospital. She stood for a moment at the top of the stairs and breathed in deeply, glad she could finally send Dre another text message even though it was very late or very early, whichever way one perceived 1 a.m. She rummaged in her bag for her phone as she walked slowly down the steps, but then a familiar voice startled her.

'Hey, Baby Love.'

Dre leant against the wall at the bottom of the stairs. With the light provided by a nearby bus stop, Emma could see that she had changed from the black ballgown she had worn at the ceremony into a grey tracksuit. She still looked gorgeous, yet it was her concerned eyes that warmed Emma's heart the most. There was a man next to Dre that Emma hadn't met before but she knew his face instantly – Dre's husband, Ricardo. Emma's mind wanted to race but couldn't get off the starting block.

'I just wanted to know that you're OK,' Dre said. 'He's driving. You just know I was making the most of that champagne before Caterina drop dung.'

Emma couldn't help but laugh at Dre's description of what had happened to Caterina. She stepped gratefully into her girlfriend's strong hug, and gradually felt the stresses of the night falling away.

'Hello, Emma,' Ricardo said. 'We don't have to count this time as our official first meeting, since I'm pretty much here in the capacity of a driver right now, like Dre said.' He smiled at Emma warmly yet tentatively.

Maybe it was the tiredness from enduring Caterina's many waves of emotion, but Emma searched her body for the jealousy she thought she would feel upon meeting Ricardo and couldn't find it. *Maybe later*, she thought to herself.

'I've heard . . . not that much about you,' Emma responded with a cheeky smile, and the three of them laughed.

They walked slowly to the car park, Dre with her arm around Emma's shoulder as if it were the most natural thing in the world. They all had questions, but for now it felt as if they didn't have the energy to be asked. There was time. Emma let herself enjoy the warmth of Dre's body by her side as they sat in the backseat of the car and Ricardo drove.

'Is Caterina OK?' Dre asked.

'If you're talking about the Ally-chip, yes. She should be.'

'That's good. Have I still got her as a client? Because I know telling her to come find you was risky on my part. I can bet you would've been tempted to tell her about herself.'

Emma smiled because Dre knew her so well. 'No, for you I held it down. Although I have to say, I don't know how you tolerate that kind of behaviour all the time . . .' Emma's statement trailed off with a yawn.

'When you're rested we will talk more. But ultimately, I can handle people like Caterina because I know I can use their money to do something worthwhile for people like us. Like I said to you before, "good money once bad". They think that's what they're doing with the Ally-chip, but this the *real* work. It's about as close as we will get to reparations for some time.'

The three of them chuckled until they fell into simply listening to Ricardo's jazz playlist on the car stereo. The neon lights of the late-night shops shone out onto the street. The cleaning trucks were already out scrubbing the roads slowly. Sirens blared past while Emma's mind reluctantly drifted back to Caterina – someone who spoke of wanting a changed world, yet who was determined to remain mostly unchanged. Emma also existed in a world consisting of Dre and Ricardo – that was a change to what *she* had known or what she had imagined for herself. Resting her head on Dre's shoulder as they drove towards Brixton, Emma closed her eyes and appreciated her own feelings being just hers in that moment. She wasn't sure how this relationship would play out, and the feelings that accompanied the many possibilities felt like galaxies themselves unexplored.

Briefly witnessing Caterina and Chuks grappling with having a voyager in one's own space, or being the person exploring someone else's complexity and vastness, seemed too arduous and exposing. Maybe the change being sought in life didn't require a donning of someone else's emotions, but rather a fearless commitment to confront one's own. Of course, people don't need to know that for now if Dre's Ally-chip rollout was going to be successful.

Emma smiled as she nestled closer to her girlfriend. Even without a chip connecting them, she hoped Dre could feel the depth of her love.

Blue

'. . . And that's it for this today's show! Thank you for listening to the Feminine Hour. Be sure to tune in tomorrow when we will be discussing whether it is a feminist act to get laser hair removal on your bikini line . . .'

Ibby very much enjoys listening to the 'Feminine Hour', having been a guest a couple of times. She chuckles to herself in the back seat of the car as the chauffeur glances at the radio in bemusement. She derives a weird pleasure from watching him not quite know what to make of the random discussions that come up on the radio show. As problematic and white-centred as she finds some of the programme to be, as a world-renowned psychotherapist she feels that there's something to learn from how women present their own issues with little direction as to the solution. Guests would come on the show to promote books and the like, and yet in all the promotions it seemed nobody was brave enough to ask, 'So what is the point of all of this?' It felt as though there was a market in *never quite solving an issue*, or at least being honest about there not being an obvious or easy solution. Instead, it seemed the show thrived on getting just close enough that people would buy into whatever was being promoted so as to feel as if they were making progress. But Ibby felt hypocritical as she observed her own thoughts on the matter. Her own career wouldn't be what it was if it were not for people seeking answers that she was not able to truthfully provide without there being some fallout . . .

The point of all of this is what Ibby has spent her career thus far researching. Why do people carry on despite the systemic obstacles placed before them? How do people navigate a world fuelled by pain? She is on her way to give a keynote speech about this very subject. Gazing out of the window at the cold, dark yet familiar London streets, Ibby takes a moment to do what she would generally advise to her clients who are always on the go: be present. Take in this moment. This is now. This is your life.

Is this my life, though? Ibby finds herself wondering. She takes in her reflection in the car window: big, brown, expressive eyes; lustrous lips tinted with a plum-red lipstick; skin deep brown and a vibrant, dark brown crown of hair with golden-coloured tips. Beautiful. Ibby knows she looks beautiful, and yet proceeds to pull out her compact mirror from her purse so she can check the lipstick hasn't betrayed her and had a rendezvous with her teeth. It hasn't. She checks her white pantsuit for dirt. There isn't any. She notes her own restlessness but has little time to analyse the cause, because just then the car stops outside the central London cultural venue where Ibby is due to deliver her keynote speech.

'So glad I'm getting a chance to meet you! I am undoubtedly one of your biggest fans. To me you are a feminist icon, and the only person I care about hearing on stage today. I probably shouldn't say that as the senior programmer, but I don't care!'

Ibby smiles warmly at the excited woman leading her to her dressing room. There is something about the way her brunette ponytail bounces up and down as she fawns over Ibby that makes her think of a cute Labrador, the kind that she wanted when she was younger.

Ibby remembers asking her mum for the dog as they walked past an old man in Burgess Park who said he wanted to give the puppy away as he could not take care of it. Ibby had pulled at her mum's sleeve pleading for them to be able to take the dog home.

'Ìbùkún, is there something wrong with you?' her mother had said. 'Do you no longer have sense? Upon all the work I do in this life to look after you, you also want me to take care of a dog? It's as if you want to kill me, you this girl! But I won't allow it.'

Ibby realises she has stopped listening to the bouncy brunette woman and refocuses in time to catch, '. . . so I'll be back in about twenty minutes to lead you out onto the stage. We will show a VT of some of your amazing research and TED talks before you come out, as well as sharing some excerpts from your books.'

'Thanks,' Ibby replies, deeply grateful that she doesn't have to sit through watching her own work being shown on screen. She has long noted the jealousy she senses when she observes people taking in her work, unaware of how deeply alone she felt in making it. Whenever she would mention these sensations in contact sessions with her own therapist, she would be told that it's normal to feel alone when charting a course of treatment that hasn't existed before. Ibby knows there is only so much that she can say in reply to that. Some things she must keep to herself.

As with most of these prestigious events, it all happens in a blur for Ibby. She walks out on stage to bright lights and hundreds of people in the audience. She smiles and begins to talk about how she has managed to help even the most troubled people with their pain.

Ibby was catapulted to stardom after taking on a male pop singer as a client; he was struggling with life, having been a child star. He told the world during one of his deep-dive television interviews that sessions with Ibby had done what attending trendy megachurches and endless hiking in LA's canyons, as well as various illegal substances, had been unable to provide him with – a deep sense of peace. Ibby's career was already well established at that point, but nothing could've prepared her for the massive shift her life took once she was mentioned by the star. Many celebrities reached out, desperate to be freed of the mental cages they'd made do with decorating instead of breaking out of, as well as everyday people who wrote to her assuming they wouldn't be able to afford her services but were still so desperate to achieve the sense of peace they had seen their idol express.

Ibby found herself in a predicament, because as much as she wanted to help people feel at ease in such a tumultuous world, she knew it would be futile to even attempt to describe how exactly she went about her healing. It was not something she could explain – perhaps even if she was at liberty to, which she was not. Instead, she crafted her advice and her books around the widely agreed consensus of helpful psychotherapeutic tools. Over the years there were a few other therapists who had critiqued her books for not being any different to the advice that they would give – however their critique was drowned out by the people who, after *one-to-one* appointments with Ibby, spoke of how utterly transformational her sessions were. As a result, the people who were unable to access such sessions nevertheless put their trust in following the exercises Ibby suggested, and reading the anonymised case studies she provided, in the hope that they, too, would find respite from their inner demons through her work.

On stage, Ibby describes her research and findings in a way that holds the audience transfixed with her knowledge and expertise. She looks at them sadly, knowing that nothing she has said can truly be actioned without her being physically present. She wonders how much longer she will be able to tolerate her own stories. As expected, when she finishes someone comes out from the side of the stage to present Ibby with a bouquet of flowers, which she graciously accepts to uproarious applause from the audience. Ibby leaves the stage, smiling when necessary as she struts back to the car waiting to whisk her away from one performance to the next . . .

'Ms Williams,' her chauffeur begins with a thick Russian accent, 'I just want to confirm, I am now driving to Solstice bar, correct?'

'Yes, I'm making a call on our way so please pop the partition up.'

'Certainly.'

Ibby unbuttons her white blazer to reveal a white lace body-suit underneath. She reapplies her plum-red lipstick and changes earrings. 'Date-night Ibby activated,' she mutters. Ibby dials a number and the inside of the car comes alive with ringing.

'Ìbùkún! So you remember you have a mother, *abi*?'

Ibby laughs at how dramatic her mum can be when communicating that she would like to hear from her daughter more often.

'How could I ever forget my sweet mother?'

The two women laugh.

'I can't believe that you have been in London for four days and didn't come and see me. Can you come over tonight?'

'I'm going on a date, Mum.'

There is silence from the other end of the phone followed, after a while, by a relieved sigh.

'Ìbùkún, I can't tell you how happy I am. Ha! I am so, so worried that with all this international-jetsetter-woman lifestyle you are doing, you wouldn't make time to pursue a husband.'

There is annoyance in Ibby's voice when she replies, 'It's funny that I grew up with you telling me to face my books and not think about boys, then almost overnight you start a countdown for when I'll settle down. Honestly, I am so busy. And it is also about meeting the right guy.'

Ibby catches herself before finishing her own statement with 'or girl', because she knows that as dramatic as her mother is, there would be even more drama to contend with should she have to explain her sexuality as well. As far as Ibby is concerned her sexuality is not something that needs discussing with her mother, because Ibby knows that the reality of truly settling down with *anybody* is something she has long since compartmentalised as an impossibility.

'Well, Ìbùkún, I hope that is all there is to it. You have always been a secretive child, but if there is anything you need advice on, you can always speak to me about it.'

Ibby giggles at the thought of discussing relationships with her mother, the same woman who refused to be with another man after Ibby's father moved out to be with the lady who ran the launderette on Choumert Grove.

'Um, sure, Mummy. If I ever have any burning questions about dating, I will be sure to run them by you. Anyway, I'm just pulling up outside the bar, so I'll call you later?'

The two women hang up, both knowing that there is so much more to say than what they've actually said, but also noting that this sensation is nothing new.

Ibby strides into the trendy, dimly lit bar to see Daniel sat in a booth, sipping half-heartedly on his mojito. Looking at him makes her feel good. It seems like such a strange and simple thing for Ibby to think, but she appreciates just how rarely she tends to simply feel *good,* and so she tries to make the most of the moments when she recognises the sensation. From their very first date, Ibby has always found it endearing just how much Daniel enjoys cocktails. They have joked many times about how attractive she finds it that he doesn't play up to expectations about the type of drinks men should enjoy. Daniel's ease with things like this is just one of the many things that make him so pleasurable to be around. As well as the fact that he carries his six feet five inches muscular frame, dark brown skin and beautifully tender eyes so effortlessly, he is also very funny and kind in a way that Ibby can sense he has always been.

'Are you drinking the mojito or is the mojito drinking you?' Ibby teases as she slides into the booth.

'You love speaking like a Nigerian aunty, innit?' he retorts. They both laugh. That easy laugh. The type of shared joviality that has made the year they've been dating fly by. As their laughter dissipates, Ibby searches Daniel's face for something, but can't quite find it. Perhaps because she isn't sure what she's really looking for.

'What's up?' Ibby asks. 'I'm getting a vibe that something is off with you.'

Daniel smiles at Ibby sheepishly. 'I'm always stunned by how easily it seems like you can read my every emotion, even before it's something I'm able to identify for myself. It is sexy can't lie, but sometimes stay out of my mind, OK?'

They both laugh again, eyeing one another. The sexual tension between them never ceases, no matter how many times they've explored each other. One of their nights laid up in Daniel's bed, he had told Ibby that he felt at times like he wore her in his skin – a weird merging he had never felt with any other person. He had pondered his own revelation for a while before concluding that it would be frightening if it wasn't so damn erotic.

'. . . Anyway, talking of sexiness and getting into people's minds,' Daniel continues with a chuckle, 'GQ want to do a profile on me, and their angle is apparently "the high-flying commercial lawyer who walked away from it all to open an art gallery".'

Ibby beams at him. 'That's amazing, D! I'm going to see you in the pages of a magazine? I'm going to have to frame that and hang it up somewhere.'

She catches a slight tone of irritation in Daniel's reply. 'You're going to hang it up, are you? In the house that I'm still not able to visit because . . . what was the reason again? You "haven't finished decorating"?'

Ibby watches Daniel's face and notices not just the annoyance, but a more familiar expression, one which she had witnessed on her partners before him: hurt.

At some point or other in Ibby's romantic relationships – sometimes sooner rather than later – the conversation always arises as to why Ibby never invites them back to her place, and why the relationship seems to stagnate once it feels like things are getting too deep. She had hoped that she and Daniel could've lasted a bit longer before this same thief came to take her joy, but as always, she was ready to put on a performance and see if she could buy herself more time with this one.

Before she met Daniel, Ibby had been of the opinion that dating men rather than women was easier, as men always seemed content for a lot longer to not know too much about her while still viewing their relationship as fulfilling. When these relationships came to their inevitable end, Ibby would be sad but never heartbroken.

The only time Ibby had experienced heartbreak was when things had ended with Amina. Amina who, just by holding Ibby, could make her feel what she never thought possible – safe. The two of them would lie languidly on the soft rug on Amina's living room floor, caressing one another's naked skin and talking about almost everything. Amina scared Ibby with her relentless pursuit to *see* Ibby, truly and deeply. Then one evening after a dinner party at Amina's place, as they cleared the dishes away after the guests had gone home, Amina had suddenly paused, placed the plates on the counter and taken Ibby's face in her hands, kissing her with immense love and passion before saying, 'I think we have to end this, Ibby. Tonight more than ever, I could feel something I've struggled to articulate in the months we have been together. There is a part of you that you don't want to share. I hear you holding back, even when we talk for hours. There's always a limit, a particular point where you stop. I feel it when you laugh so deeply, but the happiness doesn't quite make it to your eyes. I don't doubt that you love me, but I doubt that you love me enough to choose me over your secrets.'

That was Amina's superpower; her ability to see things in their rawest form. In their months together, whenever Ibby would talk about a work trip and Amina would ask to come along, Ibby knew deep down that it was not because her girlfriend necessarily wanted to come so much as she wanted to note if and how Ibby evaded her request. With Amina, beautiful Amina, who created the most incredible art from clay, Ibby could not hide. Life with her had felt ideal – from their weekends at farmers' markets to lazy evenings where Amina was stationed in the studio area of her large living room, working with clay and chatting about nothing and everything with Ibby outstretched on the sofa reading. It was bliss.

But then Amina had ended it.

Ibby had surprised herself by how suddenly tears escaped from her eyes and trickled onto Amina's hands as they continued to gently cradle her face. At that point, Ibby had known she had a choice. A choice to finally say something, or at least come up with enough to hold on to the relationship for a little longer. But she knew that Amina, who moulded life out of lifeless clay for a living, had chosen to speak these words so that Ibby didn't have to utter them herself. So Ibby had simply kissed Amina's hands and held them against her own face more firmly for a while longer, as if trying to imprint Amina's essence into her memory. She'd smiled at Amina and without saying a word, packed her things, gathered her tears and left.

Sitting next to Daniel now, Amina crosses Ibby's mind in a way that happens less often nowadays, but is usually accompanied with a gnawing feeling in her stomach, like a yearning. Daniel and Amina are different in many ways, but in this moment, Ibby feels he has a similarly unyielding desire for her to let him in, and let herself be seen.

'Ibby, you're doing that thing again,' he says. 'You can't just stop talking when things feel a bit awkward. You are the famous psychotherapist; I shouldn't have to tell you this.'

'You're right. I apologise. I just wasn't expecting this kind of conversation on date night at a bar with such low-hanging lights. Honestly, why do they make them hang so low yet they don't even provide that much—'

'Ibby.'

She sees that Daniel's annoyance is graduating to frustration. 'Sorry. I know we need to have this conversation. Could we possibly do it somewhere quieter and maybe when I'm back from LA next week?'

Daniel sighs. 'Sure. Whatever you want. Anyway, in the GQ feature I told you about, one of the questions is going to be about me as "the gallery owner still in search of the art that would steal his heart".'

She stares at him blankly.

'Ibby, they're trying to find out if I'm taken.'

'Ah! So what are you going to tell them?'

'You tell me. We've been at this for a year now, even if it hasn't felt like it with you being in and out of the country and me being busy with all my stuff. But I know we both realise that we have something here, right?'

Ibby realises they still haven't divested from the conversation she desperately does not want to have. 'Kristoff is calling me from the car,' she tells Daniel, deflecting again. 'He's so punctual, that guy. He knows the exact time I need to leave here to make it home in time to get my stuff so I don't miss my flight.' She kisses Daniel with a smile as she slides out of the booth. 'I just had to see you, no matter how briefly. You know you're my babe. I'm very much looking forward to getting back next week so we can hang out. I'll come round and cook for you, and you can show me all the poses you plan to do for your GQ shoot!'

Daniel laughs in spite of himself. 'This is the Ibby I love, I guess. Always on the move.'

Ibby can feel Daniel watch her leave. A huge part of her wishes that she didn't always have to go when she found someone with whom she would like to stay.

As Ibby bustles into the back of the car, Kristoff's thick Russian accent is cloaked with inquisitiveness. 'Ah! Ms Williams, I wasn't expecting you back so quickly.'

'Yes, I wasn't expecting myself back so quickly either, but there has been a change of plans, so . . .'

Kristoff sets off for Ibby's home without any further questions. She hates lying, but for someone who hates it as much she does, lying is something Ibby has found herself doing from a young age. She considers that maybe this penchant has contributed to her worldwide success, because she is able to spot untruths in all her clients, even when they've been unable to identify it themselves.

Ibby hadn't actually received a call from Kristoff, of course, and there had been no real reason to rush off from her date other than her no longer wanting to continue down the line of conversation that Daniel was insisting upon. That is one of the things she had found so attractive about him when they first started dating – how determined he was in everything he did. Ibby could feel that getting her to open up more had become his new pet project, and so that very same determination now unnerved her.

The drive home is quiet, and Ibby relishes it. She especially appreciates having a driver like Kristoff, who instinctively understood from the moment he was initially assigned to her that she didn't enjoy conversation just for the sake of it. Ibby began requesting Kristoff from the agency for all of her engagements, even for the day-to-day tasks. However, when her management team asked whether she would prefer to have Kristoff put on some kind of retainer so he was her permanent driver, she had declined. Ibby knew that once an arrangement such as theirs was formalised, then the talking would start and everything would be ruined. The *silence* would be ruined.

They drive further away from the vibrant London streets until they're in quiet suburban lanes. Kristoff reaches a small, tree-lined street and drives towards a looming gate, which opens automatically. The wooded lane on the other side of the gate would be pitch-black were it not for a few streetlights dotted about, and the beam of the car headlights. Ibby looks out of the car window again, taking in the mansions inhabited by neighbours she never plans to introduce herself to, not even when she happens by them on one of her early morning runs.

Ibby catches her own reflection again in the car window and thinks that she looks just as she did the last time she checked, more tired this time. Tired of what though? She decides not to think about it, not after the conversation earlier with Daniel. She notices a stain on her white trousers – a blue speck, but a stain nonetheless. This annoys her, and she's aware that it is more than just the blue speck on her white trousers that is rousing this emotion within her.

'We are here, Ms Williams.' Kristoff looks at Ibby in the rear-view mirror, with a smile in his voice that doesn't quite reach his eyes. Ibby finds Kristoff's professionalism comforting. He always shows just the right amount of attention to let her know that he is a thoughtful person, but not too much attention or overfamiliarity that it would make her uncomfortable. He seems to get her in a way that many other people fail to, because he isn't offended by her need to be seen yet unseen.

'Thank you for today, Kristoff,' she tells him softly.

Kristoff opens the car door for Ibby, gathers her bags from the car boot and helps carry them up the steps to her giant front door. He doesn't attempt to ask Ibby whether he should help her inside with everything, because he's been her driver for long enough now to learn that nobody goes inside Ibby's home except for Ibby. He must have heard the phone conversations she had with her mum during which, whenever she was asked about visiting, Ibby would have an excuse ready for why it wouldn't be a good time to come round. Maybe Kristoff even recognised that this is why she'd chosen a stunning house so far away from everyone she knew – because it would make it harder for them to just stop by.

Although they had never really spoken about it, there was a time when Kristoff had gone to help Ibby into the car after one of her speaking events in the pouring rain, only for his phone to fall from his pocket and the screen crack. He had said nothing of it and had continued to use the phone. But Christmas was a few weeks after the incident, and after he dropped her at her mum's and they said their goodbyes for the few days of the Christmas break, Ibby had made sure to leave a card and box in the back seat where she would usually sit. It was a brand-new phone, and in the card she had written:

Kristoff. You broke your phone in the rain while making sure I wouldn't get wet. I understand this is part of your job, but you do it very well. Thank you. Please let us never speak of this. Merry Christmas. Ibby.

When Kristoff had arrived to pick Ibby up from her mum's after the Christmas break, he didn't say a word about the gift to her, but had positioned his suit jacket so she could now see the brand-new phone attached to a holster on his belt.

'Good night, Ms Williams,' he says now.

Ibby watches the car pull out of her sprawling driveway and then heads inside. As Ibby closes the front door behind her, she pauses for a moment to take in everything she can see – the cream Italian marble floors across her large foyer, the doorway to her right leading to a plush living room, and the doorway to her left opening into her painstakingly designed kitchen. Ibby kicks off her heels and lets her feet press upon the comforting coolness of the floor. As she walks up the stairs, Ibby speaks out loud in her empty home: 'Aláké, call Mum.'

Her smart home system begins to call her mother instantly.

'Ìbùkún, you are home already? So you could've come to see me.'

Ibby laughs at the way her mum seems to always be on the warpath no matter what time of day they speak. 'No, Mum, I couldn't. Remember I told you I'm travelling in a few hours?'

'Ah, yes! Of course! Miss Jetsetter! Anyway, how was the date?'

Ibby knows better than to give too much information. To tell her mum that she and Daniel had been dating for a year would mean an open invitation to questions about when they would be getting married. Funny that the day she finally decided to mention Daniel to her mother at all is the day she's also realised they'll need to end things.

'The date was OK, I guess. I'm just taking my time, you know. I'm sure when I find the right one, I will know.'

Ibby's mum sighs in an exaggerated manner. 'OK oh! I hope you know sometime soon so maybe I can know my grandchildren.'

They both laugh an unfinished laugh.

'Anyway, Mum, I just wanted to call before bed. I'll come and visit you as promised when I'm back.'

'Remember you can always talk to me about anything, do you hear me?' Even when Ibby's mum is being endearing there is ferocity to it.

The two women say their goodbyes and hang up.

Ibby's mother, Fọláké, sits upright in her bed staring at the phone. She can't help but worry about her daughter, because she knows there is something – there has always been something – that Ibby refuses to share with her. The distance between them as mother and daughter was easy to ignore over the years because such emotional distance was seen in parts of Nigerian culture as 'good parenting'. In actuality, Fọláké's distance from her daughter was born of guilt, and that guilt felt more pertinent in the past few months since her recurring dream of the woman by the lake had returned . . .

Fọláké was seven years old when she had first seen the woman. Her family had gone to their home in Èkìtì, as they did every year in October for the annual festival in their hometown.

'Fọláké, you are not in the city now. Go and stretch your legs and play with the town children.' These were the orders from her mother, Ibby's grandmother.

'I don't want to play. Can't I just sit by you and watch you prepare the leaves for the soup?' Fọláké pleaded.

'No. Trust me. There will be a time when you won't be given the option and you must stay in the kitchen. The time is not now. Relish it.'

So, Fọláké shuffled reluctantly out of the house and into the woods, only to soon find herself by the lake where celebrations would take place the next day. There were a few people dotted about, but Fọláké's eye caught a woman wearing a white cloth wrapped around herself, sitting by the edge of the lake.

Fọláké took in the woman's beauty – from her glowing brown skin that looked as if it were crafted from the finest polished wood, to her intricate braids with cowrie beads entwined in them that made her look like a queen. Fọláké couldn't quite describe what was so fascinating and mesmerising about this woman, nor understand why nobody else seemed to notice her. She walked over to the woman and sat by her side. The woman smiled.

'So you can see me.'

'Of course, ma. Can you see me?' Fọláké asked.

The woman laughed an easy, soft laugh that reminded Fọláké of trickling rainfall.

'Of course I can see you. But only special girls can see me. It means that today I can give you a gift.'

'Oooh, I like gifts!' Fọláké exclaimed.

'Well this kind of gift comes with a lot of responsibility, and it means that you might not get to share the fact that you have it with many people.' The woman looked directly into Fọláké's eyes as she spoke, the gentleness of her gaze reminding Fọláké of the lulling rhythm of the river's current.

'Hmm, that doesn't sound very fun. What is the point of a gift if you can't show it off and let other people know that you have it?'

'Sometimes having a gift mostly means that you are a gift to other people, and you can help them – but only if they don't know about it.'

'I see . . . Well, thank you, ma, but I don't think I want this gift. It sounds like the homework I get in school from Aunty Bilikis, and I don't like homework.' Fọláké had made up her mind, but felt worried she may have offended the beautiful woman.

But the woman just smiled as she said, 'That is fine. You should know, though, that there will come a time when this gift won't be offered to you anymore. It will simply be given to another girl close to you.'

'That's fine. Some of my friends and cousins like homework, so I'm sure they'll enjoy it.'

The woman smiled again in a way that Fọláké couldn't quite decipher, and as she continued to take in the mysterious woman's beauty, she heard a loud splash on the other side of the lake. Fọláké looked over to see what had caused the splash, and saw a couple of boys playing. By the time Fọláké turned back, the mysterious woman had gone.

Fọláké had thought nothing of this strange encounter as she grew up, went to university, met Ibby's father and then decided to move to England. Then, the night before she discovered she was pregnant with Ibby, she dreamt of the mysterious woman by the lake. She hadn't quite known what to make of it. When Fọláké realised she had missed her period the next day, the words of the woman came back to her so vividly that she could even smell the scent of the lake where they had met.

This is why she had chosen the name Ìbùkún, because to have a child of her own in a country as dreary as Britain was a blessing – and because she had suddenly known, with a powerful instinct, that it would be her *daughter* who would be bestowed with this mysterious gift.

As Ibby grew up, Fọláké was unable to tell what exactly the gift might be, and she worried that it may have all been in her head, and that the woman by the lake was some kind of weird waking dream. Ibby was a chatty, effervescent child until about the age of twelve, when she witnessed a local schoolboy's death and everything changed. Fọláké was unable to describe it, but she'd felt her daughter begin to pull away from everything and everyone after that. Not so much that she was considered a recluse or 'weird' – she was still personable, and her aloneness went almost unnoticed.

Ibby's father saw no issue in his daughter's behaviour, and said that if anything was wrong it would've simply been the residual trauma from witnessing the schoolboy's tragedy. Fọláké could feel that it was something more than that, but she could never bring herself to ask Ibby for fear of sounding crazy, but mostly for the fear of the great guilt she would unlock in herself for passing on whatever this strange gift was to her own daughter rather than experiencing it for herself.

For years, Fọláké continued to watch her daughter excel at everything she set her mind to, and become famous beyond imagination. Yet for someone known by so many people, Ibby still held on tightly to that solitude.

When the woman by the lake started to appear to Fọláké

again, she worried that her daughter might be in some danger, but by paying attention in the dreams, she saw the mysterious woman's gentle and regal smile as reassurance that her daughter was safe. Despite this, Fọláké was certain that Ibby needed something from her, even if she wasn't sure what it was. Ibby hadn't been to her grandmother's town in Èkìtì, and had never visited the lake. Yet if Fọláké's suspicions were correct and Ibby had in fact inherited the gift she'd turned down, then her daughter would surely need someone to talk to about it all. Most especially, about how spirits moved around Yorùbáland. Fọláké considered that in the eventuality that Ibby was, in fact, gifted in this way, getting her to the lake might serve some good, since that is where it had all begun for Fọláké. Even if Fọláké didn't know what the gift could be, or all that much about the deities in Yorùbá tradition at all, she still believed that she could guide her daughter to her answers in one way or another. The torment persisted because she couldn't be sure of any of it, and she felt helpless because of it.

Now, after her call with Ibby, Fọláké puts her phone aside and lies down in her bed, turning her head to look out of the window at the eerily quiet London streets. She decides that she will go to Nigeria again at some point to visit her parents' hometown. She hasn't visited it since Ibby was born, but something about her recent dreams makes her consider that maybe the woman's presence is also a call for *her* to return to the lake, with Ibby, to gain more of an understanding this time.

She softly wades into sleep as she thinks of her plans, and yet again the woman appears in her dreams. This time, accompanied with the smile, is a faint nod of affirmation.

★ ★ ★

Ibby paces around her bedroom but then eventually surrenders to merely sitting at the end of her king-sized bed, staring at her immaculate surroundings. Every so often, she feels suddenly pulled under by a wave of loneliness forged by the constant need to keep everyone at bay. She has lied to her mother many times over the years, and although each lie may have been different, the reason has always remained the same.

There are no suitcases out, because Ibby isn't really travelling. A tingle runs along her right arm, and she smiles wanly. She has timed everything correctly. This weekend is, in fact, a Blue weekend.

At twelve years old, Ibby was happy. She would often be the one laughing the loudest in her group of friends. High school was amazing, and everything her favourite TV shows had led her to think it would be. Ibby was one of those students who seemed to do really well at everything. Every teacher had nothing but great feedback about her work and her personality, and for some reason she managed to sidestep ever being seen as a teacher's pet because she was also comfortably friendly with the other girls in her year.

That all changed one Thursday evening after netball practice, when Ibby took a shortcut home through a crooked alleyway behind the library. Ibby would take this little route often, even though her mum always warned her about *awon gbomo-gbomo,* who could kidnap her at any time. Ibby always found this hilarious but knew her mum took it seriously, so she would do her best to feign obedience. As she made her way through the crooked alleyway that day listening to R&B jams on her Walkman, she noticed a figure huddled on the ground resting against a concrete fence. As she moved tentatively closer, she saw that it was a young boy, probably a similar age to herself, and he was bleeding. Seeing the blood made her look around again, only to see the drops had trailed along the dimly lit alleyway, she just hadn't noticed them. Ibby had no clue what she could do to help as she knelt by the young boy and held him. Her ability to form words escaped her.

The boy's eyes were wide and brown, but as he struggled to take in breaths, Ibby saw sparks of blue flash across them. His hands were pressed on his abdomen, so Ibby pulled off her school blazer and pressed it on the area to stop the bleeding. As she did so, she was shocked to discover an immense tingling that overtook her entire body. She could feel and see blue sparks along her hands and arms, tracing where her veins would've been. She looked at the young boy, and even his immense pain could not disguise the shock he, too, must have felt at seeing what was happening. As Ibby shouted for help, the two children were awestruck by the swirls of light that began to emanate from Ibby's mouth, dancing in waves towards the blue flecks in the young boy's eyes.

'What is happening?' Ibby whispered.

It seemed to take all the strength the young boy could muster to answer, 'I don't know what you are doing, but it's making the pain go away. I feel like sleeping . . .'

Ibby didn't know what to do. Time seemed to have stretched itself out so thinly that it felt like forever before a passerby finally heard her shouting and called an ambulance. The police followed soon after.

Everything from that moment felt like a grey blur. The young boy didn't survive, and Ibby found out from the news coverage that his name was Jamal Onyi. Suddenly Ibby had aged by what felt like years because of that one late afternoon after netball practice. Eventually the police stopped contacting her for information, since she clearly didn't know anything more. She couldn't tell them about the blue specks and the swirling lights that took the boy's pain away.

Jamal's mother had asked to meet the person who stayed with her son during his ordeal, and so Ibby's parents had taken her to meet the woman. They all sat in the living room, which held firmly onto the memory of Jamal with framed pictures. But as Jamal's mum spoke about the pain of losing her son, Ibby was distracted by the blue flecks that danced around her eyes, just like they had around his.

Ibby could feel the tingles spreading across her arms again, and she was thankful that she had worn long sleeves this time. Her parents looked at her oddly when she would only respond with nods when spoken to. They couldn't know that Ibby's fear was that she would open her mouth to speak and they would see the swirls of light like Jamal had seen when this tingling sensation had taken over her before.

Ibby and her family were getting up to leave when Jamal's mother nervously asked, 'I know this is weird, but since you were the last person to hold my son, could I hug you?'

Ibby noticed Jamal's dad appear at the top of the stairs, having stayed out of the meeting. He looked on, waiting for the response. Ibby couldn't see his eyes from where she stood, but sensed that his pain had made him unable to join them in the living room. Ibby's parents shuffled uncomfortably, but before they could answer for her, Ibby nodded. As she hugged Jamal's mum, Ibby could still feel the soft warmth of the light in her mouth and the surge of blue currents around her body.

'I don't know what happened there but just being able to hug you has made this grief feel so . . . different . . . easier,' Jamal's mother told her. 'Thank you.'

Ibby felt the tingling subside and normality returned to her body, but overall, things continued to feel different. While it seemed like her friends were dealing with the usual occurrences of puberty, Ibby could sense that her experiences weren't in line with the normal growing-up changes everyone else was having. She gradually found herself laughing less, turning inward. Ibby knew instinctively that she couldn't afford to draw attention to herself until she figured out what was going on, and so she began to spend less time with her friends and more time at the library. She never went through the crooked alleyway again.

As much as she researched and consequently focused her studies on psychotherapy, Ibby found it near impossible to find out anything about the strange experiences that she'd had. The only way she had been able to understand this mysterious ability was through her dreams. The first night after absorbing Jamal's blue flecks, Ibby had a dream in which a beautiful woman adorned in cowries stood by a lake with her arms outstretched. Ibby saw how the woman's eyes shone brightly, and the lake behind her swished with blue flecks. As the woman parted her lips to speak, Ibby had seen the same white light that had swirled out of her own mouth come bursting out of the mysterious woman's mouth. Ibby had woken up from this first dream confused and afraid, wondering if this was all happening because she ignored her mother's warnings to stop falling asleep in church during the excruciatingly long services.

The mysterious woman appeared more frequently in Ibby's dreams as she grew older, showing her how to control the tingles and importantly, what to do with the blue flecks she absorbed. The woman pointed to the lake and demonstrated how Ibby should open her mouth; her hands were placed over her chest and she sang a melody which drew up the flecks from Ibby's body and allowed her to expel them into the water.

In other dreams the woman sat with Ibby by the lake and explained to her the duties of being what she called a Guardian of the Blue. Apparently this is what Ibby had been chosen to be – a guardian of the pain of others. The trade-off for absorbing others' pain was never explicitly mentioned in her dreams, but Ibby found that she never wanted for anything materially throughout college, university, and as she started out in her field as a psychotherapist. The scholarships, the private practice where she began her career, the clients she garnered thereafter, the book deals with international acclaim – literally everything found her with ease, as long as she collected the blue flecks whenever she saw them emanating from someone in pain.

The mysterious woman by the lake had shown her an image of the entire world one day in the reflection on the water's surface, explaining what could happen if too much pain over-took it. 'You see, my daughter, as bleak as the world may look to you now, it could be much, much worse. Your gift has been bestowed upon you so that you may guard the pain, so that it never becomes too much for the world. Myself and your river sisters will protect you as you do so. It is a lonely gift, but an important one.'

Ibby had not been told that she couldn't tell a soul about all of this, but once she had realised the magnitude of the task, she could not think of anyone she could trust enough with the information. She was certain that it would simply be too much for anyone else to bear.

★ ★ ★

Now, Ibby gets up from the end of the bed and walks over to the wall in front of her. There are three paintings hanging on it, and she moves the middle painting slightly to the right. As Ibby shifts the frame, what appears to have been a wall with beautiful wooden panelling starts to creak open, spilling blue light into Ibby's bedroom. Another room sits behind it, deliberately hidden away. As Ibby steps into the hidden room, the blue glow inside it is intense, but the whirring of the metal capsule in the middle of the space is comforting to her.

Ibby would travel so often that the blue she absorbed required release regularly. Eventually she began to recognise just how much pain she could hold for her clients, or even for random people she felt called to interact with in public. Releasing the blue required more and more time since she carried so much – that is why she had begun to schedule particular weekends into her diary where she would be unavailable to absolutely everybody, in order to release all the blue into the tank she'd had built as part of her home.

The architect had seemed rather alarmed to say the least at Ibby's requirements for a large metal receptacle tank that would be housed in a room hidden by a fake wall. Nonetheless, her specifications were met and now, as she climbs the small steps onto the mini platform at the opening of the tank, she places her hand on her chest and begins to sing the melody taught to her years ago in her dreams with the beautiful woman of the lake.

Ibby closes her eyes and sees the various memories coded into the blue flecks of pain that she has absorbed from so many strangers. Surprisingly though, today she sees her own memories too. Ibby sees the strained conversation at the bar with Daniel, noting his mention of love as she left the bar, yet choosing to pretend as if she hadn't heard it in her hurry to get back to the car. She sees the night she said goodbye to Amina, and how close she had been to a different type of bliss with her goddess of clay sculptures who refused to settle for anything less than Ibby's rawest form. She sees Jamal, for the first time in years, and she sees herself curled up on the sofa in her living room, tears streaming down her face as she considers her loneliness. The various images meld and dance with one another as she sings and the blue flecks surge out of her and into the water tank in front of her where thousands of other blue flecks already reside.

Then the tingling subsides for now, and Ibby stops singing. She looks into the tank at the brilliant blue light that the culmination of blue flecks exudes and wonders how she would ever be able to share this with anybody. She had considered many times that it might be possible to simply keep the room hidden and still have a partner and family, but as quickly as the fantasy would come is how quickly it would go. Ibby wasn't just a brilliant psychotherapist because of her gift of being able to literally absorb the pain, fear and loneliness held by her clients; she also understood that the basis of any true connection is vulnerability. What would be the point in being with someone who couldn't truly know all of her? She'd never know how they would handle the truth of her being until her moment of telling them, and at that point it would be too late to back out if they were the wrong person to tell.

Ibby steps off the platform and climbs back down the little steps. She slides out of the hidden room, and as she shifts the middle painting to the left and the wall begins to close, the blue pulsating light fades.

She climbs into her bed and looks at the time. 9.48 p.m. She picks up her phone and texts Daniel.

Ibby: Flight is about to take off, practise those poses for when I get back!

Ibby sighs regretfully as she hits send, exhausted from purging the blue flecks and from all the lies. She falls into a deep sleep almost instantly.

The beautiful woman by the lake is there in her dream, smiling at her as always. As Ibby walks closer to her, she notices that there is somebody else sat to the side of the woman. A little girl. One who seems shy and a bit guilty for some reason. The woman holds onto the little girl's hand.

The girl reminds Ibby so much of her mother, Fọláké, that she has to pause for a moment.

The woman reaches out for Ibby's hand, holding onto them both now. Then the mysterious woman by the lake turns to the little girl who looks so much like Fọláké and begins to speak.

'For too long you have both sought counsel with me in dreams. The time has come for you, Ìbùkúnolúwa, to understand the expanse of your gift. What you have achieved thus far is only the beginning. For the journey that lies ahead, you require the spiritual fortification administered by the elders, and by this lake we stand next to.'

Looking at Ibby and the little girl that she now knows is her mother in turn, the beautiful woman smiles and finally settles her gentle eyes upon the child version of Fọláké. She quietly instructs, 'Bring our daughter home.'

The School Run

Alicia leant against the gates with her hands snugly tucked away in her pockets. There was a nagging bite to the autumnal wind that blustered around her as she waited for the bell to signal the end of the school day. She didn't know where the sigh escaped from, because she was usually so good at keeping everything in. Looking around the school playground as the other parents and nannies milled around waiting and chatting, she somehow felt separate to it all.

Alicia had chosen her nice coat, the coat that James, her husband, said made her look rather sophisticated. In fact, what he had said was that the coat made her look 'like she had a job'. That had stung. Alicia felt the sting of the words piercing through the memory, and she took her hand out of her silk-lined pocket and softly stroked her other arm. She felt the carefully brushed wool kiss her fingers delicately and then sway back into its original formation.

It was while she was comforted here, in this space of quiet self-soothing, that she heard it. The laugh. Alicia's whole body felt like an electrical current was charging up to run riot through her nervous system. She deliberately put her hand back in her plush pocket, jutted her elbow out slightly, and waited.

And then it happened.

As she heard the laugh near, Alicia straightened up from her leaning posture against the wall of the school gate and made as if to turn, then – BAM! They made contact, Alicia's meticulously manicured hands flying out of her pockets and stabilising her fall against his chest.

Him.

'I am so sorry! This is, like, the second time I've barged into you. I promise you I usually have better spatial awareness,' he said. A deep voice but one infused with playful cheeriness.

Alicia caught the smile forming on the corners of her mouth before it betrayed her, as she noticed that she was still in a weird embrace with the man. Her hands remained placed on his sculpted chest and his strong arms still held on to her elbows to steady her.

'No, heavens no. It was me. I really should look where I'm going.'

They both laughed as they awkwardly let go of each other, and Alicia noticed the dancing glint in his eyes. Nothing overtly flirtatious, but . . . something. A recognition, maybe?

'Seeing as this is the second time this has happened, we probably should exchange names. I'm Hart. Emilia's dad.'

Alicia had expected an interaction, she had planned for it, but somehow she hadn't bargained for a name exchange. Her voice crept out of her throat, her shyness betraying her in a way that her earlier smile had not.

'I'm Alicia. I'm, um, I'm Jet's mum.'

They shook hands.

More contact.

Alicia directed all her efforts in that moment to preventing the outward expression of absorbing what felt like an electric current coursing through her veins. Hart's kind, dimpled smile never left his face. Alicia took this fleeting moment to drink him in: from his jaw that looked carved out of marble, with a strength to it that reminded her of oak; his taut neck leading to diligently trained shoulders, and that chest she had touched only moments ago. Hart was a little bit taller than she was. Alicia had never been attracted to men who were very tall anyway. She had never understood the allure or the purpose of their height for her day-to-day life.

The bell sounded and all the children came pouring out of the school doors. Alicia looked into Hart's eyes again, searching. But he looked past her, spotting Emilia, and then turned back quickly.

'They're here! Let the chaos ensue! Anyway, see you around, Alicia. Hopefully without the collisions.'

Alicia smiled at Hart, then waved to Jet as she saw her son bouncing towards her. *Speak for yourself*, she thought. But out loud, 'Ha! See you later,' was all Alicia could muster. Her body felt charged and her heart was racing.

She needed to get home.

'How was your day?' Alicia asked Jet as the two of them walked to the car.

'It was like any other day in an institution you've sent me to so that I could soak up their version of knowledge. We presented our science projects, and I showed my interpretation of the possibilities of time travel. Everybody enjoyed it.'

Jet scared her in the best way. He was only eight years old but seemed so much older somehow. From when he could talk, he rarely seemed to be learning things, rather, it seemed like he was merely remembering. Alicia thought back to the mummy-and-toddler groups she would go to, and how separate she felt even then. The other mums would be talking about fun cartoons and cute songs their children were learning. Alicia hadn't quite known how to explain that her son preferred to snuggle up to her and watch documentaries on astronomy and anything which addressed space and time. She knew the response would be one of two things that were typical in those mum groups:

1. They would believe her and resent her for showing off how 'advanced' her child was, eventually ostracising her from the group.

2. They wouldn't believe her, and they'd think her delusional, eventually ostracising her from the group.

It was challenging enough even willing herself to go to the meet-ups back then, knowing that the white mums had an annoying habit of seeming to talk to the other mums like they were not quite yet mothers. Some of the mums who got fed up with being spoken to like they were children eventually started their own groups, only to be met with accusations of being divisive.

At this point, Alicia had realised that even those breakaway groups weren't really her vibe, and that she'd rather go on solo adventures with her beautifully scary son as he remembered things instead of learning them.

'How was your day, Mummy?'

Alicia was driving them home as she considered her son's question. Jet was like that – gently considerate and thoughtful.

'My day was good, actually. My morning meditation was lovely, and then I went for run by the lake. Came home and did some laundry. Eventually I headed up to the attic to work on some more designs. Maybe a different version of this coat?

Then I prepped for dinner and came to get you.'

'I'm happy that you had a good day, Mummy.' Jet smiled. His matter-of-fact kindness was something that always caught Alicia off-guard, yet made her so incredibly proud.

Jet busied himself on his handheld games console for the rest of the car journey, which gave Alicia time to replay in her mind what had just happened at the school gates.

The first time it happened, Alicia had thought that she was probably going mad.

About six weeks ago, Alicia had been waiting for Jet in the exact same place at the school gates as today. She was lost in her thoughts about the possibility of setting up a website for her clothing designs when she'd heard a laugh that she hadn't heard before. She'd thought nothing of it because, while she wasn't necessarily *consumed* by the thought of showing her creations to the world, she was certainly being nibbled at by the incremental persistence of her ambitions.

As Alicia had attempted to straighten up from her leaning position and pull her phone out from where it was perched in her pocket to check the time, her elbow had jutted out so that Hart had walked into it as he greeted one of the other dads.

When they'd made contact, suddenly Alicia couldn't move. It had felt like her heart had slowed. The connection made by Hart's torso to her elbow sent painfully sweet surges of energy throughout her body. If it had stopped there, she could've probably chalked it up to a weird sensation caused by the tinctures she sometimes added to her morning teas.

It was the *visions* his touch sparked that had enthralled her.

The electric charge hurtling through her body had felt like

it soared through her spine and into the back of her eyes – and then she'd seen it. Quick flashes of a life. A life that looked like this one, but different somehow. She saw Hart in the vision before she had even seen the face of the person who bumped into her. They were holding hands and laughing, walking by the sea with the chill of the wind enveloping them and two children racing ahead gleefully. There was a house in the distance that she knew, even in this seconds-long vision, belonged to them. Alicia saw the four of them around the dining table, not quite seeing the children's faces but noting their joy as their father danced around serving dinner.

Then Alicia had felt the strong caress from Hart as he'd held her body close while on top of her as they lay on their bed. Music was playing and it sounded like Sade, singing about never leaving someone's side . . .

'I'm so sorry!' Hart's sensual, deep voice had brought Alicia back to the moment, and the air returning to her lungs. She'd looked up to see who was speaking to her, only to see that face. A face she had just seen without ever having laid eyes on it before.

'It's OK,' she'd croaked.

And then he was off, casually jogging towards his daughter who was racing towards him.

That evening, Alicia had asked Jet if there was anything new happening in school, hoping to find out if a student had joined recently, and get more of an insight into who the man was that she had seen a whole life with.

'The issue, Mummy, is that there can't be anything new really, because the school system works to a particular set of rules. But I guess if you're talking about the mundane stuff, then yes – we have a newly extended range of non-dairy milk and a new girl just started in my class. Emilia. Her family moved over from San Francisco with the expansion of some technological device made by the company her dad works for.'

That explained why Alicia had never seen the man at the school gates before, but it hadn't explained her vision.

Later that night, once Jet was tucked into bed and James had retreated to his office to do even more work, a habit that ensured minimal interaction between the two of them, Alicia went up to her studio and finally opened the box James had given her. Jet's mention that a technological device was the reason the mysterious man had now appeared in her world made Alicia newly curious. She amused herself as she considered that if nothing else, by exploring what was in this box in her studio, she would at least be able to have knowledge of some new technology by the time she saw the man next and might be able to casually drop it into the conversation.

On her birthday, Alicia had been disappointed that despite her clear request for a pattern cutting and sewing mini-bot – the Fashunn BBGRL333 to be precise – James had instead gifted her a VR headset called the Story Story 2.0, which she had no desire to ever use. He was so excited about the headset, but it felt like an empty gesture to Alicia since he was heading up its rollout across the country. It would've been nice to be gifted something that wasn't to do with his work. From what Alicia remembered as James had droned on about the gift, the headset allowed you to isolate a memory and experience it again.

She wasn't sure if it would work since it wasn't technically a memory, but she'd wanted to understand more about the vision she'd had when she made contact with the man earlier that day.

With the Story Story 2.0 settled over her head and covering her eyes, Alicia had rested back on the velvet chaise lounge in her studio.

A blue screen lit up in front of her eyes.

> Recent memory.

> Further back.

> Story.

Alicia selected 'Recent memory'.

Alicia felt a pang of guilt as she looked on in awe at how the headset had already laid out freeze-frames of all her memories so she could scroll through time stamps from different points in her day. James was actually right – the headset really was amazing.

Still getting to grips with the device yet appreciating how intuitive the system felt, Alicia had tentatively tried to locate the time of the school run – and there it was. The memory of the collision at the school gates, and then the flash of that strange montage of additional memory that she'd experienced with this unknown man. Alicia scrolled back, slowing the memory down so that she could view the walk by the sea, then scrolling past the dancing at the dinner table until finally she got to the bedroom . . .

As she watched, the man planted feather-light kisses on her neck. He traced her skin with the very tip of his tongue and worked his way across her jawline until he found her lips. With a thumb he stroked Alicia's lower lip while running his tongue across it at the same time. His eyes stared into hers, and that was perhaps the inspiration for her own hands to travel into her deep green satin pyjama shorts and further down her own body as she watched the images in the headset.

He wanted to please her – it was clear in the way he paused in between his deep, searching kisses to smile at her. Alicia watched herself get turned over onto her stomach by the man, in a firm yet careful manner. As he used one hand to raise her bottom up slightly, he used the other hand to turn her face to the side, moving his lips closer to her ear as he whispered, *'Don't move darling, stay just like this. I want you to feel everything.'*

And she did.

The short image of him caressing her as he entered her, and his moans, which told her how much he wanted to be so deeply in her in every way, were enough to make Alicia climax in a way she hadn't ever experienced. It was an orgasm so powerful she couldn't find a pitch in her throat capable of conveying it, so there was no sound – and she was glad for that, because she wouldn't have known how to explain herself if the rest of the house had heard her. Alicia surrendered to the pulsating sensation between her thighs, accompanied by an exquisite wetness and a peace that, despite having experienced it through the vision, she knew was only truly felt when body and soul meet.

Alicia had taken her time to gather herself, and eventually removed the headset. Immediately, she'd made her way to her desk and begun to draw. Summer had very much still been lingering in the air back then, but when her fingers gripped the pencil they had danced passionately across the paper, drawing a coat. She was sure that it must've all been a weird fantasy of sorts, but even if Alicia couldn't bring those feelings into her current life, she knew she could have the coat that she had seen herself wearing as she'd walked on the beach, hand in hand with that mysterious and sensual man.

The next day, after dropping Jet off at the school gates, Alicia set off to the haberdasher to buy material. She spent the next few weeks cutting patterns and stitching then unstitching, until the coat was finished and perfect.

When she'd tried the coat on and gone to show James, telling him she wanted to make more of the same design to sell, he'd perked up and said it looked great – but also made the comment about looking like she had a job.

She had learnt over the years to take James's absent-minded comments as just that. She didn't perceive him as mean because meanness required energy, and he was too emotionally lazy to be mean. The more Alicia read about the metaphysical aspects of life in order to have things to discuss with Jet, she also realised that some people were just on a different frequency. No matter how much you endeavoured to communicate with them, they could never truly tune into what was being expressed.

Prior to that first collision with the man at the school gates, Alicia had never really dwelled on the lack of passion in her relationship with James, because they were comfortable and they made a fairly decent team. After successfully completing art school, Alicia had been invited to work as a trainee pattern cutter at an esteemed tailor. It was there that she had met James, who had come in looking for an off-the-rack suit for an upcoming interview for his first job since graduating from university. They had both instantly fallen into a beautiful, easy rhythm that led to Alicia advising James to buy their cheapest suit (which was still objectively a bit expensive) and to bring it over to her flat she shared with her friends, so she could alter it privately for him to fit.

That evening, James had come over to Alicia's with a bottle of wine, and they'd talked for hours as her two flatmates came in and out of the living room, giggling at their cuteness.

Alicia enjoyed getting to know this serious man who clearly had high ambitions and the drive to get there. He talked about his interest in computer sciences and technology as she pinned and unpinned the suit on him, laughing at the moments when he'd stood in his boxers as she adjusted the inseam of his trousers.

Once the alterations were complete and James was headed towards the door, he had jokingly promised that if he got the job, he would take that as a good omen that they should date. Alicia laughed at his decisiveness about a potential relationship with her, being that he hadn't even enquired as to whether *she* would be on board with it. James was that type of decision maker.

The next evening James had called to check if she was home and whether he could come by. Alicia said yes, and within half an hour he had arrived with food from the Chinese takeaway and a bouquet of beautiful sunflowers.

'I got the job, so we should probably start dating now,' James smirked.

And so they had.

Alicia's creative flair and hard-working nature meant that any home they made together – whether it was their first flat in Camden or their current beautiful detached house in Surrey – was always gorgeously designed. James was known in the tech world as a bit of a marketing genius. He had a knack for making people want technology in their homes through carefully planned rollout events that were streamed all around the world. The public seemed to lap up his finely tuned act of self-deprecation. Initially it was genuine, but over the years it had turned into a well-timed performance. This quietly handsome man, who was tall and dark skinned with a slim frame, seemed to enamour so many people during these presentations, even if in the real world they'd usually cross the street if they saw someone like him walking in their direction. Whenever James would share his frustrations about this disparity in how he was perceived, Alicia deeply empathised with him because he was so far from intimidating.

On the day that Hart had finally introduced himself at the school gates, the car journey home seemed to drift by as Alicia considered the little snippets of a life that had flashed in front of her eyes when they made contact this time. As much as Alicia yearned to get home to the headset so that she could replay the new set of beautiful images that their bodily contact had allowed her to access, she still questioned how such an occurrence could even be real. Did she need to drink less of her herbal teas? She had so many questions, because if what was happening to her was in fact real, then why now? And why with him?

Alicia was grateful to pull into the drive of their home finally. As she unlocked the front door, Jet zoomed past her and up the stairs with a fleeting 'Hi, Dad!' thrust over his shoulder in the direction of the kitchen.

'Remember to wash your hands and face before you go and glue yourself to that computer screen!' Alicia called after her son, who had now disappeared somewhere upstairs with only the quick steps of his feet audible. 'I'll call up as soon as dinner is plated up!'

Jet's face popped around the bannister on the first floor. 'OK, Mum!'

Alicia did her best to contain her swirling thoughts until she had time alone to process them. She walked into the kitchen knowing that James would be in there, back from work at the usual time and no doubt with his head buried in his laptop as it always was until it was time for dinner.

Alicia had been right about James being back from work, but that's about as familiar as the scene was when she entered the kitchen. James was standing by the granite island in the middle of their kitchen with an unusually broad smile on his face, waiting for her.

'You're back! Great!' he said excitedly.

'What's up?'

Alicia was preoccupied with the annoyance prickling on her skin like goosebumps. She had hoped to go through the motions of their usual weekday dinner time and once the evening had wrapped up, she would head up to her attic studio and get acquainted with her Story Story 2.0 headset again. Instead, she was now considering how she would have to will herself to remain present as James talked her through something about his workday that he would eventually tell her was 'too complicated' for her to understand.

Again, Alicia was wrong.

'I got this for you.' James beamed as he pointed to a fairly large box by the dining table.

Alicia's irritation at things not being as they usually were had completely distracted her from noticing the big white box in the room.

The Fashunn BBGRL333.

'My birthday was six months ago,' was all Alicia could mutter in disbelief as she stared at the gift.

'This isn't a birthday present. I just thought you might like it.'

Alicia was still unsure what was happening, and she had more questions. He thought that she 'might' like the robot? That was strange given that she had told him explicitly that she wanted it before, and he had ignored her. Of course, now she was enjoying the Story Story 2.0 headset he'd given her instead. She was oddly amused despite herself that James hadn't initially got her what she wanted, but it turned out to be what she needed. The irony.

'I do like it. I liked it when I suggested it eight months ago, too,' she told him, trying to keep her voice light. 'Um . . . thank you. What inspired you to get it suddenly?'

That was when Alicia noticed something strangely happier about James. It was almost as if the gift was a ruse for him to talk about something else that he deemed far more exciting. He sat down on one of the bar stools by the island, but then the excitement within seemed to launch him out of the seat and over to the box containing the Fashunn BBGRL333, which he began to unpack as a way of busying himself.

'Well, this new guy joined the company to head up the User Interface Design team. I wasn't sure if I would take to him when I first heard about him, because the company he used to work for were hammering us in sales with one of their products, the Ally-chip. Anyway, they headhunted him for this position and he moved over with his family from San Francisco . . .'

Alicia's armpits suddenly felt warm and the saliva in her mouth felt like it had doubled. She gulped.

'Oh,' she uttered, trying to feign less interest in the story than she felt.

'It's nice to have another Black guy in the company to shoot the breeze with, you know? Both of us in great positions and that. We were talking a couple of weeks back at the company gym, just cracking jokes about keeping a good physique so the rest of the team take us seriously in our suits, and anyway, I mentioned that you're into designing stuff—'

'I'm a designer.'

'That's what I said.' James seemed incapable of picking up the distinction, but was undeterred from telling his story. 'Anyway, I showed him your Instagram page, with you posing in your various designs and stuff, and he starts talking about this Fashunn BBGRL333 bot that he consulted on. Apparently, the bot is meant to be amazing for integrating with your aesthetic tastes and running those trends in congruence with data analysed from the web to assist you in cutting and sewing designs . . .'

Wonderful, Alicia thought as he carried on. James was mansplaining a product she already knew about and had asked for in the run up to her birthday, only for it to be deemed worthy to him the moment another man he respected suggested it. But what had her head feeling like it was stuck in a beehive was the fact that James had said he had shown Hart her page. That would mean Hart knew who she was before their second collision today. Yet he gave nothing away in the moments she had spent trying to memorise as much of him as she could.

'I love it. Thank you.' She knew her next few words would be extremely risky, but Alicia found that she could not resist. 'And tell this guy that I said thank you, too, since he got you to see what I couldn't.'

If James was aware that Alicia was still feeling a little hurt that he had only considered the bot upon the suggestion of this new guy and not because she – his wife – had requested it, he didn't let on. Instead, James excitedly continued to chat about the man that Alicia was excited about in a different way.

'His name is Hart. Hart Nelson,' her husband was saying. 'He has a daughter in Jet's class, I think. I was thinking that since it is autumn we can't exactly have a barbecue, but maybe we could invite him and his family over for dinner some time?'

Alicia's mind began to race as she busied herself with setting out the plates for dinner. She had made spinach stew with rice and fried plantain. They might've moved out to Surrey, but Alicia very much kept the delicacies that she grew up eating with family and friends in South London firmly with her.

'So what do you say?' James had assembled the Fashunn BBGRL333 bot at incredible speed and was now introducing it to the home's wireless connections. He glanced over at Alicia, still waiting for an answer.

'Sure. Maybe give them a little while longer to settle into the area and then we should definitely have them round.' Alicia hoped that answer was enough to buy her time until she figured out what was going on. It unnerved her to think about making physical contact with Hart in her home and not knowing what the outcome would be or whether other people would notice her reaction. Alicia thought about the visions she had seen of their life together, and knew she also feared feeling guilty about the interacting with the man of her fantasies in her family home.

Dinner went by in a blur, although Alicia was very careful to respond to James or her son at the right moments with a nod or a thoughtful 'mmm' accompanied with a small smile when necessary. Finally the evening fell back into a rhythm Alicia recognised, and she was relieved when it was time for Jet to get washed, and then James hurried off into his office for a couple of hours before heading to bed.

Alicia sat at her own desk, peering at the bot that had been the object of her desires before she realised that there was more passion to feel beyond what she had known was possible. She set it aside, and instead reached for the Story Story 2.0 headset. When it was firmly in place over her head and Alicia was settled again on her favourite velvet seat, she scrolled to earlier on in the day, when visions had come hurtling into her consciousness as she touched Hart's chest.

In the visions today, Alicia saw a wedding by the beach. They seemed to have a thing for water in this alternate reality. Another vision seemed to show the birth of one of their children, as she panted in pain while sitting in a birthing pool. Hart sat behind her, holding on tightly to one of her hands and repeatedly telling her how proud he was of her. Even that pain felt like bliss.

The time stamp that Alicia lingered on, though, was the one she had been anticipating all evening. Hart and Alicia were in their candlelit bedroom, and she was standing with one leg perched on a seat similar to the one she was laying on right then. She had just come to the end of another incredible climax orchestrated by his sensual attention. Alicia looked down as Hart got up from his knees and hugged her tightly.

Alicia watched herself say, 'Do you wonder sometimes what would've happened if we'd never met?'

'Why do you ask that?' Hart guided her over to their bed.

As Alicia lay on her back, Hart rested his head on her belly.

'I just think to myself, like, wow, life is so perfect with you, and every day I'm grateful for you and our family. I just wonder if we would've always found each other, or whether we just lucked out and this is a happy coincidence. What if you hadn't been in the coffee shop I stopped at during my artist residency?'

Hart stayed quiet for some time, as if he was happy to be caressed by the rise and fall of her abdomen.

'I guess if there ever was a timeline where somehow we didn't meet on a random day at a coffee shop in San Francisco, then I hope you'd still be with someone who wants you to feel as loved as I do every day. If not, then I hope somehow your heart calls out to mine and we find each other.'

Alicia felt overwhelmed with Hart's answer, but persisted still. 'That would only be as easy if we were single though, right? Imagine that when we met, you already had all of what we have now but with somebody else?'

'Alicia . . . please get some sleep.'

They both laughed as Hart ran his hands lovingly on her thighs, and Alicia began to stroke his neck . . .

Battery Low!

Alicia hadn't thought to charge the headset despite the number of times she had used it to re-live those visions from their first encounter for her pleasure. She had surprised herself by how quickly she had taken to using the headset. The first couple of times she'd felt a bit guilty when she thought of James downstairs in his office or already in bed. Then she reasoned that it was no different to how he probably pleasured himself when she wasn't around. It was not like Hart was aware of all of these visions either . . . or was he? She hadn't really thought about it until now. For Alicia, the pleasure she derived from the visions was rooted in the sheer passion and devotion she saw in the alternate life with him. She wanted to hold on to that.

Once the headset was charging alongside her new bot, Alicia headed back downstairs to shower with even more questions in her mind than when she had encountered these visions the first time. The warm shower powerfully massaged her skin with jets of water. All Alicia could think about was the possibility that the visions she had seen weren't just some weird fantasy that she harboured for this handsome American stranger. She was beginning to believe that these flashes could be a real alternate timeline where they had both chosen differently – chosen each other. She had absorbed enough of these theories from the documentaries she watched with Jet. Although they had stressed the impossibility of such a phenomena, Alicia couldn't help but think that there had to be truth in such a theory.

But why now? It's not as if she could have this random man come to dinner at her family home and begin to tell him over her West-African-meets-Jamaican fusion food that she saw visions of the two of them being together in another dimension.

Alicia refused to let herself believe that there was any merit in thinking too deeply about the visions, since their small collisions had more than likely only sparked these visual snippets in her mind's eye and not Hart's. He didn't seem to have acted any differently from the first time they bumped into each other to the second time.

It was as if the water droplets from the shower touching her skin offered new perspectives, though, because for a moment, Alicia let herself consider that Hart *might have* felt the sensation too but just hid it well. After all, it wasn't as if she had made it particularly obvious herself.

No. No. What would that even mean for my life now?

Alicia turned the shower off, along with any thoughts that Hart could be feeling and seeing the things she had.

While drying herself off, Alicia looked in the mirror and took a moment to see herself – something she usually avoided doing on most days. There she was, naked and glistening. Soft brown skin all over, with a slight darkened line above her pelvis where Jet had been brought into the world. Alicia gently ran her fingers over the scar and thought to herself: *in this lifetime I have Jet, and so I would always choose this lifetime even for this love alone.* Not being able to have the life she had seen flashes of was one thing, but maybe there was something in this life that wasn't so far from what she had there – her love of design. Alicia now had the coat she had seen herself wear as she and her alternate timeline family walked by the seaside. She'd been able to draw it from memory. And now with the help of her new bot, she could replicate the designs and modify them much more easily to start selling them. Somehow, that would have to do.

She smiled to herself as she moisturised her body and slipped into her golden silk nightdress. Alicia took her time to savour the warmth that she felt all over her skin knowing that at least somewhere in time, a version of herself was loved beyond anything she could've ever imagined. This thought lingered with her as she got to the end of her bedtime ritual by braiding her hair into medium-sized plaits and wrapping everything up in a bronze-coloured silk headscarf.

Alicia walked into the bedroom to find James already asleep and gently snoring. Comfortable. She had just plugged her phone in to charge for the night when it pinged. Alicia turned her phone over to see her lit-up screen.

Hart Nelson has requested to follow you

Almost as a knee-jerk reaction, Alicia looked over her shoulder to confirm that James was still sleeping, even though his snoring would've confirmed this anyway.

With her heart pounding in her chest, Alicia accepted the request. Before she could begin to scroll through the pictures of Hart's sunny life prior to moving over to Britain on his page, the screen flashed with a message notification.

New message from Hart Nelson

Alicia let out a soft exhale as she realised suddenly that she had been holding her breath. She opened the message not quite knowing what to expect, and irritated by the way her stomach felt like it wouldn't stop flipping over from excitement. *Keep calm. James showed him your page, it could literally be about anything.*

Hart: Hi Alicia

Alicia: Hi Hart

Hart: Fancy bumping into you here.

Alicia: James mentioned that he'd shown you my page. Thanks for the bot suggestion, it is perfect.

Hart: Ah! Glad you like it. I thought you would. But that's not quite what I meant . . .

Alicia stared at her phone screen, convinced that her heart would surely leap out of her mouth if what she thought was happening was truly happening. As she grasped for words, pretty much all of them eluded her. All Alicia could manage was a whisper to herself as she lay next to her husband in this reality, while talking to someone who was clearly her husband in another.

'Oh my . . .'

UteruStar

Because, you see, without you there can't be an us. It is the greatest thing you could do for the greatest race. Consider the request, understand the command.

'Aaliyah, you need to check your page!'

Aaliyah's phone rang at 2.48 a.m., waking her up. That was all she could think about – that she had been woken up at *2.48 a.m.* by a phone call. It was her best friend, Beth.

'Hang on,' Aaliyah said groggily into the handset as she trudged from her previous dream state into reality. Her phone light blinded her as she logged into her UteruStar account. 'What am I meant to be looking at?'

Beth was getting impatient. 'You're meant to be looking at the comments for your most recent video. Look at them!'

It took a moment for Aaliyah to realise what had happened during last the few hours she was asleep. The UteruStar moderator had commented on her video:

UteruStar: Congratulations! You are our new UteruStar of the Month UK!

Aaliyah squealed with excitement and in disbelief. 'Oh my God. I can't believe this!'

'You'd better believe it. This is going to be life-changing!'

Even though their screams were tempered due to the fact that it was the early hours of the morning and they both lived with their parents, the girls still could not contain their sheer glee. When their whisper-screaming had subsided, the two young women stared at the comment on Aaliyah's UteruStar page in awestruck silence in their respective bedrooms.

Eventually, Beth spoke again, teasing her best friend, 'Bet you're proper grinning with all of your teeth right now.'

They both laughed.

'Me? I'm happy, not *mad*, Beth. Teeth grins are creepy. Looking like a clown.'

Aaliyah and Beth had been friends since primary school, back when people could still meet and touch each other. So many things had changed in the world since, but one thing remained the same and that was the way Aaliyah was still creeped out by a book their teacher had read to them at story time. It featured a clown with a big toothy smile, known as 'the happiest clown in the saddest town'. It was a random book and an odd story in the way that some children's stories were, and it had been an inside joke for the best friends ever since.

'What are you going to tell your parents?' Beth asked.

Aaliyah took a moment to ponder the question. 'I guess I'll say to them, "See? It paid off that I didn't go to university!"'

The two best friends giggled. They had both spent hours rehearsing together the speech they gave their parents about why it didn't make sense to spend so much money trying to go to university. These days, so many more things were valued as equal to a degree – and one of those things was being a UteruStar of the Month.

Technology had advanced greatly in the years that the young women were growing up. A decade earlier, when they were eight years old, a chip that would come to be known as the

Ally-chip was created, and used as a means to share the burden of oppression when implanted into people's brains. But when the chip was unable to fulfil the task of ending racism, governments decided that it could instead be better utilised to collect as much information about each individual as possible. For this reason, the chip was renamed as the HomeostaChip. The location of where the HomeostaChips were implanted in the brain was revised slightly, so that it wasn't just picking up emotional responses from an individual, but also noting every cellular change in the body.

Although the chip installation was mandatory, to avoid what governments deemed would be unnecessary pushback it was initially presented to the masses as a great way to target diseases and diagnose them before it was too late. This led to more people having HomeostaChips installed. However, the majority could not afford treatment for the illnesses and diseases the HomeostaChip diagnosed, so the rich remained very healthy and lived longer, while poorer people continued to die. But at least they were aware of what exactly killed them. Silver linings.

Governments used the data they had access to for the formulation of incentives, which initially made underserved communities believe that they could work their way out of a cycle of poverty. One year, Wilma Hench – a prime minister who stepped in after her predecessor was exposed for possessing of an extensive collection of explicit videos involving cows – insinuated that the poorer areas of the country were only that way because the residents didn't work hard enough. She insisted that physical and mental activity needed to be visible twenty hours a day as part of a pilot scheme titled: Do Better. The rewards for 'doing better' varied from a 0.3 per cent increase on residents' annual universal basic income to an extra piece of fruit in the governmental monthly food stipend. The most exciting reward that people vied for was an extra hour of heating, since this was controlled by the local authorities on behalf of the government.

After three months of constant physical and mental activity for twenty hours a day from 92 per cent of the residents across these more deprived boroughs, nothing changed economically but many people became mentally unwell due to sleep deprivation. Crime also rose in those areas, and a 19 per cent increase in deaths were also recorded.

Wilma Hench was forced to resign after protests erupted at the egregious nature of the Do Better pilot scheme. Three months later, she was announced as the head of prisons for the country and her predecessor with a penchant for cows returned to his position as prime minister amid mumbles across the country that, 'I'd rather him who's not quite right than her who hasn't got a clue.'

It was schemes such as Wilma Hench's Do Better that made the public become more sceptical about the ways in which their biomedical data was being used against them. Something that was purported to create an equitable society only brought about more socio-economic disparity. It seemed that no matter how much technology moved ahead in leaps and bounds, the humans in charge of the technology were unable to evolve at the same pace. 'Old injustices, new technologies' is what the phenomenon was called by an amazing campaigner known as Huda, who spoke on behalf of a mega-activist organisation Edge of Here.

The scepticism about the use of personal data with no

obvious reward was all the more reason why UteruStar took the world by storm. The app seemingly popped up overnight, and the premise was simple. If health inequity was to truly be addressed, then the app creators argued that everyday people deserved monetary incentives for staying healthy, which would in turn help them to work their way out of poverty.

UteruStar quickly became beloved by its thousands of users. It collected extensive data from the users' HomeostaChips to work out what they were physically capable of, based on what the algorithm charted as pre-existing conditions. The app would award the user points for their efforts to stay healthy in relation to this information – specifically, in relation to their reproductive health. Then each month, alongside lesser monetary rewards, the individual with the healthiest UteruStar data was awarded the top prize of becoming UteruStar of the Month. Anybody could use the UteruStar app, as long as they possessed a uterus. The UteruStar creators refused to be dragged into asinine debates fronted by who they deemed 'malevolent authors and celebrities'. Instead, they focused on the basic fact that people with uteruses faced systemic and institutional hardships due to a patriarchal society, so had an incentive to download it.

UteruStar functioned as an app to be linked with an individual's HomeostaChip. The app would then monitor the health of the individual's uterus based on blood flow, oxygen levels and hormonal patterns. Nutritional information as well as physical activity could also be input manually, which was crosschecked with barcodes on food packaging and geolocations combined with elevated heart rates that one could be expected to have during exercise. Many publications across the media landscape seemed to agree that this was the fairest use of the chip that they had seen since its emergence in the past decade. Even expected detractors were surprisingly supportive. This might or might not have had anything to do with how well UteruStar was doing financially.

UteruStar's social media interface was where the allure to participate firmly resided. This was a section of the app with a public leaderboard showing the health points being accumulated by each individual user. Those with the most health points over a thirty-day period had a chance to become the UteruStar of the Month and win an all-expenses trip to paradise. With so many people living hand to mouth, there had been some grumbles about how unfair it was that only people with a uterus could win such luxurious prizes. In answer to this, it had been announced by the company that they were working on TestiCool – an app that allowed people with testicles to also win great incentives. The release date had not been specified, but it quelled the grumbles.

To participate on the existing app, an aspiring UteruStar of the Month (or USM, as they were affectionately known) would post the food they were eating, as well as their wellness activities. The longer the streak of physical activity and good nutrition, the higher the points that an aspiring USM could accumulate. Every person with a uterus who was enthralled with the social media craze did their very best to become a USM.

Each month, when a new winner was chosen, Aaliyah and Beth would excitedly watch the videos the USMs posted as they arrived on the dreamy island with white sandy beaches to enjoy their time in paradise.

For the sake of fairness, UteruStar would then deactivate the USM's page so other aspiring USMs didn't try to copy the winner's exact pattern of success. The USMs then moved onto a very cool level of UteruStar that was only visible to the most exclusive people. That is what Aaliyah wanted for herself – a life where she could do exactly what she wanted and be rewarded for it. To her, UteruStar didn't feel like a chore because she loved being active and enjoyed most of the foods that scored the highest points on the app.

Beth was very proud of her best friend's high scores on UteruStar because she was well aware it wasn't a system that the average person could easily rig, so work had to be put in consistently by the aspiring USM to gain their points. While she enjoyed using the app and keeping up with what others were doing on it, Beth preferred to immerse herself in software coding. All the more reason why her parents had been somewhat shocked by her decision to not attend university.

Beth was so clearly talented when it came to digital technology. Beth's parents would often joke about how she could seek an apprenticeship with Tòmíwá Fọlọ́runshọ́, who had created the brain chip that had eventually evolved into the Homeosta-Chip when she was just a teenager. Dr Tòmíwá Fọlọ́runshọ́, as she was now known, had graduated from Harvard and initially worked with William Bunker on ways to alter the use of the Ally-chip, but then suddenly parted ways with the mysterious billionaire's company with the world being none the wiser about what caused the rift. It *was* clearly a rift, though, because Tòmíwá had given a press conference simply stating that she no longer wanted to be affiliated in any way with the chip and the manner in which it was being altered. It was all very vague, but news pundits concluded that an ironclad non-disclosure agreement was probably the reason for such a statement from

Tọ̀míwá. That was five years ago. Since then, the twenty-nine year old had become president of technological innovations at Edge of Here.

'Check your inbox, they would've sent you a message about what to do next,' Beth prompted Aaliyah now.

The gold and red envelope icon on the UteruStar app pulsated softly to indicate she had an unread message. Aaliyah tapped on it eagerly.

'Hello, Aaliyah,' she read out loud to her friend, grinning. 'We are so proud of you! Congratulations on becoming UteruStar of the Month! We know how much dedication it takes to earn the top points and we want to celebrate this. Our team would love to whisk you away to an exclusive island where you can meet the other international UteruStars and be inducted into the next level of our programme. Our flights and onboarding have a quick turnaround, so please do confirm that you will be ready to go on an adventure with us in the next twenty-four hours and we will do the rest!'

Aaliyah still couldn't quite believe what was happening. She had put so much effort into getting such high points on Uter-uStar but she hadn't considered the reality of actually winning, and what she would do with herself once she had completed that task. There were thousands of aspiring USMs in the country, so the chances of Aaliyah winning were all the more incredible.

'Say yes!' Beth said excitedly.

'I want to, but I definitely need to tell my parents first. I just know they're going to have something to say about me going alone to wherever this paradise place is.'

'So you won't go if they say no?'

'Ha! Now I didn't say that . . .'

The two friends laughed at their own mischievousness.

After a few more low squeals of excitement, Aaliyah and Beth ended their call. Aaliyah crept into her parents' room to tell them the news.

'Aaliyah, it is almost 5 a.m., why couldn't this wait?' Aaliyah's mum croaked.

'Your mum is right, love. The open-door family policy still stands, but surely that could be after 8 a.m.,' her dad chimed in.

Among the many things Aaliyah loved about her parents, she really enjoyed their united front – but depending on the situation, like now, she could also very much dislike it. She would often hear them around the house talking and laughing like the best of friends, because ultimately that is what they were. It seemed that they had come to an agreement well before she was born that they would prioritise their friendship above all else, and somehow that worked for their marriage. In the same way that they made space for each other to be their individual selves, they also raised Aaliyah to ask questions and to have her own say in the decisions that pertained to her life.

That is why when Aaliyah had announced that she wasn't going to university – not even on the basis of the many sports scholarships she had the potential of acquiring – her parents knew that they had to respect her wishes, even though they would've rather she chose differently.

'It's important!' she told them through the crack in the door to their darkened room. 'I'm the UteruStar of the Month! Out of everyone in the country, they chose me! They've sent a message about my prize. I get to go to this amazing island and learn about the next stage of the programme. This could be big for me!'

Both parents sat up in unison. Aaliyah's mum was aware of the UteruStar app and had it downloaded herself, but didn't put much effort into it because despite being a fit and active woman she could never seem to accrue many points. She would enter her activities and nutritional intake whenever it crossed her mind to do so, but otherwise she didn't think about the app too much.

'Wow, love, that is huge. Congratulations! You and Beth will have a great time, I'm sure. When do you go?' Aaliyah's dad beamed as he spoke.

'Beth doesn't get to come. It is just me. It's a super-exclusive programme, only the actual UteruStars of the Month get the trip to the island and induction to the next level.'

Her parents furrowed their brows in synchronicity. Although Aaliyah was eighteen and seen in the eyes of the law as an adult, to her parents she was still a young woman who needed protecting.

'I know it sounds weird,' she continued quickly, 'but you've seen how big the whole UteruStar movement is. A lot of the things they reward the UteruStars of the Month with have to be top secret and super exclusive, but c'mon it's a massive company. What could possibly happen to me? I'd also only be gone for about a week! You'd know exactly who to contact if there were ever to be an issue.'

Aaliyah knew she had made a convincing argument from the way her parents deeply sighed and looked at each other. Yet again their daughter was about to get her own way. She beamed. 'That looks like a yes! OK, I am going to reply to them now.'

Aaliyah rushed out of her parents' room gleefully as they tried to salvage what was left of their sleep.

Aaliyah: Hey guys! I am so excited to have been chosen.
I would love to take up the opportunity to go to the island
please!

Within a couple of minutes, Aaliyah received a message back
from the UteruStar moderators.

UteruStar: Hello, Aaliyah. This is great! We are looking
forward to having you join us. In fact, as a stroke of luck
there is a flight leaving tonight for Star Island. Would you
like to join?

Aaliyah's mouth was agape. She could not believe how quickly
everything was moving for her suddenly. She considered what
her life currently entailed. It had been totally consumed by
UteruStar so she had no real plans outside of it. This felt right.
She replied without thinking.

Aaliyah: Yes I can join tonight's flight.

UteruStar: Perfect. You will shortly receive an email from us
with the agreements you are required to sign. After that, you will
receive an email with your holiday details!

Aaliyah couldn't help but to squeal with delight once again.
This was really happening!

The hours after her messages with UteruStar flew by in a
haze. Aaliyah rushed to pack as concerned questions from her
parents, like, 'Will you be the youngest person there?' or 'Why
can't you have a chaperone or friend come along – lord knows
I need a holiday!' floated around her. Beth dedicated her entire
day to speaking with her friend via video call as Aaliyah buzzed
around getting ready. The two friends looked through Aaliyah's

wardrobe and picked bits for her to take, even though she had been instructed not to bring many clothes.

Later on that evening, a red and gold hued computerised shuttle pulled up outside Aaliyah's home to take her to the airport. Aaliyah excitedly took a picture of the shuttle to send to Beth so her best friend could be part of the experience in some way. She settled comfortably inside as her parents waved her goodbye and insisted that she send plenty of pictures and call daily during her week-long trip. Aaliyah could see her parents were nervous for her, but she was giddy from the fairy tale type wonder of her UteruStar of the Month experience so far, and she hadn't even gotten to Star Island yet. As the shuttle pulled away, the screen lit up and a voice began to talk to Aaliyah. *'Congratulations, Aaliyah, on becoming our new UteruStar of the Month. We are delighted to be able to welcome you to the luxury you deserve for the hard work you have put in on our app. Please relax and help yourself to the snacks and drinks available to you.'*

Aaliyah looked around the shuttle and actually began to take it all in. It had a slick, matte-black interior that was cool to the touch. The shuttle was spacious; the compartments had red lights and glass doors in which she could see her favourite snacks and drinks carefully curated and ready for her enjoyment.

'This is unreal,' she whispered to herself.

Without further prompting, Aaliyah chose a chocolate bar and soda, then settled snugly into her seat to scroll the shuttle monitor for something to watch. She didn't get very far with scrolling through the choice of TV shows before she found herself feeling rather sleepy and her surroundings blending in and out whenever her eyes managed to drag themselves open. She roughly made out a motorway, then what seemed to be a forest, a big black tunnel . . . there was lots of darkness and loud metal clanging . . .

Then nothing.

Aaliyah woke to find herself in a bed.

The room she was in was spacious and well designed. Her suitcase had been placed to the side of a wardrobe, which had red and gold tracksuits hanging up inside it from what she could see through its glass doors. There was a desk on the other side of the room with a red metallic computer sitting atop it. As she looked around the room, a large television screen appeared in what Aaliyah had assumed to be a big mirror.

'Hey, Aaliyah, glad you're awake and, from reading your vitals provided by the docs, you're feeling great! Welcome to the UteruStar incubation facility. Here you will learn how to be greater than you ever imagined. We already see the dedication you possess, as well as a ready and willing body, which you'll put to good use as part of a global movement to restore greatness among us all.'

Aaliyah was only half listening to what the man on the screen was saying, because she was still processing how she ended up at whatever facility this was and what all of it meant. She realised that she recognised the guy as the disgraced rapper Rico Miller (known by his stage name of Million-R) who went off the grid after a slew of exposés revealed him to have close ties with white supremacist groups.

It was all over social media and the news channels for a long time. Some speculated that he might no longer be alive, while other conspiracists thought he had simply disappeared to a remote island with other rap legends who were reported dead.

Many Black women activists had been calling Million-R's rhet-oric dangerous long before his disappearance, having started to see a pattern in the earlier part of his musical career. Fans across the globe often shouted this down, claiming that these Black women were 'bitter' and 'trying to bring a Black man down'. When news reports came out that the rapper had attempted to attain political power by donating millions to a couple of white supremacist groups so that they would publicly endorse him, Rico embarked on a press tour.

'How do you expect us to have power as Black people if we don't take it from white people first?' he'd argued. 'The thing is, if you try to take it in an aggressive way, you might get killed. I am *buying* the power for us.'

Again, activists and academics who had seen such patterns throughout history pointed out that Black representation in spaces of white violence was redundant. The fans were having none of these arguments though, and insisted that they saw the logic in Million-R's reasoning even though the rapper had provided no previous help within the Black community to back up his argument. What *had* been noted, however, was his many attempts to skew and undermine the long history of Black oppression. One example that went viral involved Rico visiting a plantation and picking the cotton plants for twenty-five min-utes to prove that 'slavery couldn't have been that bad'.

Again, his fans, who called themselves the 'Millionaires', set about berating any critical commentators who they found damaging to their favourite artist. When Rico's disappearance was announced, the most prominent voices who had spoken out about his various scandals were forced to go into hiding because the Millionaires found their addresses, vandalised their homes and sent endless threats as they grieved the disappearance of their lauded 'genius'.

Yet here he was now, on screen and smiling at Aaliyah with a mouthful of expensive metal tooth caps shaped as different currencies, an aesthetic that had always formed part of his notoriety.

'It can take a while to get your bearings,' Rico was saying, 'so to help you get acquainted with what is going to be the greatest achievement of your life, just watch the video that is going to appear right here on your screen now.'

Rico's face disappeared, and what looked like a promotional video replaced him.

'*Welcome. If you are watching this, then you are at the UteruStar incubation facility. You have been chosen from many candidates to help further the only power that has ever provided centuries of stability to human civilisation. You have proven yourself to be dedicated to your health and to the growth of UteruStar as a movement to save the world from demise.*'

The sinking feeling that Aaliyah had been struggling to make sense of anchored her to the bed as she sat upright and watched, her eyes wide. Her heart began to race faster, yet she was suddenly also aware that this change in her body was being monitored, so Aaliyah silently willed herself to remain calm as she scanned the room for some kind of exit. Despite her desire to escape, her eyes felt tugged back to the cartoon drawings of white people now moving across the screen holding hands and multiplying all around an animation of the Earth.

The voiceover continued to cheerfully narrate a manifesto that sent chills creeping up Aaliyah's spine.

'*Thanks to the incredible vision of William Bunker, Plant8Con has spearheaded innovation within the biotech industry for decades. The Ally-chip showed the world the endless ways that white people have sacrificed themselves in order to help humanity. Unfortunately, this has left the white race at a deficit. From risking our lives to traverse the entire world in order to bring civilisation to all, to orchestrating centuries of systems that allowed our global economy to thrive. This has all come at a cost of white lives. If we are to have any chance of saving the world that we know, then we must utilise the most promising uteruses to bring about a resurgence of the white race, and thus maintain white power.'*

Aaliyah could not believe what she was watching. She looked away to scan her eyes over her own body, then pinched herself to ensure that she wasn't in a terrible nightmare.

Despite her horror, the video continued:

'Millions have been spent to build this state-of-the-art facility, and the USMs who have come before you have done brilliantly to help Plant8Con bring about a world we can all truly be proud of. The agreement you signed stipulates that you give Plant8Con authority to use your body and its likeness to further the agenda of UteruStar as a product of Plant8Con. These wonderful warriors that you will help us incubate and birth will then go on to live in another one of our facilities so they can be raised to be the truly deserving inhabitants of this Earth.'

Aaliyah's mind raced. Yes, she had signed the agreement . . . but everything had happened so quickly and she hadn't thought too much of the terms she was signing up to at the time, which could've only been a few hours ago but now felt like days. She stared at the screen as the faces of thousands of UteruStars now flashed across it, a few that she recognised and many that she didn't.

'The way our UteruStar algorithm is designed means that although it may appear that you are the only UteruStar of the Month in your

country, a number of fellow USMs are selected at any given time. You mainly compete with those in your geolocation radius, but that doesn't make this any less exclusive. You are all the best of the best, and have shown sheer determination to support the movement to save the white race . . .'

'This isn't what I signed up for!' Aaliyah said aloud, her voice quaking. No answer. The chilling video now popped up with pictures of previous USMs sporting strained smiles, tired eyes – and pregnant tummies.

'The next level of your UteruStar journey is exclusive for a reason. Be here with us and allow your uterus to host the greatness of our future. Because, you see, without you there can't be an us. It is the greatest thing you could do for the greatest race. Consider the request, understand the command.'

A beat later, Rico's face appeared again on the screen.

'So . . . Aaliyah, right? Now that you're up to date on what this is, it is time for you to meet the rest of the new intake and start your assignments. You might be feeling all feisty, as girls like you tend to be, but understand that it is an *honour* to be here. You're part of this now, and there is no going back. Your parents will be concerned at first, but we've been doing this for a while. After a couple of initial video messages explaining that you're going to be gone a little longer than they thought, they don't notice when things move solely to written messages and maybe a voice message from our AI that sounds like you.' He chuckled. 'You will tell them how much you're loving it here, how much you're learning. Some of the USMs have been here for two years! Blame the parents, they clearly let the internet raise their children.'

Aaliyah felt rage shoot through her body and out of her mouth. She had been rather indifferent to the discourse around

Rico in previous years, considering him to be more of a star during her parents' time. To think that he was somehow part of the reason she was in this facility made her blood boil.

'And who are you meant to be, exactly?' she spat at the screen. 'Why are you acting like this is even normal? Can you see that you're not even white, you idiot? What could you possibly be getting out of this?'

Rico smiled in a cold way that wasn't related to the 'ice' on the caps covering his teeth.

'Your reaction is exactly why I am a part of this cause. We can't continue to have angry women like you out there in the world. We need order. We've always needed it. I recognised that, which is why I was able to become so successful in a white world. I learnt their rules and played by them. Being the face of this movement shows how unity is possible. This way there is a steady control on who has the power, and they don't plan on leaving me behind after everything I've done for the cause. Of course, you can't be where I am but you can do your part. *This,*' he said, gesturing at her room through the screen, 'is you doing your part. We aren't expecting this to run forever. We get a specific number of babies raised in an undisclosed location and the future of white power is guaranteed.' He scoffed. 'Thinking anyone would want to be around your attitude indefinitely is the real joke. Your genes won't have anything to do with the baby thankfully. A perfectly white baby. We just need your uterus to accommodate it to term.'

Aaliyah didn't ever consider herself to hate anybody. That wasn't how her parents had raised her. But Aaliyah decided that she hated Rico.

'What if I don't want to?'

'Like old girl said in the video – *consider the request, understand the command.*'

Now Aaliyah understood that she had no choice. She had signed the documents and wherever she was, she doubted that her parents would be able to locate her. Tears began to pour from her eyes as she fought back the pain of not seeing her family for a long time – if she'd ever see them again.

'Of course you'd want to cry, but it isn't all bad,' Rico said, then shrugged. 'Anyway, my part here is done. That door will open and you'll begin the adventure to the best achievement of your life.'

Aaliyah heard a beep and then the door slid back and a wall of noise rushed in. She jumped up, noticing she was still dressed in the clothes that she had left home in. That brought her a small comfort. Aaliyah stepped out cautiously into the hall, and it seemed that she was in a massive hangar. There were about twenty other USMs wandering out of rooms looking as bewildered as she surely did.

An animation of a blonde-haired woman with a broad smile appeared on more screens overhead.

'Welcome USMs!' she said perkily. 'In the last couple of hours you will have taken in a lot of information. Don't worry, there is still time for you to process everything. This next stage of your programme will take a few weeks before you're ready to be Ultimate UteruStars and be implanted with greatness. This is true diversity at work, because it doesn't matter about your race, religion, sexuality or how you identify gender-wise – as long as you have a uterus that can carry a perfect white baby then you are a star to us. You'll have assignments leading up to this which will let us know that you're up to the task. To begin, there are phone handsets over to the side of this space, each labelled with your names. Please collect your phone.'

The USMs located a wall with docks that had phones plugged into them, and each lit up with their names. Aaliyah found the one assigned to her. She wondered to herself what had happened to her own phone. Her family would be worried that they hadn't heard from her by now, but she wasn't sure how many hours had passed since she left . . . The voice of the animation intruded on her thoughts and brought her back into the large space.

'Around this time is when your family – if you have one – will be expecting you to land in paradise, and that is what we are going to create. Shortly, the floor in this space will fill with sand, and the walls around you will project an image of a beach. Simply stand on the marker points on the floor, and when given the cue you will post a video to your UteruStar page saying, "I can't believe I'm here. I am in paradise." Big smiles all around please. And remember – there will be consequences for non-compliance.'

Aaliyah looked at the faces of the other USMs, and most seemed just as distraught as she felt. A couple of others, amazingly, seemed somewhat excited. Aaliyah made note to steer clear of them and tried to think quickly. From what she could remember, the video in paradise was usually the last thing seen on a USM's page before it was taken offline. She needed to ensure that somehow her video let Beth know that she wasn't OK.

Aaliyah saw the marker point where her name shone on the ground and stood in position.

What would make Beth suspicious? If Beth could figure out that things weren't right, then with her amazing mind for technology, she might just be able to find a way to help her. Aaliyah knew it wasn't worth trying to communicate with her parents because they didn't really know how UteruStar worked. Her only hope was her best friend. From what she could gather, she wasn't extremely far from home but she also knew that she wasn't above ground. From the little that she remembered as she fell in and out of consciousness on the journey, the shuttle had taken her through a tunnel, and then she had felt the sensation of veering downwards as if on a rollercoaster . . .

Once all the USMs were on their marks, pipes protruded from the sides of the room and began to cover their feet with sand. Above them, yellow lights shone and the walls began to emit projections of blue skies and water. Aaliyah couldn't believe how real it all looked.

'Remember everyone! Big smiles!'

That's exactly it. Big smiles. Here goes.

Beth watched the video of her best friend over and over. Something wasn't right. It had been a day since they'd last communicated, and Aaliyah had only sent a picture of the shuttle that had picked her up before her phone had gone offline. Beth had assumed that it was because of the flight. Since then Aaliyah's phone was still offline, yet she had somehow posted this video of herself on a beach, just like the other USMs before her . . . It didn't feel right, but Beth couldn't quite make out why.

Then she watched again.

It was the smile.

Aaliyah never smiled showing her teeth. Ever. *The happiest clown in the saddest town* – the moment Beth made the connection, a panic set in. Something was definitely wrong, and she knew that however she was going to go about helping her best friend, she would need to think quickly.

Beth stared at the picture of the shuttle she had received from Aaliyah, trying to take in anything that might be of use. The monitor at the front of the shuttle had the Plant8Con logo on it, and a small barcode that she could just about make out. The barcode acted as the vehicle registration number, which all vehicles were required to have. Beth looked it up on the national vehicle registration database, but she could only find basic information. The shuttle was one of many registered to Plant8Con.

An image of a car zooming down the street next to the shuttle prompted Beth into another line of investigation.

Cameras. There would be street cameras.

It didn't take long for Beth to hack into the street camera system. Starting with those around Aaliyah's street at the time her friend had sent the picture, Beth began to track the movement of the shuttle through the streets and roads as it progressed to its destination. The shuttle appeared to have driven for approximately two and a half hours on the motorway, before veering off onto a slip road and into vast woodland where there were no cameras – and seemingly no more roads.

'Aaliyah is still here, somewhere,' Beth whispered to herself.

Once she'd gathered enough information to confirm that she wouldn't just be worrying Aaliyah's parents needlessly, she called and urgently told them what she had found. Together, they alerted the authorities, but they were told that currently all that had been provided was speculation and that there was no real proof that Aaliyah was in danger. They seemed more curious as to how Beth had managed to log into the city's camera network to locate the shuttle that took her friend away.

They're not going to help us, Beth thought. She had to do something herself.

Aaliyah couldn't tell how much time had passed, but she knew she had slept and woken up four times. There was no natural light in the facility and no clocks, so her sense of time had become skewed. Walking around her cell, as she now preferred to view the space she resided in, she was confronted intermittently with updates on the screen, showing her predicted ovulation days and other biomedical vitals.

Every time Aaliyah considered how much trust she had put into the app, she couldn't help being angry with herself. How could she have let herself fall for something so sinister? Instantly her mother's voice came to mind, soothing her and telling her that she wasn't to have known. Then her dad, confidently saying what she imagined would be something like, 'Well now that you're in this mess, how are you getting out?'

That question played on Aaliyah's mind constantly. How would she get out? Did Beth see her unspoken message?

Everything was so regimented within the facility, and the USMs weren't allowed to communicate with each other. Aaliyah knew she would definitely need some help escaping. Panic created a lump in her throat as she considered that her insemination time would soon arrive.

For the time being, the USMs spent a considerable amount of time doing various fitness exercises, then forced meditation as the mission statement of Plant8Con played on a loop: 'The advancement of the greatest race guarantees the advancement of all. To commit to this calling is the honour of a lifetime . . .'

Aaliyah did her best to block out the words, and instead focused on willing her best friend to find her before it was too late.

Beth knew that time was running out. Poring over every detail she could find online about Plant8Con, she now could see dozens of stories of missing USMs and wondered why it hadn't made it onto mainstream news.

The pattern Beth could see was that regardless of the ethnicity of the missing USMs, the one thing they seemed to have in common was families who were from lower socioeconomic backgrounds. Aaliyah didn't quite fit into this category though, so their algorithm must have glitched somehow when they chose her. It seemed to Beth that there was clearly a way that the UteruStar app was using the information from the HomeostaChip to determine who would be less likely to be listened to if their child went missing. She wasn't going to let that happen to her friend.

The blogs and independent news sites that showed any sort of interest in the disappearances seemed close to making the connections, but they never quite got there.

Plant8Con's statements remained the same for each case. 'We are disappointed to learn of the accusations of ill treatment of participants in our various programmes. We can confirm that they arrive to us safely and are treated with the utmost care. Some have progressed to stages in our programme requiring very high levels of secure knowledge. Others have chosen to leave and not inform us of their whereabouts. Plant8Con remains committed to spearheading innovation.'

While trawling around for clues on how to help save Aaliyah, Beth came back across the press conference where Dr Tòmíwá

Fọlọrunshọ had announced she was parting ways with William Bunker. Suddenly it dawned on her that if anybody would know the shady ventures of Plant8Con, she would.

Beth went straight to her email, and desperately started to type.

To: TomiwaF@Edgeofhere.universe
From: BethBotKilla@KOworld.universe
Subject: HELP! I think Plant8Con has my friend

Hi Dr Tọmíwá,

I need your help. My friend Aaliyah got chosen as a USM on UteruStar, and I just know she is not OK. I have been scouring for more information and it seems that this isn't the first time someone has suspected that something isn't right with Plant8Con.

I know it is a long shot that you will even see this message, but I have attached files to show the ways that I tracked the shuttle that picked Aaliyah up, and the woodland that it seems to disappear into. They're not above ground, I know that for sure. I've asked her parents to find the serial number of her HomeostaChip because that might prove useful in finding her geolocation, although I suspect that this is the reason they are underground, so it is harder to pick up the signal.

Whatever is happening, I know our time is limited in being able to save my friend.

Please help. Please.

Beth.

Barely an hour passed before Beth received a response. She clicked on it urgently.

To: BethBotKilla@KOworld.universe
Cc: Huda@Edgeofhere.universe
From: TomiwaF@Edgeofhere.universe
Subject: RE: HELP! I think Plant8Con has my friend

Dear Beth,

I am so sorry to hear of your concerns regarding Aaliyah's safety. Having looked at the files you attached, I must say that your knowledge is extremely impressive.

You have every right to be concerned. Plant8Con is a very dangerous entity and we must move quickly if we are to get to the bottom of what has happened to your friend and many other UteruStars in this process.

I have a very worrying idea of what these developments with the UteruStar app could mean for Plant8Con's agenda. My team are gathering further data to track all the construction work that has been happening in the woodland area over the past few years, as well as getting people out there to begin investigating.

Please find my number below for yourself and Aaliyah's parents. Call me immediately when you receive this message.

We will find Aaliyah and put a stop to whatever it is William and Plant8Con are up to.

In solidarity,

Tòmíwá

Beth logged the details Tòmíwá had supplied and proceeded to call and patch Aaliyah's parents in too. She was determined to save Aaliyah.

Dr Tòmíwá answered immediately, and shared revelations about Plant8Con and UteruStar that made Beth's blood run cold. Aaliyah's parents chided themselves for not realising the amount of information that their daughter had been providing to the app, having assumed it to be harmless. Aaliyah was healthy and active and didn't have many friends outside of Beth. They were astounded by the sinister way the app had mined information through the HomeostaChip, based solely on the chip-logging activities and friend networks. What did they plan to do with it all?

At Beth's request, Aaliyah's mum had rifled through medical records and eventually located the HomeostaChip serial number assigned to her daughter. Within minutes of Aaliyah's mum providing the serial number, Tòmíwá had passed this information onto her team to see if they could track Aaliyah's location.

For the first few hours, no signal could be found. Then suddenly, a very faint signal popped up in the woodland where they had suspected Plant8Con's facilities to reside.

'That's her!' Beth exclaimed. 'It has to be!'

'There must be quite a few floors to the facility so whenever Aaliyah ventures to a floor closer to the surface for instance, we can pick something up,' Dr Tòmíwá said excitedly. 'My team have sourced construction permission for something that resembles a massive multilevel bunker in this region of woodland. There is a tunnel, but I have asked the team to hold off from approaching it in case the surveillance in that area sees us coming.'

She went on to explain that with the information they had, the best thing was to go public. That would force the authorities to react immediately. An operation such as Plant8Con's couldn't have persisted for so long without help from some corrupt officers who would conveniently write off the concerns of USM families as unsubstantiated, but there would be others, too, who would be more worried about saving face and avoiding a wider scandal.

An hour after their call, Beth and Aaliyah's parents watched as the exposé went live on Edge of Here's daily news platform to millions across the world.

Dr Tòmíwá looked soberly into the camera with Huda by her side. 'It is with rage and urgency that I address our comrades around the world to a disaster happening that we must all be aware of. UteruStar is not a safe app. We've suspected as much for some time, and now we have proof. Numerous people have gone missing since being allegedly whisked off to paradise. Based on the focus of the app, we have reason to believe that these people are held in order to make use of their uteruses in some way.

'We are urgently trying to locate the places these so-called UteruStars of the Month are being held. We have already found one site, currently showing on your screen, in this forest area. For legal reasons, there are certain names that cannot be mentioned as part of this broadcast, but you know who you are and what you've done. Just as we've located this bunker, we will bring down another, and another, until they are all found and these people are returned to their families.'

Beth watched Dr Tòmíwá in awe. She wanted to learn more from this woman and be part of something as great as Edge of Here.

Within twenty minutes video images circulated on all news channels as police special units located the tunnel that Beth had helped discover and made their descent into the facility. Live video footage showed bright searchlights shining and helicopters overhead. Beth's face was inches from her screen, desperately willing them to find Aaliyah, and that she'd be OK. The dread hadn't completely left her body, but tingling hope began to seep in as she watched.

'Hold on, bestie. Help is on the way.'

Aaliyah was woken up by the alarms and chaos. Something was happening and it wasn't good for the facility, clearly. Surprised to see her door open, she got up from her bed to look into the communal space. The staff, who had seemed so poised in the time that Aaliyah had found herself in captivity, were now running around erratically and pouring water over all electrical devices.

The blonde animation onscreen urged them on: 'All evidence must be destroyed!'

Aaliyah felt nauseous from the sudden wave of hope that she might escape this place. She looked around for the other USMs and saw a couple of them running towards exit signs, which were now illuminated due to an emergency procedure being activated. Three other USMs were beating up the member of staff who came round to do their daily intrusive physical checks.

Still trying to make sense of everything, Aaliyah's thoughts were distracted by Rico's voice blaring over the speakers.

'Guys, the police are surrounding this facility and my fucking door isn't opening for some reason! Let me out of here. I know you're not trying to make me the scapegoat in all of this. Open the fucking door! They're gonna think I came up with this shit. I was just tryna help y'all be great and this is how you do me? You clearly don't care about Black people! Wait, wait, the floodlights are turned towards my window, they can see me from out there! Guys! Fucking answer me! William Bunker, if you can hear this man, fuck you!'

Aaliyah felt immense joy at hearing Rico in distress. It fuelled her to move her feet and get to running towards the exit. Without warning, armed police began to enter and guide the USMs, who were easily identifiable by their red and gold tracksuits and nightgowns, out of the facility. Meanwhile the staff, who wore medical uniforms, were put straight into handcuffs.

'Come this way! Come with me!' a police officer wearing a visor instructed. Aaliyah followed with urgency. As she ran up the seemingly endless flights of stairs, she couldn't believe how far underground she had been. She found herself colliding with so many USMs who had been locked in other areas of the facility and were visibly pregnant. Some people jumped into the fleet of available shuttles to make their way up the dark tunnel that linked the UteruStar incubation facility with the outside world. Aaliyah ran instead. There were officers ahead with flashlights and LED strip lights on the sides of the tunnel, allowing her to find her way, and she just let her legs carry her as fast as they could. She couldn't bear to think of sitting in the shuttle that preceded the nightmare she had found herself in.

While the shuttles whizzed by back and forth on the track, with police shouting orders and USMs screaming from the panic of it all, Aaliyah continued to race determinedly towards her freedom.

The first thing she felt was the cool breeze of the night air.

Then there were bright floodlights with the glare that made her shield her eyes with a hand. Police and helicopters and firetrucks and reporters were everywhere.

Aaliyah gulped in the outside air gratefully as a medic came rushing towards her with immense concern.

Not quite knowing how it all happened, as Aaliyah allowed herself to be checked over and provided contact details for her parents, she knew that somehow Beth had something to do with freeing her from the clutches of UteruStar. Just the thought of this set the tears of gratitude and relief spilling from Aaliyah's eyes.

She was free.

The Other Man

Eve wondered why they'd opted for a pink hue inside the pod. That was where she was sat. Inside a big, white, plastic pod shaped like a massive egg.

It was perched alongside other pods in a large space that reminded Eve of a convention centre. People didn't really gather like that anymore.

She jumped slightly as the silhouetted avatar on the screen in front of her began to speak. 'Welcome to the Ancestry Experience, Eve. You can call me Mia. I am your guide this afternoon.'

Eve felt a nervous itch in her armpits despite all the Ancestry Experience had clearly done to make the process comfortable.

'Remember, Eve. You can talk to me at any time. I must make it clear that I am not human in the way that you are, however I believe with my breadth of knowledge I will be able to assist with any questions that you might have.'

Believe is such a funny word, Eve thought to herself. This thing wasn't human, yet it had beliefs.

'Will they know that I've watched?' Eve asked. 'Like, um, will they get my details or anything?' Her voice croaked out of her throat.

Mia's programmed gentle voice responded, 'No, they will not know you have watched. They have consented to their LifeSnap being watched by anybody with a DNA match above 10 per cent, as this usually signifies a tangible ancestral link. They will only know you have watched if, for instance, you express to us that you would like to make contact.'

Eve stroked the furry, baby blue cushion next to her on the seat while taking in the information.

'I detect that your heart rate has risen slightly, Eve. You have nothing to worry about. These videos have been readily shared by people who have taken the Plant8Con Ancestry Experience just like you. They've willingly provided a little snapshot of their life to hopefully help the process of meeting a stranger who is actually family a bit easier.'

'And these matches could be from anywhere in the world,' Eve mumbled to herself. So she knew that unless she made the special effort, she was highly unlikely to just bump into any of them in her everyday life. That was comforting and disappointing at the same time.

Eve's mother had passed away when she was a teenager and she didn't know much about her father other than that he moved back to Jamaica when she was eight years old. Taking part in this Ancestry Experience was a chance for Eve to see what other family she had out there in the world, but while she had chosen to do this, it still made her anxious. Being moved around in the care system for two years until she was considered grown enough to fend for herself had been sufficient chaos for a lifetime. Then again, therapy had shown Eve that she still found little ways to be immersed in chaos, even if she didn't immediately see it as such.

But this decision isn't really that chaotic, Eve promised herself. *If anything, this Ancestry Experience might bring me closer to a sense of peace.*

The pink hue in the interior of the pod had become comforting; there was something rather womb-like about the whole vibe. Eve couldn't be sure that if she had been given a choice of colours for the ambience in her pod, she would have chosen anything other than pink. It was sometimes liberating not to have a choice in certain matters.

She swiped across the screen in front of her while Mia's silhouetted avatar remained in the background.

Loading . . .

The screen shifted and Eve saw it start to populate with many empty squares, and only one square that showed a short video compilation available to watch.

'As you can see, there is currently only one person who has closely matched your DNA and who also has LifeSnaps available for you to watch,' Mia told Eve. 'Therefore, there are only these videos currently available to you. Should you have more matches who upload LifeSnaps, they will be available here and you will be welcome to return to watch them.' Mia was so informative, and it gave Eve a small sense of ease.

Eve touched the play button on the video compilation, and it began with the most recent short clip – a video recorded literally through somebody else's eyes. Participants who chose to film LifeSnaps were given computerised contact lenses to wear that would capture everything they saw. The footage was then remotely uploaded to a server and looked after by the Ancestry Experience, and processed into clips that their DNA matches would have access to.

Eve was trying to make out what she was looking at. A front door to a house with a driveway to the left where a car was parked, and Eve was proud of herself for recognising the make and model. Fourteen – that was the number shown by a brass plate on a forest-green door.

As the door was unlocked, the person recording the LifeSnap stepped inside the house and looked down as they did so. Cute shoes. Then they looked up again. The view now was of a narrow hallway and family photos in copper picture frames above the radiator on a terracotta-coloured wall and—

'Wait . . .'

'Are you OK, Eve? Would you like to stop watching?' Mia asked.

'No. Sorry, I'm just being weird. I thought I recognised someone in the photos. We can continue.'

The video began playing again. The person looked towards the sound of running footsteps on the stairs getting closer. A teenage boy came bounding down the stairs, followed closely by a much younger girl. 'Hi, Mum! Did you get everything?' the boy shouted excitedly.

'Mummy! I want give Daddy my own card. Not share a card with Taj.'

'Yes, Joy, you have your own card. Did you help your brother with the balloons like I told you to?'

These were the woman's children and it was her husband's birthday, Eve concluded. She continued to watch, noticing a tight smile creeping up on the side of her lips as her jaw clenched.

Must be nice.

'Your dad will be home in about half an hour, so let's get the balloons and presents out of the garage and I'll start setting out the bits from the caterer.'

Eve hugged the furry blue cushion closer as she watched this faceless woman and her family put decorations up, laughing and preparing everything for this lucky man. Then a swift look towards the window let Eve know that the person this family was waiting for had arrived. A car seemed to be pulling into the driveway.

There was a very brief running around in the room towards the light switch, and then the room went dark. Whispers could be heard as the family shuffled around preparing for the surprise.

'Hide by the kitchen counter,' Taj said in a sharp whisper.

'No! I wanna stay with Mummy and shout first to Daddy!'

'Shh, the both of you! Dad is about to open the door.'

Eve could now make out the door starting to open into the darkness, and light from the hallway crept into the living room. The silhouette of the man filled up the doorway as his arm reached into the room to feel along the wall, and then the room became reacquainted with light.

'Surprise! Happy birthday!'

Oh shit.

Those words were all Eve could hear over and over in her head as she watched the family embrace each other excitedly.

'Eve, I've paused the video. Is it bringing you some distress? I've noted an elevated heart rate and a dilation of your pupils. Can you talk to me about what you are feeling right now?'

Eve couldn't quite find the words to describe the prickles of emotions that were cascading through her body in that moment. How could she explain any of this without making the sting of embarrassment that had lodged itself suddenly and with certainty in her chest even worse?

POETRY NIGHT — FOUR MONTHS AGO

Eve had taken a chair with her on stage for her performance this time. She'd decided that she hated the way she swayed stiffly when reading her poems if she was standing up. Looking in the mirror in the days leading up to the poetry night, Eve had observed herself. Straight. That was the only word that came to mind. Athletic, yes. Ironically, her years of yoga and contemporary dance had somehow set her posture in such a way that the only word to describe it was 'straight'. She secretly envied the women she would see who seemed so much looser than she did, who seemed to flow effortlessly in their movements. In the videos people would share of her performances online, Eve had a way of ignoring the comments praising her eloquence and talent, but instead honed in on descriptions that highlighted her stiff sway. *Looking like a twig blowing in the wind*, she mocked herself. She had told her therapist she would stop speaking to herself in this way. Then again, therapists generally couldn't really want you to stop all your self-sabotaging behaviours because surely then they would be out of a job. Eve felt like this justification bought her some more time in her life for a bit more negative self-talk.

As she waited for her performance to begin, Eve was quietly grateful that she could not see the audience due to the spotlight facing the stage and the way that entertainment pods were constructed these days: clear plastic casings, varying in size depending on how many people they needed to accommodate. The pods at this performance night where Eve was reading her poetry could accommodate around six people in each from what she could see.

At the bottom of each entertainment pod were two big tubes, one tube bringing in sanitised air and the other taking out dispelled used air. The pods could be booked for family who lived together, for work colleagues, and for friends who'd had their bio-chips scanned as being free of any infections. As much as Eve felt like the pods had impeded on her dating life throughout the years, she did appreciate that random people couldn't now accidentally spill their drinks on her at a reading or a night out.

Eve's performance began, but the swaying didn't stop even though she was seated. Her mind had wandered as she started to speak, and she willed herself not to feel so self-conscious and to simply flow with the rhythm of her own making. With her legs slightly crossed, she started to read out carefully crafted line after line of her poetry, taking gentle pauses to allow the audience space for their audible admiration. Their claps and *oohs* and *mms* transmitted through the pod's speakers to Eve.

However, there was an added sensuality to the energy she felt on the stage on this particular night. The audiences were pretty much always receptive at her readings, but on this particular night the atmosphere felt charged for some reason. Eve found herself stroking her own knee as she read, realising that she was starting to feel turned on from sailing on the wave of words she had set in motion. For once, she wasn't too bothered about whether the audience noticed her movements or not.

Yet, as soon as her performance was over, the spell seemed to break for Eve, and the heart-warming applause left her face feeling hot from the thought of having allowed people an insight into her own longing. Her yearning. Her desires. *Could always say I was just taking artistic liberties,* she thought to herself, but there wasn't as much comfort in the thought as she had hoped.

Don't know if you are out there
I know you are
Stumbling searching seeking something

Can it be someone
Doubting if I exist
I do
In quieter moments listening to your heartbeat
And hearing me
I fear we are worlds apart
Hurtling through life
Waiting
For our worlds to collide.

Eve could tell that the audience had loved that poem in particular. Those who were looking for love could hold out hopefully, and those who were in love could hold on righteously.

After her reading, she stationed her individual pod by the bar, smiling coyly and modestly as people sent over videos and messages from their pods congratulating her for such a brilliant performance. They offered to buy her drinks as she sat alone by pinging over requests to add Eve to their drinks tab, but she declined. Those who she was able to spot in their pods would get a short shy wave and smile, but Eve was happy to nurse her one glass of gin and tonic courtesy of the venue and promoter until she felt ready to book her taxi home. Unwinding after a poetry set always felt necessary to her. The rest of night would be live music, and she allowed herself to enjoy the different artists as they took to the stage.

There had been a national uproar when people had been informed they would need to be situated in pods when in public for the foreseeable future. There were protests about how people would be able to socialise effectively, and promoters and club owners bemoaned how much it would affect the upkeep of their businesses. In order to keep the arts and people's social lives going, the government had artists like herself register onto a national scheme where they would be paid a monthly stipend, with all other utilities subsidised, in order to ensure there was always entertainment available to keep up the public morale. Eve was required to perform at least once a week to earn her payments, and this suited her fine as she loathed the idea of having to get a job that required her to be initiated into pods with work colleagues. This was one of the few things that Eve felt the government had got right in the recent years of biochemical chaos, which people generally felt uncomfortable thinking about nowadays.

Eve's pod screen lit up again as a musical act ended. A message.

@J-Roc: I'm sure you're tired of people sending messages to tell you how brilliant you are and I want to stand out by saying something different, but that would mean I'd have to say something like, 'oh you were terrible' and I wouldn't want to say that.

Eve clicked on the avatar picture that accompanied the message to see a man in a blue suit smiling gently at her – well, at the camera. He wore a white shirt underneath his suit jacket, which was unbuttoned at the collar. No tie. His dark beard seemed to glisten in the sunlight wherever the picture had been taken. His head was bald but not excessively shiny like some men who went with that look. Eve decided that he was sexy. It was rare that she would receive a message from such a cute guy at one of these performance nights. It was rather low key and not flashy at all. She mainly interacted with other artists or the club owners at her readings, but she could tell that this guy in a suit wasn't a regular at this type of place. Eve was unsure whether it was the G&T's effect or the curiosity she felt at having received a message from such an attractive guy in this venue of all places, but she felt braver than she usually would've. Eve placed her glass to the side and responded.

@EveNoApple: Yes, I don't think saying I was terrible would be very endearing, to be honest. I might be tempted to write a poem about you, and not a nice one.

@J-Roc: OK, feisty! I wasn't expecting that after such beautiful poems.

A flirtatious playfulness. It was definitely there. Eve could sense it.

@EveNoApple: Well, still waters run deep and all that.

Eve attempted to return the playfulness in her tone, too, but wondered if it would come off as brooding.

@J-Roc: I bet . . . I see you sat alone in your pod, would you like me to send over a video of myself? Just to show you I'm not some weirdo scammer?

@EveNoApple: Sure, send one over, but even scammers know how to use video functionalities in pods these days.

Video received from @J-Roc. Open?

Eve opened the video, which had clearly been recorded by the man only a few seconds before. He was dressed in a suit like the one in his avatar, shirt buttons undone like they had been that picture, but unlike his static avatar there was more mischief in his eyes in motion. He was smiling and talking.

'You're brilliant on stage. I'm sure you could just be there and say nothing and still be told that, but something about how you speak . . . It moved me.'

Oh wow. There was no mistaking that. Flirting. Eve searched around in her brain for why she was making such a big deal of this particular interaction, as if she wasn't familiar with men flirting with her. Of course she was, but not in this type of arty and flighty venue, and it had been a while since she had sensed such open interest in her. This felt intentional, not clumsy. There was a spark, there was . . .

A wedding ring.

As the man had reached towards the camera to stop his record-ing, the glint of the black metal band on his finger had caught her eye. Eve took the final sip of her drink before typing back.

> **@EveNoApple:** I appreciate the compliment, but I'd better be going.

She stood up and made to leave the suddenly awkward situation, which had saturated the air in her lonesome pod.

> **@J-Roc:** OK. Well it was nice to meet you and to have the honour of hearing your poetry. Only came in here by chance because a colleague is leaving and insisted this is what she wanted us all to do with her on her last day. My name is Jordan by the way.

The name suited him, but Eve was tired of being impressed by this clearly married man.

> **@EveNoApple:** Enjoy the rest of your evening with your colleagues, Jordan.

Eve managed a smile at her screen, as she wouldn't have known which direction to turn to send her smile otherwise. As she exited the club, the pod that she had been inside for most of the evening opened up so that she could step out. A few seconds of air and then Eve's personal pod was activated and encompassed her while she moved towards the street where her taxi was waiting.

When Eve returned to the bar to perform again a week later, Jordan was there. No suit this time. A white T-shirt is what Eve could see of his outfit as she looked out into the audience. He was sat in a pod by himself this time, no work colleagues. He had chosen to sit slightly off centre, which meant that Eve could see him without the glare of the lights off his pod's surface. Poised. Waiting. Eve tried not to be distracted by his ever-steady gaze as it rested upon her.

> What was that?
> That thing.
> The thing.
> That moved
> When you fell into my world
> Or
> Did I fall into yours?
> Sometimes
> Fate writes words
> Sometimes she mixes herself
> In with my tonic . . .

Eve didn't have her usual post-performance G&T this time. She headed straight towards the door, saying thank you and smiling with people who wanted to gush over her performance. Usually she liked to sit by herself at the bar in a solo club pod while reading their encouraging words and watching their reaction videos to her performances as she sipped her drink, but she felt too impassioned to do that this time. Their messages would show up in her pod space later on to read through anyway. For now, Eve was on Operation Avoid the Married Man. She wanted to be out of the bar as soon as possible to avoid any conversation with Jordan. Thinking back to their first conversation, Eve hated the way she still felt an electric surge in the meeting of her thighs even after she had noticed his wedding ring. *Best to leave well alone,* she told herself.

She felt a sense of victory as she stepped out of the bar having managed to avoid Jordan and how good he looked in that white T-shirt. However, the thought didn't last long, because just by the taxi rank she noticed a tall man in the same white T-shirt, looking over at her.

Jordan.

'You were great again tonight. No round-about compliments this time,' he called over to her from his personal pod.

He stood by the virtual valet sign, which meant he was probably waiting for his car to drive itself over from the car park. Clearly, Jordan had a bit of money, since the cars that most people had, like those of Eve's friends, required a human in them at all times to operate. It made it even funnier that a man like this would be at her performance night in such a dive bar. That work colleague's leaving do must've been fate.

'I appreciate it,' Eve responded as she walked towards him. The whole time her mind was attempting to formulate every possible outcome of this conversation, while her pod rotated around her from underneath, allowing her to move closer. She was aware that as straight in figure as she found herself to be, she was letting her hips sway more in her wedge heels and making the most of the movement that her red minidress allowed.

Eve liked this dress. She liked the way the red popped against her brown skin. It wasn't so short that she couldn't sit comfortably on the stage as she performed, but it was short enough to complement her long legs, which were further accentuated by her black leather wedges. She suddenly caught herself questioning whether she had worn this particular outfit in case she saw Jordan again at the bar. She hoped she hadn't. *What would that make me?*, she asked herself.

'I wanted to see you perform again,' he said. 'There was something you said about waiting for worlds to collide that spoke to me. Different poems tonight.'

The two stood side by side, as much as their pods would allow, looking out into the street. Eve loaded the taxi screen inside her pod to make as if she were about to book a cab, but she wasn't yet committing to pressing the buttons that would make that a reality.

'New poems this time, yes,' she replied. 'But I tend to just flow with whatever poem feels right for the moment, you know? I know you said you were here last week because of a colleague, but are you into performance nights generally or . . . ?'

Eve trailed off, hoping she could get some clarity as to what this pull was between them.

'Or,' Jordan responded without missing a beat or taking his eyes off Eve's.

There it was again – that surge, followed by a tingle deep inside her. Eve refused to let her shyness stop her from getting the clarity she wanted.

'Does your wife enjoy poetry?' she asked with an air of defiance, although all she heard was the clunky way the words made their appearance into the summer night air.

'No, actually. She isn't into much, outside of reality TV shows and her job.' A mischievous smile crept out at the side of Jordan's mouth, like he was waiting to see what Eve would do with this information, which felt like a dead end and, at the same time, an invitation. *An invitation for what?*

'Well, it was nice seeing you again. I'd better get going.' Instead of attempting to book a taxi on the app integrated into her pod, Eve waved down a taxi by setting her pod to an amber colour as one drove near. She wanted to get away from Jordan, and quickly. She needed to get home and into the shower, where she could more comfortably process why she didn't want Jordan's eyes off her.

As Eve made to get into the taxi that had pulled up, Jordan moved closer. The first change in position Eve has seen him make since spotting him outside.

'Look,' he said. 'I know this seems weird, and I'm not trying to be a dog or anything. It's awkward trying to find a way to talk to you about how random it is that I would come to this bar for a work do and see you perform a poem that was like you were speaking only to me. Life does feel like I was waiting for a collision. Like I was waiting for *this*. That sounds more fucked up when I say it out loud, but there you go.'

Eve could only muster a 'thank you', as all other words seemed to have failed her and the impatient taxi driver had already started the meter. Determined to fight whatever energy was building between the two of them, Eve waved goodbye to Jordan as her taxi door closed. Her pod fell away into a flat disc once Eve was sat in the taxi, since it was partitioned and only circulating sanitised air. Her phone pinged.

@J-Roc has expanded your communication parameters to Headsets and Devices

Eve caught Jordan's facial expression through the taxi window, wondering if she would hit 'accept' as the taxi sped off and away from the city's Art Quarter nightlife.

As Eve showered in her studio apartment after the performance that night, she finally had the space to consider what it meant for her to find this married man so terribly attractive. *Am I attracted to him, or am I attracted to him being attracted to me?* she asked herself. It was something her therapist had encouraged her to question whenever she felt those tell-tale butterflies at the very beginning of a relationship. 'Not that this is going to be a relationship,' she gargled out loud under the shower head.

She chose not to think any more deeply into the question swirling around in her mind. Instead, Eve thought about Jordan's eyes travelling across her body and she traced their imagined path with her fingers until they ventured further down, right to the site where she felt her excitement about him most. She took her time rubbing gently and rhythmically as she visualised Jordan's dark beard and soft-looking lips, lightly lingering on her navel and travelling downwards. Although physically standing in her shower, Eve let her spirit float on the orgasmic waves she was able to conjure for herself . . .

After drying off and getting ready for bed, Eve stared at her phone screen debating whether or not to accept Jordan's request to expand their communication. The online universe had become more regulated, and so telephone numbers weren't exchanged anymore because people didn't have them. Most people who chose to have social lives had avatars, and everything was done using these. The avatars were linked to bio-chips that most people had embedded in their wrist. This logged everything from biological data to employment and shopping lists, as well as dating profiles.

Permissions for communication and data would be granted by the individual based on whether it was, for example, a work colleague or shopping clerk that required interaction. Activists had protested for years about how corrupt such a system could become, but for the most part the majority of people seemed to have adapted to it, including Eve.

Although she very much wanted to head to bed, her brain still felt too preoccupied, and so instead she sat on her sofa, finding herself looking around her studio apartment. It was cute. Lots of pre-loved things were the summation of the place she called home; furniture acquired from car boot sales or friends getting rid of things they no longer needed. Eve liked knowing that her sofa, bed, table, lamp – all of these things – had a home before she came to own them. Something about the way they were already lived in freed her of the pressure of being their only home. Maybe that was part of the appeal of being with Jordan?

Sighing, Eve restlessly scrolled the dating app she had installed to see if anybody else caught her eye and . . . nothing. Flicking back and forth between the dating app, her social pod comments and the request waiting from Jordan was a dance of deliberation she didn't manage to keep up for too long.

Request accepted

From that moment on, it felt as though everything moved at a breakneck speed.

Jordan started sending Eve video messages throughout the day, and text messages at night. He would attend her performances and talk for ages afterwards with her, each of them sat alone in their separate pods.

Eve learnt that Jordan was an architect, and a really successful one at that. He didn't just work at a company the way he had made out when they'd first interacted – he had founded it with his friend. The colleague who was the reason for the leaving do was actually his PA, Grace, who was retiring having worked for him for ten years.

Jordan was forty-five, which meant he was ten years older than Eve. Somehow, this made him more alluring to her. He was someone not of her world, but seemed intrigued by her all the same. She convinced herself that they were doing nothing wrong really, because they had never physically touched. As much as they had both wanted to, that would require extra permissions, which would then potentially be visible to other people – in this case, Jordan's wife, April.

Jordan would often send Eve gifts, though, and one happened to be a headset that allowed them to at least feel as if they were together. The Story Story 2.0 headset connected to the chip in Eve's wrist and synced with Jordan's own headset and chip, so if Eve stroked the right side of her body it felt to Jordan has if she were stroking him. The two of them would mainly use the headsets when Jordan was away for work and could use it freely in his hotel room, or on the occasions when the temptation got too much and he would take it with him to the guest bathroom in his home.

'Doesn't April wonder where you are when you just disappear in the house for long periods of time?' Eve asked one night as they stood outside a bar she'd just performed at.

Jordan's jaw seemed to clench momentarily before he answered. 'No. I told you she's in her own world most of the time. She hardly shows any interest in me. Ever since our daughter was born, it's like I don't exist to her. I've tried with her, I really have, over the years. I just think it's over but neither of us has set things in motion officially. And I think about the kids and how breaking the family up would affect them.'

Although Eve knew from the scenarios she watched on TV that many men said similar but later turned out to be lying, she believed Jordan. She felt his sadness, and that he wanted more passion in his life. Maybe he truly had been waiting for his world to collide with hers.

'I am sure your kids would prefer seeing two happy parents.'

It felt like the right thing to say, but Eve felt like a fraud because she could only think about what their life might be like if he finally did leave April. She desperately wanted to feel Jordan's touch properly, feel the warmth of him in every way. There was no technology yet that could give her that.

Mentioning Jordan to her friends seemed off-limits, so Eve channelled the feelings and sexual tension into her poetry instead. The comments sent through on her social pod referred to a new sultry confidence in her, and she liked that. Knowing he was in the audience on some nights, and knowing all the things they'd said and tried with each other through their headsets, ignited a different type of creative passion within her that she'd never felt before.

Jordan was the first person Eve had told when she decided to sign up for the Ancestry Experience. She rarely spoke of what it was like growing up in her late teens without her parents or any family, forced to figure out the world on her own. She wanted to share these things with Jordan, but all she could manage for the most part was just explaining how much nicer it would be to know that somebody out there could be her family in a real way.

'It sounds cool,' he'd said, 'but it's like, haven't we given out enough of our information? Now it's like you're asking them to trace absolutely everything connected to you in this life and the next.'

His reaction implied that Jordan was less than enthusiastic about the idea. He didn't seem to fully understand the void Eve felt existed within her from not being able to pick up her phone and call a sibling the way he sometimes mentioned that he did.

She decided not to delve deeper into that conversation, though, and instead watched as Jordan sat in his office at work, telling her about his plans for the rest of the day.

Time spent together in this way felt normal and comfortable, until Jordan would get home and the messages would become fewer. For somebody who was as unconcerned as Jordan claimed to be, he seemed to take an awful lot of precautions not to trigger any suspicion on April's part.

Maybe he wants to stay married, Eve thought to herself. This made her wonder what the future truly meant for them. The two of them would often joke about being not quite in a relationship, and when Eve mentioned this joke to her therapist, although she didn't say so, Eve could tell she was not impressed.

'As you've mentioned yourself, Eve, situations such as these don't tend to progress further than affairs.'

Hearing her relationship referred to as an 'affair' stung, but Eve was also aware that her therapist wasn't incorrect. 'Trust me, I know,' she'd said. 'If it were someone else in this situation, I would tell them the same thing, but he is different. He is truly saddened by their marriage not working, he says he has spoken to friends and family about it. These days you can't just up and leave, you know, the data clearances and life overhaul you have to undertake just to untangle your lives, it's not easy at all.'

Eve found herself flailing, trying to explain and defend Jordan – or rather, defend her own actions. Her therapist was a little older, and that made the interaction more challenging because Eve assumed she probably had her life together while guiding Eve through her own chaos. That's what it was after all: chaos. The one constant that she was trying so hard to get away from.

'So from what I am hearing you say, he has told everyone about how unsatisfied he is in the marriage, but he hasn't talked to his wife about it?' There was a delicate pause before Eve's therapist continued, 'Eve, you are an incredibly intelligent woman who paints with words for a living. Do Jordan's words truly all match up to you?'

Eve felt a flash of anger course through her at that. She knew it was her therapist's job to ask these questions, but she hated the answers they brought up. Eve was now very conscious of the rollercoaster four months she'd had so far with Jordan, and how flimsy the plans were that she had made for his birthday, for example. Actually, for two days *after* his birthday.

'Well, our time is up for this week, Eve. I would like you to consider my offer for you to participate in a study I'm working on, and how we could progress in your healing journey with a different type of therapy. It would require meeting in person.'

Eve was hesitant about her therapist's offer, because these days it seemed as if nothing in life was free and she couldn't quite figure out what she would be giving over of herself in return for this alternative therapy. Jordan was right; she had already given out a lot of information about herself in order to have different chips inserted over the years as they were modified and upgraded, or even to use the Ancestry Experience services.

The monthly government stipend for Eve to continue working as poet, although generous enough to meet most of her needs, would not have allowed her to afford a therapist like the one she had, if it were not for the initiative her therapist ran to provide a sliding scale payment structure for Black people. It was something known as The Blue Project, and Eve definitely appreciated it, but apparently this new study that her therapist had asked if she wanted to participate in would require no money on Eve's part. Instead, there would be in-person therapy sessions, because apparently physical contact was required to map where trauma resided in the body. Eve's reluctance to talk about her mother's death or her years of loneliness had been the catalyst for her therapist's offer, yet Eve could not imagine being able to write her poetry without her pain.

'If I give that up, what do I have left to write about?' Eve had asked.

'*Life*, Eve. You'll be able to write about living. Think about it.'

THE PRESENT — THE ANCESTRY EXPERIENCE POD

Back in the womb-like environment of the pod, Eve continued to stare at the paused LifeSnap video. Without a doubt, she was seeing Jordan's family. They were in the midst of shouting 'surprise' with glee. His wife, April, must clearly be someone that Eve was related to somehow, or she wouldn't be able to view her LifeSnaps.

It all felt like something out of an exuberant soap opera, but there Eve was, reaching out to press the screen for the images to begin moving again. She watched April jump into Jordan's arms and shower him with kisses all over his face. Jordan kissed his wife deeply and then, through the lens worn by April, Eve saw Jordan hug the kids as he looked deeply touched by their gesture.

'I love you, baby,' Jordan whispered to April, but to Eve it sounded like he was shouting. She felt nauseous from the confusion and hurt, which felt like clanging pans in her chest.

April's hand came up to stroke Jordan's face. 'It feels like we've been out of sync these past few months especially, so I wanted to make sure we did something extra special for your birthday.'

Eve's eyes began to water as she saw Jordan's own tearing up as he looked at April. 'I'm sorry. I have a lot on at the moment,' he replied to his wife. 'There's this bar in the city's Art Quarter that's going to be knocked down soon. It's pretty much a done deal that we'll get the contract to design the new building that will replace it. Something way more accommodating to technology. Anyway, I've gone over there a few times and I've fallen in love with so many things about what the bar currently is, and what could be carried over design-wise in the new building . . .'

Eve dug her fingers into the blue cushion as she listened to him speak. The rage she felt made her want to leap up from the seat and run straight out of the pod, but she continued watching. Wanting to know everything about the other side of this man she thought she had been getting to know.

'Eve, are you sure you'd like to continue watching?' Mia's programming prompted her to ask, clearly still concerned by her bio-data.

'Yes. Definitely.' Eve seethed.

The clip Eve had watched was April's most recent upload. She scrolled back through the other LifeSnaps to see two additional uploads on the server, one which showed April out at dinner with her friends, then another of April at a spin class. Although Eve couldn't see the woman fully in any of the clips, she did not seem like the sour person Jordan had described. April *had* a life and she seemed to love it.

And they were related somehow.

Eve had been extremely excited to take a glimpse into the life of this relative she had discovered through the DNA mapping, and had been looking forward to telling Jordan all about it at his birthday dinner. The odds of the only person matching with her in DNA so closely and also having LifeSnaps available to watch being *her boyfriend's wife* felt like a cruel joke. Eve was beginning to wonder if she was being punished for allowing her curiosity and habit of collecting pre-loved things to get the better of her.

It now seemed clear to Eve why the caution was so tantamount on Jordan's part no matter how laid-back he tried to appear. It was possible, for instance, to be in separate pods and go out to dinner, yet Jordan had insisted that it would feel better to actually be in one pod together when they'd finally go out to dinner. Now it seemed obvious to Eve that sitting at the same table in separate pods would indicate a date, and he had tried to avoid that.

She thought through the past few months of their relationship, but she still couldn't bring herself to believe that it was all some weird game. Had any of their relationship really been due to Jordan having some romantic magic, as opposed to just her poetic imagination?

Eve wanted to send a message to tell Jordan that she knew he hadn't been honest with her. She wanted to get him on the headset so she could tell him directly how deeply he had hurt her, and watch his face crumple with shame. She knew she wouldn't do any of these things, though, because they felt hollow, and because the person she was truly angry with was herself. She had wanted a romance and had built it from an unromantic situation.

Later that night, as Eve attempted to distract herself with writing, her phone lit up. Another message from Jordan.

@J-Roc: Are you OK, babe? I haven't heard from you since morning. How did the ancestry thing go? Don't tell me, they took you in your entirety to clone you?

@J-Roc: And are we still on for my belated birthday tomorrow night?

Eve hadn't cried since leaving the Ancestry Experience pod, and seeing Jordan's messages didn't bring up any tears either, only a rolling rage in the pit of her stomach.

In one swift motion, she swiped the message notification off her screen. Instantly, another notification popped up from the Ancestry Experience. Eve opened it, and a mellow voice began to speak.

'Hi Eve, It's Mia here. I hope you enjoyed your time with us today using our LifeSnap technology courtesy of Plant8Con. Now that you've had some time to think, would you like to make direct contact with the Ancestry Experience connection whose LifeSnaps you viewed today?'

Two buttons popped up underneath Mia's computerised silhouette.

> Yes

> No

Eve was unsure of what to press. Instead, she closed out of the Ancestry Experience application and opened Jordan's profile to respond to him.

@EveNoApple: April seems to have thrown you a wonderful birthday surprise. Let that be enough.

The message showed up as 'read' almost immediately, and Eve noticed a pause before three dots popped up to let her know Jordan was responding to her. Almost as if her fingers moved without her command, Eve selected *Settings* above Jordan's profile.

Remove @J-Roc's communications: ALL

Eve clicked on it and instantly Jordan's dots disappeared, because he would no longer be able to communicate with her.

She doubted she would see him at any more poetry nights, and it stung her deep inside to consider how much she had enjoyed seeing him at them. Maybe it was the idea of someone like him being there and *seeing* her. Did he really see her, though? Clearly not, if he was willing to string her along knowing that he was happily married, and not even giving her a heads up that she would need to find a new place to perform since he was in on the publicly undisclosed plan to change a fundamental part of the city's Art Quarter in such a major way.

Instead of dwelling on it any more, Eve picked up her pen and pad and began to write.

I'm packing you see
Packing away who I thought I was
Before you
Realising she was better than who I've been
With you
Packing away all the things this couldn't be
I'll open the boxes one day
And find nothing
Because
I pack and pack and pack
Yet everything is still here
In the open
Waiting to be seen.

Eve's screen flashed once more with Mia's face waiting for her response on the Ancestry Experience app.

```
Would you like to make contact with your Ancestry
Experience connection?

> Yes

> No
```

Broom

Nikki rested her head against the car window as she looked ahead at the long, winding road. Her body felt weary – maybe for more reasons than just the nine-hour flight from London, but she decided to attribute it to that for now anyway.

Every time she wanted to doze off in the passenger seat and make the most of the long drive they were on, the sun seemed to beat down even more menacingly through the windscreen. Nikki forced her eyes open to a partial squint, reluctantly taking in the endless lush greenery and dusty roads leading to their destination.

'Maybe you should stop forcing the sleep, Naks. We are almost there.'

The comment interrupted Nikki's moving of her sunglasses, which were perched on her forehead, down over her eyes. She had told Luke how much she disliked the nickname, but he seemed to insist that her annoyance with the moniker was just down to her 'sassiness'.

Looking over at Luke as he confidently drove down the increasingly narrow road, her heart spread a warmth around her chest, maybe a mix of irritation and lust. *It's complicated,* Nikki thought to herself. She cast her mind back to the day she'd posted a picture of Luke in the group chat and was met with shock and horror from her friends.

Melissa: Nikki 😱 a white guy?!

Doyin: Nikz . . . nahhh . . . not you, my G! An oyinbo man?!
I didn't even know you rolled like that

To be fair, Nikki hadn't really thought she rolled like that either. She had never particularly been *against* dating white men, yet in her mind's eye of what her future looked like she hadn't ever really pictured her future partner's skin colour. Growing up in South London in a Nigerian household, she had seen a couple of her male relatives with white women, but never an aunt with a white man.

Throughout college and university, Nikki mainly dated Black men. Well, except for Anwar, the one South Asian man she'd been out with who, after three weeks of regular dates *at Nando*'s because his cousin was a manager, had asked Nikki if he could say 'nigga' with an 'a' because it was 'more of a hip-hop ting'. Needless to say they didn't go on anymore dates after that.

Luke had shown up in her life almost as a surprise. He had matched with her on Stars Align – a dating app that used astrology to suggest potential matches. Nikki had seen the dating app advertised for months, but took very little interest as she wasn't really into astrology. She'd read her horoscope in passing a few times before, but she struggled to see how the millions of people who had the same star sign could have a weekly foretelling ring true for all of them. Nikki prided herself on her logic. If something couldn't be explained, then she wanted no part in it. She thought this to be the inevitable outcome of growing up with a mother who was heavily religious, not to mention superstitious. Her mother attended celestial churches, where they wore white garments and called the Holy Spirit forth with rapid drumbeats and high-pitched singing. Surely the aim of such devoted worship was to bring one peace, but instead Nikki's mum consistently prayed and fretted in tandem.

'Ọláníkẹ, I am imploring you to join me in church,' she'd say whenever they spoke. 'Every prayer man who has prayed for me over the last four years always sees you, even if I have not mentioned that I have a daughter. I have told you time and time again that they keep saying you have a connection with the dead. The message won't stop coming, and I have done every offering they have asked of me. You should join me in church so they can pray for you in person.'

Her mother's lament was ready on her lips anytime that Nikki visited her family home in South London. The messages that these prayer men brought forth from the Holy Spirit always seemed to require that her mum part with money in one way or another, and Nikki didn't like that. Death seemed to be the clincher. Any mention of it and people would throw their money at these men to ward it off. To be fair, they had never said *she* was at risk of dying per se, just that she had a connection to the dead – but didn't everybody in one way or another?

It all just felt too vague and non-factual for Nikki's liking, but she would simply smile and nod whenever her mother spoke, placating her with a promise to attend church some time when she wasn't so busy with work. This seemed to appease her mother somewhat, because the only thing she loved as much as church was knowing that her daughter was gainfully employed.

Given her scepticism, Nikki was surprised when a Stars Align advert happened to catch her attention one day.

'What if we told you that logic is also a construct? Take a chance on what defies your understanding. Stars Align. Download now.'

It was the way it was phrased, as if they knew what her hang-up was about their app. Then again, that was what focus groups were for, right? Either way, the message felt like a challenge and Nikki was inclined to disprove it, in the same way she explained away her mother's white garment church shenanigans.

Nikki had been in the middle of shooting what was tipped to be the cover of the year for the most renowned fashion magazine in the UK, *Sophley's*, when the distinct tinkling sound of the notification on her phone let her know that she had a match. She couldn't help herself. As the philanthropic billionaire cover star went to change outfits, Nikki grabbed her phone and was amazed at how handsome the man was when she opened the app. LukaszNowak82 had dark brown hair playfully flopped over his right brow, which matched his deep brown eyes. Somehow, Nikki found his prominent nose and slightly full lips enticing.

Her curiosity had to take a back seat once the cover star stomped hurriedly back onto the set and expertly assumed a pose in keeping with the feisty persona the world knew her for. Yet, with each angle she shot the highly anticipated photos from, Nikki found her mind lurching back to the dating profile.

She waited until she got into her car to whip out her phone, eager to check out the page that had distracted her in the latter part of her photoshoot. His face was still as handsome as she had first thought. Nikki scrolled to read his page.

Name: Lukasz (woo-cash) but you can call me Luke

Age: 40

Height: 6'2"

Venus sign: Virgo

Location: London and NYC

A bit about me: 'Let me upgrade you.' OK I'm just joking . . . but kinda not. Hi, I'm Luke - born and raised in Connecticut but I've spent the last ten years based in London. My job requires me to travel quite a bit (I know you'll likely miss me when I'm not around 🥺) but I always make sure I spend time with people I care about, preferably around good food and laughter and a brilliant wine list. I am not trying to convince you, whoever you are, that I'm some kind of saint, but I am considering getting the Ally-chip so I can show my support for people that need it.

Stars Align compatibility rating: 83%

Nikki had sat with her feet up on her dashboard wondering if maybe the site had made a mistake, because there was nothing in what this man had written that could warrant such a high compatibility score – especially since this was the highest score she'd had with anybody since she had joined the app two weeks prior. The whole Ally-chip thing wasn't even sexy, it just seemed like something that people suffering from white guilt were doing in their droves. Having a chip inserted into your brain so you could feel Black people's racial trauma for them? It very much felt like appropriation from the beginning, but Nikki refused to be the bearer of bad news for this guy. Instead, she clicked on the star-shaped icon to find out why the dating site thought she and Luke would get past a 'hi', talk less of a relationship.

The aspects of your Moon, Venus and Mars mean a
very passionate and nurturing romantic environment
with Lukasz. Your Sun signs are opposing and,
while this might be a challenge as it represents
very contrasting core personalities, Lukasz's
Jupiter is conjunct your Midheaven. This is an
indication that your connection will impact your
destiny in a major way, and it is also a chance
of expanding your horizons.

Do you accept this match?

Nikki hesitated for a few moments longer while awkwardly
flashing quick smiles through her car window towards the
colleagues she had just shot with. She sat in the gloomy car
park with her driver's seat half-reclined, staring at her phone.
Finally, Nikki clicked 'yes', and within minutes she had received
her first message from Luke.

LukaszNowak82: this is the highest I've matched with
someone, do you think we should just get married?

LukaszNowak82: I am joking, in case that wasn't funny.

NikkiG: Maybe let's hold off on the marriage, but yes, this is the
highest I've matched, too. This is all very new to me.

LukaszNowak82: I've been on here for a little while but
you're definitely the cutest lady I've matched with.

NikkiG: Here we go . . .

LukaszNowak82: No, I'm serious! 😌 Of course, you're
not my usual type but maybe the stars have something to
do with that.

'Nah, this guy is annoying,' Nikki said aloud to herself.

Yet she continued typing.

NikkiG: You're not my usual type either.

From what Nikki could gather from the rest of their messages, which continued way into the night, long after she had finally driven home, Luke wasn't used to not being a woman's type. He also seemed fascinated with even the most mundane things that Nikki would mention about her life.

'So your mum would go to those churches with the white gowns and walk barefoot through Peckham? That's so cool. I lived in Peckham for a while. Did you grow up in Peckham, or did your mum just sort of walk there barefoot on the church days?'

Luke was talking to Nikki via video chat by now. Talking with each other was so natural that their differences seemed to exist simply as a playful backdrop to their growing connection. Maybe Stars Align was onto something. It was because Nikki could see Luke's face that she knew he was pulling her leg about her mum walking all the way to Peckham barefoot, but it still annoyed her slightly.

'I grew up in Peckham, yes. And no, my mum owned shoes, Luke, don't be annoying,' she replied curtly.

Luke, trying to pivot from his badly executed joke, switched on his charm a bit more. 'Wow! So at some point we could've very easily bumped into each other on Rye Lane.' He seemed excited at the thought of their paths having crossed in real life without them realising.

'I highly doubt it. My Rye Lane and your Rye Lane wouldn't have been the same.'

'Ah! Because of gentrification, right? Yeah I know, it sucks. I am one of the good guys, though. Whenever I would see those little Black kids at the cafés running around while their mums braided hair, I'd say hi.'

Nikki couldn't believe that Luke was serious about doing the bare minimum and thinking it was what made him one of the good guys. 'Oh wow, you acknowledged their existence without contempt? You definitely deserve a Nobel Peace Prize. Also, here's a tip, men who say they're good guys are usually not good guys. At least not in the way they think they are.'

Nikki expected a retort akin to the defensive statements she had heard white people make throughout the years whenever race, class and consequently gentrification was discussed. But to her surprise, Luke nodded.

'You're right. I've gotten by on the bare minimum. I'll do better. I'm listening and . . .'

'Learning?' Nikki finished Luke's statement for him.

Laughing in surprise, Luke asked, 'We must have a lot going on astrologically, because how did you know I was going to say that?'

'It's just something I've heard white people say a lot, is all. It's passive. Listening and learning endlessly, but no action.'

'Action? I thought you'd prefer being taken out to dinner a few times before that happens.'

Looking at Luke's irreverent smirk made Nikki chuckle despite herself.

'You have an incredible smile, Naks.' Luke's voice was softer, and Nikki knew that he meant his compliment.

'Naks? What kind of name are you trying to give me please? Let's just stick to Nikki.'

'It's like Nikki Naks Paddy Whack.'

'Yeah, Luke, and how does that last part go?'

Luke thought for a second and responded, 'Give the dog a bone?'

'Exactly. Go back to the drawing board on that one.'

Their relationship continued with the same playful irritation for the next two months, while Nikki anticipated the release of the highly coveted cover of the *Sophley's* September issue she'd been shooting when she first matched with Luke. The shoot was destined to catapult Nikki's career and pay grade significantly, and the thought of it gave her butterflies in a way that Luke didn't, but he was still very pleasant to date all the same. Their dates were varied, and Nikki couldn't deny that their lives complemented each other in a way that she really enjoyed. Luke was a sports agent, and his clients included footballers in the UK as well as NBA players in America, hence his location being split between London and New York City. There was an understanding between the two of them about how their respective industries and the world of celebrity operated, so going to events together flowed with a sexy ease. Luke had already recommended that his clients request Nikki as their photographer for their magazine features, and Nikki appreciated it – found it to be a turn on, actually. A man was actually taking an active interest in her career and not seeing it as frivolous just because she wasn't a doctor or a lawyer – this hadn't been the case with some of the other men she had dated.

They looked great together as a couple, and Nikki enjoyed seeing people take them both in. It wasn't simply about their differing races, but rather that individually they were both attractive – both tall and athletic in physique. Nikki's brown skin, high cheekbones and big brown eyes glistened next to Luke's permanently tanned skin, which seemed to be the standard for certain athletic men who had grown up with some wealth and thus participated in numerous outdoor activities.

Nikki hadn't known what to expect from dating a white guy, and while she would often stress that Blackness wasn't a monolith, she somehow felt the urge to assert the signifiers of her Blackness even more so that she didn't feel like 'one of those girls'. She would suggest that they order Nigerian takeaways, or she would try her very best to attempt cooking the foods her mother used to cook. When she wrote about her conflicting feelings in the girls' group chat, the responses were as varied as her own inner dialogue over the issue.

Doyin: what do you mean by 'one of those girls'?

Melissa: D, why are you trying it? You know exactly what Nikki means! Those Black women who start dating white guys and suddenly their accent changes to an obscure part of Chelsea via Essex and they love a straight shiny wig.

Nikki: LMAO! I wasn't even going to describe it like that, but Mel isn't all the way off and you know I love my middle-part mid-length units, I could easily get mistaken.

Doyin: Nah, you lot are actually ridiculous. Haha! I can't lie, I've seen those types of girls around, but I've also seen the swirlers with the braids and afros and varying accents. How am I the one even backing the chat? Nikki, stand up for yourself, against yourself!

Nikki: I just don't want people to think I've lost my Blackness because of this guy. You know how people like to chat. My profile is growing the more people see my work, and the last thing I want is my name trending for anything other than my great photography.

Melissa: I've got to agree with D on this one, you can't let random opinions measure your Blackness for you. We know you're smart enough that if some wild shit happens with this guy, you'll bounce.

Doyin: Mel's right, Nikki. It's not because of this guy that you'd have to question how Black or how Nigerian you are. In my opinion, you lost a lot of your cookout credentials when we went to Joshua's barbecue and you were eating chicken wings with a knife and fork.

Melissa: OMG! I remember that! HAHAHAHA!! If anything you'd already given people the heads up that you were on the way to swirl-ville!

'Swirling' described (mainly) Black people who dated outside of their race, usually when dating white people. Nikki and her friends had often discussed the Black female influencers who had gained notoriety online from their interracial relationships. Nikki had often wondered how the influencers tolerated the constant scrutiny from strangers on the internet. She considered whether that might've been the reason that she was interrogating herself in such a way about her relationship with Luke.

Chatting with her friends had helped Nikki to see that she could just take the experience with him for what it was, as long as she kept her wits about her. Worrying about how people would perceive her for dating him was also something that seemed too far removed from the present moment to continue to fret about.

Stars Align had predicted 'sizzling sexual tension and long conversations' between Nikki and Luke, and it didn't lie there. The sex was great. Luke was attentive in a way that didn't come burdened with hang-ups about whether it was 'masculine' to go down on her or not. He seemed preoccupied with wanting to pleasure her for as long as it took.

Sex couldn't be everything in a relationship though. There were other tensions that Nikki found hard to shake. Like how Luke, as a white man of Polish heritage born and raised in the USA, could move around the world with much more ease than she could. When Luke described his life and his 'hardships', it felt to Nikki that the things she thought were all a part of growing up just weren't experienced by certain groups of people. Of course, Luke told her about his grandfather moving from Poland to America after the Second World War, and how hostile it had been for him and his family. The way Luke spoke of his grandfather's experience felt to Nikki as if he were describing folklore and not something that was immediately connected to his own experience. Yet whenever Nikki mentioned experiences she'd had as a Black woman, like being followed around the store no matter how well-dressed she was, conveniently Luke would bring up his immigrant grandfather who'd also had it tough as proof that he identified with her struggle. It wasn't the worst thing in the world but it wasn't ideal, and Nikki wasn't sure how long she would want to continue dating someone who, despite what the dating app had said, felt rather middle-of-the-road to her.

On her own Stars Align profile, Nikki's birth chart breakdown described her as 'someone who would go with the flow for as long as possible, until life shakes the courage within her free'. She didn't quite know what to make of the cryptic description because she was fairly new to astrology and had tried all the other dating apps that she'd come across at some point. On the other apps, she had always matched with overtly opinionated people who pushed for their own way, and who were rather uncomfortable to be around – perhaps because they made her question a little whether she should be speaking up more herself.

I got this far by playing the game, and I could maybe one day win it, was what Nikki regularly told herself whenever doubts crept in about whether she needed to say more about the unfairness that she sometimes witnessed in her industry. Messaging with guys who seemed so sure of their outlook on life and society unnerved her. She couldn't imagine herself ever going against the grain so emphatically when it was clear that it was much easier to get on by not kicking up a fuss.

So playing the game is what Nikki kept in mind when Luke invited her to a client's wedding in North Carolina. The soccer player Mark Timson was getting married to his fiancée, actress Melissa Cross, and the lead up to the wedding was the talk of the celebrity blogs.

'This would be a great way for you to meet a few of the big movers and shakers across the pond. Joan Crow, the editor-in-chief of *Sophley's US*, will be there, since the magazine will feature the wedding. Good chance for you to meet her, right? Then boom – you could have a chance at the September issue of a US edition of *Sophley's*!'

Luke made a great point, and that is why he was such a good agent: he thought ahead about how to pull several seemingly unrelated bows together to get the best opportunities for his clients. It was admirable. Where Nikki saw herself playing the game, Luke saw himself as *being* the game, and those were two separate ways of viewing the world. Thus, the two of them experienced the world differently.

'I dunno, Luke,' Nikki had said. 'Obviously, I appreciate you inviting me, but it feels a bit weird. I know he is your client, but Mark has some very wild political views. And fine, he has all these trophies, but how do people overlook him voting for that racist dickhead?'

'A racist dickhead as president? You're going to have to be more specific,' Luke chimed in. Nikki could tell that he felt he'd just made a rather astute joke, but it wasn't people like him that were affected by those racist presidents. The glare from Nikki must've made Luke realise he needed to redeem himself somehow.

'For the record, I see the issue with the way that Mark votes and sees the world. I mean, *I* voted properly the time we got to choose a president who wasn't like the rest, and I would do it again. Sports is sports, though. I can't hold his political views against him, especially when he's currently one of the best players in the soccer world. It's just business.'

Nikki still wasn't at ease.

'Sports *isn't* just sports, because nothing is simply just as it is,' she said. 'Everything is political, and his perspectives and voting choices don't just happen in a vacuum, because others who think and vote like him end up putting very horrid people into power. But whatever. His fiancée is also iffy, by the way. Isn't she the one who keeps playing non-white roles even when people tell her that it is erasure?'

'But if that's who the producers want to cast, should she turn down the role and be broke? I mean, I get it, but at the same time, I think you're being extremely judgmental. You already know what this industry is like.'

Yeah, Luke didn't get it. Nikki felt consumed by impatience. She wondered whether dating Luke for a long time would entail even more back and forth about the basics of politics and privilege. But maybe he had a point about keeping it separate. Maybe she was beginning to sound like those men on the dating apps that she found so annoying, who seemed too sure of a world that is largely unknown.

'She absolutely wouldn't be broke,' Nikki had countered, still unable to help herself. 'Her family are rather wealthy and well connected in the industry, hence the roles being offered to her instead of actresses who are of the ethnicity and race described in these screenplays. They're the ones who end up being broke, because they're not being cast in things!' She knew she sounded exasperated, but she simply couldn't tolerate how Luke viewed the behaviours of individual people as unrelated to world events, and disregarded the clear nepotism that helped many.

'Fine, you don't want to go to this wedding because they're ter- rible people. At least come along with *me*, even if it's just because it would be our first time away – not to mention the fact that you'd meet Joan. That could only be a good thing, right? Surely you don't want the potential work opportunities that could come of this to go to the equivalent of Melissa in your line of work? I'll take care of everything, flights and stuff. We'll be staying at the wedding venue since it's a large home. Oh, and I'll sort out car rental and snacks even! But I can't take care of that bonnet thing you wear at night though, so make sure you pack it. Ha!'

Luke clearly still didn't get it, but Nikki was uncomfortable hearing herself spouting things she had previously not been as impassioned to speak about outside of her WhatsApp group. He clearly wanted to lift the mood of the tense conversation, even if it was with a bad reference to her hair-care regimen. Nikki considered it all. It *would* be nice to go away on a road trip with Luke. It would be something different to what she'd experienced before, and if she was going to play the game of moving up in the industry, she was definitely being offered a golden egg in meeting Joan Crow in more jovial surroundings.

'OK, fine. I'll come.'

It was only now, as Luke drove through the looming gates of the wedding venue, that it dawned on Nikki the type of place that would be sufficient to accommodate all the guests and serve as the venue for such a luxurious wedding in North Carolina.

'Is this . . . is this a plantation?' Nikki sat up straight as she saw the massive white mansion come into view the further they drove into the estate.

'Err, maybe. I guess so. I didn't look into it. It isn't any more, obviously,' Luke responded distractedly as he attempted to follow the directions for guest parking on the massive plot of land.

Instantly, Nikki was annoyed with herself for not asking for more information in the lead-up to their trip. She had been so consumed with the buzz around her since the release of the September issue of *Sophley's UK* that she was relieved when Luke said he had everything in hand. Of all the potential high-profile events that would align with the current chatter about her and her talent, being a guest at a wedding on a plantation would not be one of them.

It irked Nikki that Luke's initial response was that the plantation was no longer operational, as if that took away from the atrocities of slavery that would have been perpetrated there. It wasn't even like the place had been renamed; as they pulled up, she saw on a sign that the place was literally called 'Beau Feu Plantation'. That would mean that the couple who booked the venue and those who were attending who (unlike her) had paid attention to the venue details, would've also been aware that they were attending festivities on land where likely many people were kept in enslavement and tortured. Nikki felt nauseous at the thought of it all, but her discomfort with their location was disrupted by her inability to ignore how beautiful the grounds of Beau Feu were. Acres of beautiful plush green land sprawled out before them, where stunning, stooping trees let their branches drape downwards as if they were caught in the middle of a contemporary dance piece inspired by grief and longing.

Once Luke had found a suitable place to park in the designated areas for the guests, the couple were able to take in the magnificence of the mansion set within the grounds. The height of the building loomed over them menacingly. From the numerous windows that Nikki could see from the outside, she guessed that there would be many rooms, and considered once again how such a grand home of dazzling white could represent so much darkness. As if her hands had a mind of their own, they found Nikki's camera in her bag and raised the viewfinder to her eye.

Snap.

'Welcome, you gorgeous duo!'

No sooner had Nikki's camera captured an image of the house before her than a couple flung open the front door. Mark and Melissa stood on the spotless porch, waving for Nikki and Luke to come up the steps.

185

'Thank you for having us! Long ass journey, but worth it for my star client and friend!' Luke chimed back, as he and Nikki followed the couple into the mansion.

He's already started, Nikki thought. Luke had switched on his game mode, and was likely planning to treat the four days like one long networking event. Nikki was already exhausted by the thought of it. She had initially agreed to this trip because of the potential career benefits of being in attendance. A plantation though? *Sheesh*.

Melissa beamed at Nikki. 'Hey girl! Nice to meet you! So looking forward to us getting to know each other for a couple of days before the wedding. I never get to meet cool people like you. I mean, I don't get to chat much with people from . . . Where are you from?'

Nikki knew what the question meant, and also understood the assignment she and Luke had at this wedding. 'I'm from London,' she replied with a stiff, overly enthusiastic smile.

Noting the momentary confusion on Melissa's face, Nikki offered nothing else about her geographical background. Glancing at Luke quickly, she noticed that his gaze was fixed firmly ahead with his own exaggeratedly friendly expression still stuck on his face, and so she knew he had picked up on the weirdness of Melissa's comment, too.

'By way of Nigeria!' Luke added on Nikki's behalf after a beat of awkward silence. Nikki was annoyed that Luke could clearly tell that she hadn't planned to give into Melissa's silly line of questioning, yet he still offered the information anyway.

Melissa's face brightened up even more. 'Ah-ha! Now *that* makes sense! Your face reminded me of a little child I saw when I volunteered in Kenya as a teen.'

In that moment, Nikki was glad to have her deep brown skin, because the irritation she felt at Melissa's asinine comment would certainly have made her face red if she were lighter. She saw Luke's jaw clench ever so slightly as he realised that he shouldn't have given Melissa an opportunity to be more ignorant. He probably would've expected Nikki to say something about the exchange, but she was determined to prove to him that she could play nice, especially since Mark was an extremely important client for Luke's career.

Nikki wracked her brain for something neutral and painless that she could potentially connect with Melissa on and move away from the tension that she and Luke clearly felt, but the other couple seemed blissfully unaware of.

'I can't wait to get to know you more, too,' Nikki said at last. 'And it is such a pleasure to be here. I feel like I know you already because one of my best friends is named Melissa. But of course, not all Melissas are the same.' Nikki added a small laugh at the end of her words to convey her faux enthusiasm.

'Your friend's name is Melissa? Oh wow! Is she Nigerian too, though? Is that her given natural name?'

Nikki was stunned by the flippant nature of the loaded question and the odd use of the word 'natural', but again she reminded herself that within celebrity circles there were games to be played, and she didn't want to cause Luke to lose. 'Yes,' she replied through gritted teeth. 'Her grandmother named her when she was born.'

'Well, you live and you learn!'

With that, Melissa and Mark twirled around and led the couple inside. They showed Luke and Nikki around the mansion, with its dazzling marble floors, grand staircases and imposing chandeliers. Each room was palatial in size, but Nikki could not shake her disgust for the history of the place. Only a couple of centuries back it would've been absolutely normal for enslaved Black people to be moving meekly through this house and its vast grounds, ensuring its upkeep while they were denied their humanity in every possible way. She needed to get to a private space to work through her thoughts, lest she end up saying what was truly on her mind.

Just then, Melissa chimed, 'Nikki, you must be exhausted from that long journey. A nine-hour flight and then three hours in the car with this one?' She patted Luke's arm. 'I wouldn't blame you if wanted to sleep through dinner!'

Nikki managed something of a smile to disguise the annoyance that had built inside her from the moment she and Luke entered the gates of Beau Feu. 'You are right, a nap would do me some good right now.' She glanced at Luke. 'Don't worry, though, I will definitely be down later to meet everyone else at dinner.' The snacks Luke had promised for the journey had run out rather quickly as he'd gorged on them while he drove. This meant that if Nikki was going to get some food, she didn't have the luxury of hiding in their designated room until tomorrow's activities, which she had learnt was going to consist of a historical tour of the grounds before lunch served in the garden. The day after that would be the wedding itself. Nikki was already fretting about whether she could stomach being in this house for the next few days.

Luke excused himself to join her in their guest room, and when they were finally alone, in what felt to Nikki like a suite rather than a mere bedroom, she could finally let her shoulders droop and the smile fall from her face. 'You do know I would've never come to this place with you if I'd known this is where the wedding would be.' Nikki stared directly at Luke, ensuring that her anger was clear even without a raised voice.

'I'm sorry,' he said with a sigh. 'It was an oversight. I didn't think it would be that big a deal, especially since you're from the UK and this is about America's history.'

Nikki's disappointment sat like a rock in the pit of her stomach. 'While you might only know of the way it affected America, it went far beyond that and started way before that. Also, even if it *was* solely America's history, as a Black British woman of Nigerian heritage – which you were so keen to share with Melissa – why would you think I would be okay with knowing other Black people suffered here?'

Luke couldn't hold Nikki's gaze, which sizzled with conviction. His head bowed, he mumbled, 'Babe, I am truly sorry. There are clearly things I still need to learn. Maybe this is why I should get the Ally-chip, so I can understand what this feels like for you.'

'First off, I don't want that fucking chip, and we don't know each other like that yet. And second of all, you don't need the chip to know how I am feeling because I am literally telling you now. I don't need you to feel my feelings for me, I just need you to hear me that this is a mess. I wonder how the other guests feel about this.'

Even as Nikki said the words, she had a sneaking suspicion that everybody else had been well aware of the location of the wedding and had no qualms with it. Luke had no answer to Nikki's question, and it must have been clear to him that Nikki had answered it herself by the way a cloud of disappointment cast itself over her face.

While Luke was in the shower – a decision he had probably made to give Nikki some space and to let the tension between them dissipate – Nikki found herself unable to nap as she'd planned. Instead, she checked her pictures from their arrival. Taking photos for brands and magazines paid the bills and came with a lot of esteem, but Nikki enjoyed the candid pictures that she took of the day-to-day and of her travels more. She wondered if the positive aspect of being in a place with such a terrible history might be the opportunity to capture something that at least felt respectful of those who had lost their freedoms and lives there.

As Nikki flicked through to the pictures she'd taken that afternoon, she stared at the image on her camera's screen, confused. In the image of the front of the mansion, a big broom was propped against the wall of the porch. An old-school type of broom with a long piece of wood for a handle and bunched-up, thin sticks attached to the bottom to sweep with. It was odd because Nikki didn't remember seeing the broom at the time of taking the picture.

'Babe, do you remember seeing a broom on the porch when we arrived?' Nikki called out to Luke as he shut off the water in the shower.

'Nope. Everything is pristine, right? Like, clearly they clean the hell out of it constantly but it's almost as if these little elves tidy everything up when you're not looking,' Luke's voice chimed back from the bathroom.

'Elves aren't what they were known as, but whatever . . .' Nikki muttered to herself.

While Luke was moisturising his entire body, something he credited Nikki for getting him into doing, Nikki showed him the picture on her camera, searching his face for the same confusion she had felt.

'So why did you ask me about a broom?'

'Because it's right there.'

Nikki turned the display screen of her camera back to herself, and to her shock there was now no broom in the picture.

'Looks like somebody really needs that nap,' Luke said with a chuckle. 'You've got two hours before dinner anyway, so maybe just chill out up here and I'll get on with some calls downstairs in the meantime?'

'Yeah, sure,' is all Nikki could manage as her mind rushed back and forth trying to figure out how she could've seen a broom in her photo one minute and then it was gone in the next. Perhaps Luke had a point, she could do with some rest. She put her camera away, and allowed herself to be caressed by the gorgeous sheets on the bed, falling into a much-needed deep sleep.

Nikki stood on the grounds of Beau Feu Plantation, then moved inside one of the shacks that she guessed was the accommodation for the enslaved people who resided on the plantation once. But the scene surrounding her now was clearly from a long time before her arrival. The stove inside the shack was of an earlier era, as was all the rest of the minimal furniture. She saw Black women in white cotton dresses preparing for some sort of special occasion. Some cooked while a few others fussed over a young woman with excitement.

A wedding.

'Now you know we have to keep this hush hush. If they catch onto this, we gon' feel the wrath of them up there in the house,' a much older woman warned.

The sun was setting, and the women ushered the young woman into another shack, where Nikki saw that a group of men were gathered, faces shining in the candlelight with expectant smiles glistening. There was a young man in the middle of them all who looked slightly older than the bride and equally as excited.

Nikki looked on as the group sang hushed songs harmoniously, and a broom like the one she had seen in her photo was placed on the ground for the couple to jump over, a symbol to formalise their marriage.

Suddenly the door to the shack swung open with a bang.

'Now what are y'all disobedient animals getting up to?'

A red-faced, dirty-looking man stood in the doorway with a whip, menacingly glaring at those in the shack. Nikki realised he must be the overseer, employed to watch the enslaved and ensure that they remained compliant at all times on the plantation.

Chaos erupted as the group attempted to disband and run past the dirty, angry man.

Nikki turned her head in the dream, and immediately found herself elsewhere. She was now in the middle of the grounds, where a wooden beam-like structure had been erected. The smiling bride from earlier was on her knees sobbing, her arms tied around a stump of wood.

'Marriage is forbidden and you know that, you whore.' The last word cut through the air, at the same time as the dirty man's whip made contact with the young bride's body.

The despair Nikki felt at witnessing this made it harder for her to breathe . . . she was desperate to wake up.

And as she willed herself to, the young bride looked directly at her . . . and smiled.

Nikki's eyes flung open and she leapt up from the bed, sweating as if she, too, had run away from the overseer. The smile of the young bride haunted her, because it didn't feel menacing. It was *assured*. Yet, Nikki couldn't fathom what she could have been so sure about in the midst of all that pain.

She checked the time on her phone, but what had felt like hours time-travelling in her dreams had only been around forty-five minutes. Her annoyance with Luke had faded somewhat, since he had clearly left her alone in the room to get a good enough nap. Notifications of messages in her group chat blinked at her from her phone.

Doyin: Girl, can you let us know that you arrived safely? This one that you're going on your first trip with an oyinbo man, we have to make sure you're still alive.

Melissa: Yes, confirm! Ever since I got into them true crime podcasts I've been feeling very somehow about this partnership. Of course not all white men are the same, but at the same time also share your live location with us!

Nikki loved how much her friends cared about her and how hilarious they could be even when worried.

Nikki: Hey girlies, I'm alright you know. The trip was lonngggg and the couple are as you'd expect 😶 but the maddest thing is that the wedding is on a plantation.

Melissa: A PLANTATION NIKS!? PLANTATION!! So Luke took you over there to go and serve food or work the land or what?

Nikki: He seems to think it's not a big deal and I imagine the other guests feel the same way, but this place is really not a bit of me. I think he and I have some serious discussions waiting for when we get back to London.

Doyin: Well, whatever you decide we are here for you. A plantation wedding will always seem very strange to me. Like would they go to a concentration camp to have a wedding?

Melissa: Exactly this! Anyway, take it easy. It's literally a few days there and you're back. Avoid any group photos though. You know you'll get dragged on social media for months if those pics ever make it online.

Nikki could not bring herself to mention the broom she had seen in her picture to her friends. She prided herself on her logic, and there was nothing logical about being able to see a broom in a picture that Luke could not see, and then dreaming about the people who she just knew were part of the memories of this large house, somehow.

Sighing, Nikki realised it must be dinner time. She freshened up and headed downstairs to the culmination of the voices she had been hearing from the bedroom as she got ready. Everyone was already sat around a large dining table ready for the evening's meal. Nikki was aware that apart from one Black man, sat with his white partner, she was the only Black person in this group of roughly fifty people.

'Hey, girl!' Melissa chimed from the other side of one of the two dining tables. 'So lovely of you to join us! I wasn't sure if you were working to that, uh, what do they say when a certain type of person is always late? That CP time—'

'Babe, why don't you come and sit over here?' Luke interrupted.

Almost as a reflex action, Nikki had sought the eyes of the Black man in the room as Melissa spoke, but he just stared intently down at the cutlery on the table. Given he'd averted his gaze, Nikki eventually shot a glance towards Luke, who offered an embarrassed smile as he indicated the seat again, but Nikki was unable to work out if he felt the embarrassment for Melissa's ignorance, or for her discomfort.

Just play the game.

That's what Nikki heard over and over in her head, but she couldn't help a slight jab. 'Ha! Yeah, the jet lag really got a hold of me. So you know quite a bit about *the culture*?' she asked Melissa. 'Did that inform your choice of venue?'

Melissa looked confused. 'I'm sorry, what? I am not quite catching on.'

'Never mind!' Nikki wanted desperately to get right into the painful choice of wedding venue, but then she also noticed Joan Crow, the *Sophley's US* editor, smiling over at her. She bit her lip and sat next to Melissa, with Mark at Melissa's other side.

The evening bustled with various topics floating across the two tables, yet somehow the main one that the guests wanted Nikki's input on was the death of the queen of England.

'You must be devastated!' proclaimed a woman a couple of seats away from Nikki. She recognised her to be a very popular country singer who had risen to fame via one of the franchised televised talent shows. The woman continued, 'She did so much, and she reigned for so long. I can't imagine how it must feel for the nation. Couldn't have been an easy decision to miss the funeral to be here.'

Those within earshot of the country singer's comments looked over intently at Nikki in anticipation, as if she were some kind of correspondent for Britain's affairs. Nikki went to answer, but couldn't help being distracted momentarily by the two large brooms that had appeared by the fireplace in the large dining room. Instinctively she knew better than to ask if anyone could see the brooms this time. Instead, she forced herself to focus on the conversation at hand, while in the back room of her mind she tried to make sense of what was going on at Beau Feu that apparently only she was privy to.

'It wasn't too hard a decision, as I wasn't personally asked to take part in the funeral.'

'Oh no! You didn't even get a chance to queue?' interjected the Black man who had earlier tried his hardest to avoid her eyes. 'Honestly, it was so beautiful to see all that dedication. But truly, for reigning that long she deserved it!' From his athletic build and fashion choices, Nikki had deduced that he must've been one of Mark's teammates.

'Well . . . she deserved something, that's for sure.'

Nikki's smile had become non-committal because she was irritated, not to mention distracted by the random brooms appearing. She already wanted to go home. The entire vibe of the place and people felt oppressive and eerie. Of course, the people who saw no issue with attending a wedding on a plantation would also be unable to fathom how she, as a Black woman of Nigerian descent with a modicum of critical thinking ability, cared very little for the death of a coloniser monarch.

Conversations bounced around the room while rather bland versions of food she had seen in Southern cooking social media posts were presented to the table with flair. Yet Nikki felt stiff, and desperate to stand up and stretch, because everything about the atmosphere in the room felt tight around her body, crushing in on her. Nikki was making do with simply stretching her long legs out a bit underneath the table, when—

Tap.

Nikki knew what her feet had touched without seeing it. *Another* broom, lying underneath the table. She allowed her shoes to trace along the length of the handle to be sure, and a cold chill gripped her heart. *Something is not right with this place,* she thought to herself.

Determined to not lose her mind in front of white people, Nikki honed in on the conversation being had by Joan Crow and some of the others, promising herself that she would do her best to participate, if only to take her mind off the weird brooms and her unsettling dream from earlier.

'So, I actually just got in on my helicopter,' someone was saying. 'Yah yah, it's at the airport now, but can be over here in about thirty minutes if a news story breaks and I have to head out.'

'Oh, mine too,' Joan replied. 'No news stories for me, but I couldn't imagine doing that drive from the airport. Way too ghetto. You never know who is going to pop out at a stop sign and say "*Yo yo yo gimme all your money*" around these parts.'

The 'ghetto' comment from the mouth of Joan Crow felt like it had yanked Nikki's ears. She wasn't shocked, and not really even disappointed. She had come to tolerate hearing these kinds of comments quoted often in her industry, but usually they would at least have been more elaborately veiled. Nikki assumed that the nature of the festivities and the type of people in attendance meant that Joan perhaps felt more comfortable to share her unadorned opinions. She gritted her teeth. Part of playing the game meant that Nikki knew she'd have to avoid drawing any attention to Joan's awfully racialised comment, and instead feigned neutrality and a deep interest as Joan moved on to her thoughts and aspirations for *Sophley's US*. Nikki laughed at all the right points, and added her own quips and anecdotes for good measure, ensuring that nothing was 'too political' for the table.

Still, the evening dragged and Nikki wanted nothing more than to retreat to the bedroom and be done with performing an ease she did not feel. Her subsequent conversations with Joan Crow seemed oddly positive, considering that Nikki had decided that she disliked the woman now. She wondered whether her lack of reverence contributed to Joan's interest in her. Maybe being invited to such an exclusive wedding weekend made Nikki worth considering working with in Joan's eyes, in just the way Luke had anticipated. That was something, at least.

'If you'd both rather not drive back after the wedding, feel free to leave the rental car and jump in the helicopter with me. I would *love* to hear more about you,' Joan was saying to Nikki now. 'The UK cover you shot was very urban, and that might carry over well in the US now and then. Can't have it *too* often, of course!'

Nikki willed her face to move into something vaguely resembling a smile as she tried to move past another of Joan's racially loaded comments. There had been nothing particularly 'urban' about Nikki's cover for the UK issue of *Sophley's*. It hadn't been shot at outside of a social housing estate, for instance. Although the cover star was Black herself, all the clothing she'd worn for the shoot was actually by white designers.

Yet Nikki was acutely aware of how rare it was for a Black photographer to shoot any major magazine covers, much less the coveted September issue of *Sophley's US*.

'That would be lovely, Joan,' was all that Nikki could muster as she felt her mask of tolerance slipping. She was relieved when Melissa's annoying voice rang around the room.

'Thank you so much to everyone for being here with us. Please do get some rest now, and I look forwards to our tour tomorrow!'

Nikki turned and left the room, leaving them to coo about wandering around the plantation grounds the next day.

As they got into bed for the night, Luke seemed to have resigned himself to Nikki's spikiness towards him and clearly thought it best to weather the weekend as pleasantly as possible without addressing the disrespect of his client friends in any depth.

'I am not excusing their comments,' he said, 'but you have to understand, these people live a pretty closed-off life. I'm sorry you're upset, but it's not your first time at this rodeo, Naks. You deal with people like this all the time from what you've told me, so what is the problem with holding on for the weekend?'

'Yes, you're right. Ignorance and bigotry is nothing new to me unfortunately, and I knew there would be aspects of that when I chose to come along with you. However, the problem is that having it all take place on a *plantation* is even more triggering. Just because I have to deal with something frequently doesn't make it any less distressing. That is why I don't want to hold on.'

'Well, it would be rude to leave at this point. The drive to the airport is three hours. Please let us just get through this weekend, and I promise not to invite you to another wedding again.'

Nikki could not believe that someone who prided himself on being so aware seemed to struggle to understand her current plight. Turning over and switching off her light, she fell asleep with her disappointment covering her. But as she drifted off, Nikki found herself back at the version of Beau Feu from centuries earlier . . .

Nikki watched as the bride from her previous dream sat constructing brooms with the elders. It was night-time, and they were gathered behind the shack that was their home. Nikki looked on in awe as hazy images of weddings throughout the years swirled in the air around the women as they put the brooms together and chatted in whispers.

What was happening?

Suddenly one of the elderly women looked up, directly at Nikki, and gestured for her to follow as she rose from her low stool. Nikki obliged and walked into the swirl of countless wedding memories – those of white people from the 1900s to Nikki's present day, all beaming with joy as they said their vows on blood-soaked grounds.

'Your mama done told you that you have a gift and that is why you see us,' the woman said to Nikki. 'That is why you need to leave, child. The time is almost here.'

The elderly woman swooshed a broom in the air as if swatting away a fly, and Nikki saw decades of other brooms being placed all around the house and grounds of Beau Feu.

It was hard to tell whether they were in the past, or the present, or the future now.

'Every time these devils celebrate here, it is like we never mattered,' the elderly woman continued. 'We saw things that no human shoulda seen. They don't care. They will keep coming unless we stop them. Now that we don't have but our spirit and no body to move in, we're able to put these brooms everywhere. On the blessed day, a match will

be struck and this will all be taken down to nothin' but ash. So you have to leave before that happens, child.'

Nikki felt herself panicking in her dream state yet fighting to understand everything she was being told, because she knew this was no ordinary dream. 'The broom,' she said. 'I could see the broom in my photograph, but Luke couldn't. And then in the dining room, there were more brooms and nobody noticed, and—'

'Why would they child?' the older woman interjected. 'Maybe that lil' ol' picture contraption you got helped you realise it the first time, but you could see the brooms in the dining room because you can see with our *eyes. We're connected by ancestry. You probably always have been able to see so much more but you chose not to, just to get by. We could see you in that dining room. Looking like a church dress worn on a Friday. Girl, you ain't never getting on with any of them folks.'*

Nikki felt overcome with amazement at being able to talk with this old woman, and trusting that it was meant to be, as she would not have ever been privy to this information otherwise. For all her love of logic, she somehow knew that much.

'You better get back. That floppy haired boy you carrying on with is about to wake you. Leave soon, child, because another wedding ain't gon' happen here. We makin' sure of that.'

Nikki was indeed woken up by Luke's gentle shake. It was morning, and their room was bathed in soft gold light shining through the large windows.

It was time for the tour.

The hum of excited and varying conversations followed closely behind the Beau Feu tour guide as he led the wedding week-enders towards the repainted shacks in which the enslaved people of the plantation would've once lived. Nikki was startled by how clearly she had seen the shacks in her dreams without ever having visited anywhere like Beau Feu. One could argue that there were more than enough films depicting slavery that she could have gleaned this knowledge passively, but in spite of the sceptical part of brain wanting to say otherwise, Nikki really had seen it all in her dream. Even the way the shack the bride had lived in leant to the right side ever so slightly. *How could this be?*

'OK, ladies and gentlemen, I thought we would take a moment here to check out these beautiful little homes that the workers on the plantation used to occupy,' the guide was saying. 'They were kept quite a distance away from the main house to allow the workers to foster their own community and have some privacy.'

Nikki felt nauseous at the blatant whitewashing of such a violent history, and even more sickened by the nods of interest making their way around the group as they seemed satisfied with the explanation given by the tour guide.

Joan Crow moved closer to the nearest shack, taking in the texture of the exterior by stroking the front door with a single finger. 'Just so quaint, isn't it? I'll brief the photographer when they arrive tomorrow morning. Would be great to get some shots of you both by this backdrop, Melissa and Mark.'

The couple cooed and nodded along with Joan. Nikki looked for the Black man from dinner the night before. His name was Malik Hayden and he was in fact Mark's team mate, as Nikki had guessed. A quick internet search had informed her of his stance that racism had never affected him in his career, even though his father had been imprisoned when Malik was very young and his mother had been forced to raise him on her meagre wage while living in the projects. It seemed from Malik's interviews that he viewed being poor as a personal failing as opposed to the highly probable result of racial injustice. His reluctance to fully acknowledge her when they were the only Black people at Beau Feu still felt rather absurd to Nikki.

When she did finally spot Malik standing further back in the group, she was surprised to realise he was looking at her, too. As their eyes locked, Nikki hoped that this would mean an affinity at last, and a chance that they would be able to talk to each other about how wild the trip had been thus far. But Malik tugged his eyes away and reached out for his white, auburn-haired girlfriend's hand. There was a desperation to him that Nikki found sad. She looked over at Luke as they walked side by side and noticed that she felt a pang of sadness about her relationship, too.

'Now what do we have here! A broom! I have never seen this before at Beau Feu. Did one of y'all bring this with you?'

The tour guide made out as if the question was to the group, but his eyes landed on Nikki. She was too focused on the growing panic within her to take much notice of the tour guide's intended disrespect. Her dream state had clearly merged with the real world somehow. The group laughed along with the tour guide cheerily, and Nikki wondered if they could even identify what exactly was funny about his comment.

The tour guide started to move on, gesturing around the plantation as if bloodshed, rape, torture and enslavement were perfectly normal, but Nikki found herself asking, 'Wasn't jumping the broom a Black American practice? Something that would've been observed by those who were once enslaved here?' She was fighting to keep her tone measured.

The subtle hum of chatter amongst the group ceased immediately, and the atmosphere became thick with resistance. The tour guide took a moment to choose a smile to wear before addressing Nikki. 'Now, Ma'am, we do have a policy here that we don't use terms such as enslavement, because it can make others feel very uncomfortable. While we acknowledge that some unfortunate things have taken place in history, we believe in moving forward with beauty, and dreaming of a better world.'

Nikki was unable to stop herself. 'Maybe it is time to stop *dreaming* and wake up! People were literally tortured here and had to live in these "quaint" shacks against their will. Who in their right mind would think it was OK to celebrate any occasion here or any place like it? It is disgusting, and I can't bear to think that all those who died could be forgotten in history because you feel uncomfortable to use the exact word – ENSLAVEMENT – that describes their experience!'

Nikki could not believe that all these words had come tumbling from her own mouth, but she'd felt them coursing from her heart and she couldn't hold back any longer. The audacity of the tour guide and the apathy of the group had ignited the passion in her to say something.

Once she stopped speaking and looked around the group, the eyes that could bear to look at her cast judgement, as if she had ruined a beautiful moment. But it was Melissa who for some reason began to cry, and instantly the tension from the group towards Nikki seemed to intensify. She reached for Luke's hand, which felt cold in hers. He was clearly reluctant to clasp her hand tightly in return. Looking up at Luke's face, Nikki realised that he, too, wore an expression of discomfort.

He removed his hand from Nikki's and whispered, 'C'mon,

Nikki, you promised to make this work for the both of us. Not everything is about you. This is really unfair.' He then turned away and gathered with the rest of the group to console Melissa while glancing over at Nikki and willing her with his eyes to understand his predicament.

She felt her anger spark hot tears of her own, which sprang from her eyes suddenly. Walking away from the group as her eyes blurred from crying, Nikki chastised herself for not being able to hold her tongue long enough to see the weekend through. It is not that she believed herself to be in the wrong, but rather her rightness and conviction left her severely outnumbered in this environment.

As she wiped her tears from her eyes, she looked up to view the woodland around her on the lengthy walk back to the house, and saw that she was suddenly surrounded by brooms.

They were everywhere.

Turning back to look at the path she had been walking on since leaving the group, Nikki realised with breathless shock that brooms were also placed all across the ground where she had just passed.

The message from the elder in her dream had been clear, and Nikki understood with complete certainty now that it had been real. The spirit of those who had suffered on these grounds could not rest while people continued to behave as if the atrocities committed in this place meant very little.

'Another wedding is not going to take place here. You must leave.'

Nikki understood now that the wedding wouldn't go ahead. She didn't know how the fire would start, but once it did there would be no saving Beau Feu.

She broke into a run towards the house.

★ ★ ★

Luke found Nikki in the bedroom, packing in a frenzy.

'We need to leave this place. Something weird is happening and I can't give you a logical explanation right now, but we need to go.'

'I think it's best you go on without me.' Luke stood back observing Nikki pack, clearly resolute that he would be staying.

'What do you mean go without you? You drove. How would I get to the airport? What are you even saying? Do you not realise how wild it is that they're carrying on as if all of this is perfectly normal?'

Luke's gaze was steely and uncompromising. 'We get it! You're upset by the location, but it's not Mark and Melissa's fault that these places happen to be the ones available for the type of wedding they want to have. They didn't build the plantation, for fuck's sake! You talk about all of this stuff and how you can't stand the Queen and this and that, but you still play the game. You still want the accolades. Doesn't that make you a hypocrite? Not everything has to be a struggle, Nikki.'

She noticed Luke had chosen not to call her Naks, and also understood that something between them had severed completely now, even if it was flimsy to begin with. He wasn't wrong about her hypocrisy, but even that cold hard truth could not make her budge on the necessity of saying what she had during the tour.

'Maybe you're right and I am a hypocrite, and maybe not everything has to be a struggle and I wish it wasn't, but hey ho – welcome to the world! It is easy to frown on struggle when you've been aligned with the victor for so long. I shouldn't have tried to play along, but sometimes you have to play these people at their own game. But as a Black woman, I have to draw a line somewhere. I cannot choose to simply opt out of participating in society, even if the very construct of it requires me to betray myself at many turns. I have tried to teach you about these things, but clearly the listening you claim you were doing didn't get very far into your brain.'

Luke stared out of the window, the corner of his eyes creased as he contended with himself. When he spoke again, his voice was quiet. 'So, look . . . we all had a chat out there and they think it's best you go. You know this is awkward for me, and I imagine now even more awkward for you. You have hated this place since we arrived, and I feel terrible that I asked you to come along, but we can chat about all this when I get back to London in a few days. I thought you'd be talking about leaving, so Chet Harris, the newscaster guy, has kindly offered for his helicopter to come get you and take you to the airport. I've checked the flights back to London and I've been able to move yours to tonight. You have to understand how difficult this is for me, Nikki. As much as I love the time we spend together, this is my client. This is my life.'

Nikki's disappointment pressed down on her shoulders and caused her to sit on the bed next to her suitcase. She had no words left.

Her tears continued to fall as she walked with her belongings towards the helicopter as it hovered down to the ground outside the mansion. The group gathered on the front porch to look on as she walked away, Melissa remaining committed to her worthless tears even when Nikki called over her shoulder one last time to the group to suggest that they should consider not seeing the wedding through at this location. Melissa wailed even more at this, and Mark began to get visibly irate. After giving Nikki a lacklustre hug, Luke moved back to stand awkwardly on the grass between the helicopter and the wedding group, clearly conflicted by his choices.

Joan called out to Nikki, barely audible due to the loud whizzing of the helicopter propellers as they started up again. 'Nikki, I'll be in touch!'

Nikki did not know what to make of Joan's comment. Would she really see any of these people again? She had little time to process it, trying desperately to ignore all the brooms she could see placed carefully all around the mansion and literally everywhere her eyes could see on the plantation grounds.

Once she was sat in the helicopter and her ear protectors were secured, the pilot informed Nikki they were taking off. As they rose into the air, she felt a relief that melted her initial humiliation away. Looking out through the window as the ground drew away from them, Nikki took in the stooping trees once again. As the branches swished, Nikki thought she caught a glimpse of white dresses in among them.

The women gathered, waving, and then Nikki saw the sudden spark of a flame . . .

Councilwoman

Simi woke up and *remembered*. That is how she knew that today she would die.

It was not a painful realisation either, because Simi considered herself to have lived a full life. Did she have any fears at the age of ninety-two, having just celebrated her birthday two weeks prior with her children and their children, and their children? No. She felt no apprehension about knowing this day would be her last day alive.

The first flash of remembering happened just before she opened her eyes to begin this final day. Simi saw in her heart's eye what looked to be a vast amphitheatre hovering in the middle of space, surrounded by stars and with planets barely visible in the distance. Simi noticed a translucent pillar made of light and cascading water at the centre of the amphitheatre. She looked around and saw shapes that resembled people, but they were made of light. Simi could make out that these light figures were clothed in robes, and that each being was a unique entity. As Simi witnessed them all, she realised that they were murmuring words she knew she had not heard on Earth before, yet still understood. She also knew that this place was not merely of her imagination.

The pillar of cascading water and light pulsated in a mighty manner, calling the attention of the light figures. In a language that sounded like crashing waves and tinkling wind chimes, the pillar asked, 'And what has the council decided?'

In the most bizarre occurrence that made Simi catch her breath and caused her to open her physical eyes, the entire amphitheatre turned to look at *her*.

What could it all mean? Why are they turning to me? These thoughts careered through Simi's mind as she awoke fully and gently lifted herself up from her bed, setting her feet down on the woven rug she had bought many years ago during her travels.

Travel.

Although she was now awake, Simi saw another flash in her heart's eye and became certain that she was remembering a time before the one she was currently living. In this vision, Simi watched herself confidently speaking among the council entities who filled the enormous amphitheatre, all of them facing the pillar made of water and light.

'*For as long as you have dreamt us into being, Spirit, most of us have resided here, ruling on the completion of soul tasks without having experienced what the Soil-beings go through. Divine wisdom is one thing, but in order to ensure that we decide fairly in the case of a being such as this one whom we are judging today, I volunteer to enter one of the dimensions as a Soil-being myself, so that I may experience what they do. I am aware that this would strip me of all celestial memories until the day that it is time for me to return. It will be the equivalent of but a moment here in this realm, but if I am able to incarnate into a life similar to this being's earthly one, then we would have a conclusive answer for our judgement rather than making it solely on the basis that "this is the way it has always been". Look at the many souls that wait for their judgement as to whether they have satisfactorily completed their tasks. We owe it to this being, and to the many souls who wait for news of completion of their tasks, that we are just and swift and make our judgements from an informed perspective . . .*'

Before Simi could finish her speech in the vision, an uproar of dissent broke out from the council entities.

'*I respectfully object!*' shouted one of the ethereal voices from what sounded like miles away. '*We have watched over the lives of the Soil-beings in every dimension since the beginning of time. This being that appears before us now has been instructed to return to Earth because, by the very rules we have abided by since we were brought into awareness by Spirit – and that are written into the Book of Souls for every Soil-being – he should have met specific assignment targets. One of those assignment targets included leading a nation with love. The Soil-being met all other requirements, but instead of ruling or leading a nation, he merely led a small town to freedom from governmental tyranny. That wasn't a nation! The appeal to conclude this Soil-being's earthly quest as complete should not be entertained. Our rulings as to whether Soil-beings would need to return to complete assignments have never been incorrect, so why should we question or test our judgements now?*'

This appeared to be an incredibly important celestial council, and Simi was one of the council members. The hundreds of thousands of council members gathered in the amphitheatre swished their robes of light forward to show their support of the sentiment shared by the far-away voice. Then, the pillar of cascading water and light that had brought them all into being began to speak, and all the swishing of robes ceased.

'*Councilwoman, you are correct,*' the pillar began. '*When I dreamt all things into being, granting free will was integral to observing how all things find their way back to this place. I already have my answer, but there would be little purpose in yourselves if I were to decide on all matters. I hereby create an entry for you in the Book of Souls, permitting you to assist in the decision regarding the completion of this Soil-being's soul tasks, and thus the council's collective ability to adapt your judgements for the completion of tasks in a broader manner. This Soil-being's task in the Book of Souls specifically stated that he must lead a nation, and that is not what was achieved, yet the impact seems to have allowed for the liberation of other Soil-beings, empowering them.*

'*Thus, your own task will be about power. You will enter into the form of a Soil-being, and your assignment includes only one thing: to gain immense power and change the world. You will have no recollection of this once you have taken the form of a Soil-being, and you will not have the advantage of being a councilwoman with timeless knowledge to aid your journey. This ensures that your experience is as close to those of the Soil-beings as possible. If you achieve the assignment as dictated, it will mean that it was also possible for this Soil-being and all others to complete their task exactly as written and thus any abstract completion of tasks will continue to require the being to return to Earth to finish their assignments exactly as written.*'

Simi was seeing this vision while still sitting awake at the edge of her bed. She wasn't sure if she could trust herself to stand while seeing such vivid images of the most breathtaking celestial place. Eventually, as the vision dissipated, Simi pushed her toes into the rug with intent and stood slowly, determined to continue with her last day on Earth.

She made her way to the kitchen while attempting to make sense of the images that had begun to return to her in that strange, liminal space between dreaming and waking. As she walked to the kitchen – or rather, the kitchen formed around her as the construct of the bedroom folded itself away and into the ground – Simi smiled, thinking about the many milestones in her life.

This was how things were now. Everything was automated and called forth with a mere flickering thought of the mind.

She had seen it all develop over the decades. From being a young girl and waiting for her mother to get off the landline before she could go on the internet, to the rise of mobile phones and then social media. Now this – living in a house that was perfectly sized for her at her age, because the majority of it was constructed using augmented reality, with basic and minimal furniture all decorated to one's taste using computer coding. Appliances, folded away underneath the floor and into the walls, were triggered to emerge by thought patterns and homeostasis recognition, which were perceived by chips everyone had implanted into the right side of their skull.

Life felt easier now for sure, but Simi could not deny missing the days when technology was not so embedded in her day-to-day life, and before global outbreaks of disease had led to stringent measures prohibiting physical human interaction. Now people required permits to see loved ones, otherwise everything was done through holograms. Unless legally permitted to live with someone, most people could only physically interact with other households on special occasions, which were cross-checked by extensive databases to ensure the reasons for meeting were valid. For example, it had taken two months to have Simi's last birthday party approved. Her eldest daughter, Mariam, had meticulously sourced all the family's skull chip identification numbers. She had begged family members who insisted on being off the grid to avoid sharing their personal data with the World Surveillance Agency to apply for temporary passes to travel into Simi's zone. You could only reside there if the WSA felt that all the required personal data they had asked for was satisfactory. It had been quite the to-do.

While waiting for the kettle to boil for her tea now, Simi

looked at the accolades projected onto her kitchen wall. One of them caught her attention: Zonal Medal of Achievement for Services to Equality. Simi smiled to herself as she gripped the sturdy handle of her kettle and began to pour hot water into her cup. From as far back as she could remember, Simi had felt somehow separate to the world around her. Perhaps that was starting to make sense now. As a little girl, Simi would often ask her mother if she was sure about how she had arrived into the world.

The more she asked, the more offended her mother became. 'Of course you are my daughter, Simisọlá. It can't be that terrible to have me as a mother that you are looking for another origin story.'

Simi wasn't trying to be rude with her enquiries. It was just that in her dreams she would often see herself walking through purple velvet curtains and suddenly appearing into the life she was told was her own but felt quite foreign to her. Simi's father did his best to assuage her concerns about where she came from by encouraging her to write about what she saw in her dreams. As far as Simi's parents were concerned, her imagination was immense – something that scared her mother and excited her father.

This feeling of not quite being of Earth didn't leave her for many years. Even as she made friends in high school and proved herself to be charismatic and popular, as well as a gifted writer, it always felt to Simi like she was on the outside looking in. The outsider's role paid off for her in many ways as she grew up, because it allowed her to have a perspective on life that many who were very immersed in their own experiences were unable to possess. Her writing of poetry and fiction was so intriguing that it earnt her a place at the University of Edinburgh, and that is where she met Huda.

Freshers' week had been an absolute bore for Simi. She was hours away from home, in another country, and Simi wasn't quite sure how she would cope with the endless bar crawls and overbearing dorm mates.

Then one evening, sitting listlessly at the student union bar willing 'Summer of '69' to finish blaring out of the speakers, Simi felt a hand on her arm.

'You seem like you want to dissolve like the ice in your glass. Do you want another drink?'

Simi didn't quite know why her words seemed incapable of forming a sentence as she looked up at the person talking to her. She was firstly enamoured by the smile formed by full, light brown lips and round, gorgeous cheeks. As Simi took in more of the face of the person in front of her, her eyes met theirs, which were filled with mischief in their deep brownness. She had immaculately arched brows and luscious, jet-black, wavy hair that had been adorned at the hairline with tiny gelled swirls of hair studded with tiny rhinestones.

Incredible, Simi thought to herself.

'Or have you actually dissolved and all that is left is your body, since you're not answering?' the woman teased.

Simi could feel her face getting warm. She wanted to say something, but her throat seemed to have shut down along with the part of her brain that was usually so good at threading words together. Instead, her chest and stomach ached from excitement and awe, and she considered why it had never occurred to her in all these years that she hadn't fancied anybody in particular until now. Simi's mind quickly started trying to play back any occurrences of crushes, even when attending an all-girls' high school, and she could think of nothing. She had always found other girls interesting to look at, and was sometimes curious about one or two of the boys she would see at the youth centre; but as Simi began to think about it, nothing had ever come close to sparking this emotion before.

'Sorry. I . . . um . . . You're just really pretty, and it threw me off. Sorry if that sounds weird.' Simi let the words tumble out.

'It's not weird at all. I don't usually offer drinks on the house since I'm trying not to get fired. I still have another two years of uni to survive after all. But you're pretty, too, so I'll take the chance. I'm Huda.'

And that was the beginning of their love.

For the next two years that Huda studied at university, the two women melted their lives together and lived in the concoction that formed as a result. As soon as Simi's first year was done, she and Huda found a cheap flat together and dedicated their time to orbiting each other while fulfilling the tasks that university and family required of them.

Huda was of Sudanese heritage and had been born and bred in East London. She was incredibly insightful, in a way that Simi had never experienced before. She had received a scholarship to study Politics and International Relations at the University of Edinburgh, and she took the opportunity very seriously. Huda worked at the student union bar to earn extra money since her father could not provide financial support while raising her two younger sisters. Her mother had passed away when she was eight, and from what Huda could remember, she had died from tiredness. Her father had told her later that it was from a cancer that hadn't been diagnosed in time, even though her mother went to the doctors with complaints about her symptoms frequently. Huda understood this yet still maintained that it was tiredness that took her mother away. Fleeing Sudan only to arrive in a country that showed her daily that she was unwanted, her mother would wake up every day and dress her daughters for school, reminding them that to survive in England it was important to be *wanted*.

Huda cared very little about being wanted by the society that had tired her mother out, though. Instead, she wanted to be *heard*. Studying politics was Huda's way of understanding how the country operated, and she hoped that one day she could impact change in some way. In her first year of university, she had stumbled upon a student activist group that would regularly meet to discuss the effects of British imperialism. Her understanding of her own Sudanese heritage became even more clear once she comprehended the sociopolitical role that Britain played in the 'war-torn' countries that resembled the land her parents migrated from.

The only times Simi didn't see Huda would be when they were both at lectures, or when Huda was working or meeting with her activist group: RS.

'What does RS stand for?' Simi asked one night when Huda had returned out of breath from either passion or walking up the hill that their flat was perched on.

'Restless Souls. I think it sums up how it feels to be in this world and know that you can't truly have peace when it is denied to so many others. When we are together, in here, I feel like peace is possible. But then I get this sort of electrical charge when I think about my mum and other families who struggled in this world and didn't deserve to, and I think to myself – what can I do about it? How can I help? I want to make things better, and when you want to make things better your soul can't rest.'

Simi loved to listen to Huda. Not only was her voice the softest raspy conjuring of her inner light, but she spoke with such conviction and passion that it really was no surprise that she was often asked by RS to speak on their behalf at marches and in video campaigns that were shared all across the internet. The activist group was well aware of the disparity in viewership when one of the other group members presented their points on video compared to when it was Huda. Her stunning features, her incredible intelligence delivered in a casual manner that felt accessible, with that enamouring voice? That was a combination that kept people engaging with the work of RS. Huda's impact was undeniable.

Meanwhile, Simi had got a part-time job as an administrative assistant in one of the UK government buildings. She couldn't believe her luck when she was approached by a man handing out flyers for a recruitment drive.

'Hey, in case you're looking for work alongside your studies, consider this.'

Simi had taken the flyer from the man. He appeared to be middle-aged and rather serious looking, even though he spoke with a smile throughout their conversation.

'What kind of work is this?' Simi queried. 'Students can't work many hours.'

'Yes, it's fine for students. Ideal. They're mainly administrative roles to help in various governmental departments. For those who are about to graduate, there is a different recruitment scheme. Do you know anybody who is about to graduate?'

'Yeah, my girlfriend is about to graduate, actually. She studies Politics and International Relations. I'll show her this and see if she's interested.'

'Well, since you're still studying, these roles might be better suited to you. Maybe I could grab an email address for your girlfriend and I'll send details through for the graduate scheme?'

Simi wrote down Huda's email address and took off home to sort her own application. Within a couple of hours of applying for the role, Simi had received a response – they'd offered her a part-time job and a start date, just like that.

'Simi, don't you think that is so odd?' Huda had asked. 'Government buildings require a lot of security clearance, and they just said they're recruiting *students*, people who spend most of their time nursing hangovers?'

Huda continued to be sceptical of her girlfriend's new role, and Simi wondered if there was a bit of jealousy there, since Huda had mentioned only having a choice between retail or the student union bar as job prospects throughout her time of study.

'Maybe things are changing,' Simi had told her. 'That is what you say all the time that you want to see, right? If more young people are being invited to work in these institutions, albeit in menial roles, their impact will be felt eventually. Anyway, I gave the recruitment guy your email address since they have a whole different thing for soon-to-be-graduates.'

Huda had smiled at that. 'You're so sweet, babe. I appreciate that, although I don't think I want to work for the government. I want to see more of the world and figure out how I can really be of service.' Her face had turned more serious. 'I'll be graduating soon, and we haven't even talked about what that means for us.'

Simi had known the conversation would have to happen at some point, and it made her anxious. Since her first week at university, all she had known was Huda's world. Neither of their families knew about their relationship – they only described themselves to family as 'best friends and housemates'. It just felt easier. Huda had mentioned moving back to London and back to her family home after she graduated, so she could decide what to do next. That meant a year left for Simi at university without Huda, and with the task of finding a new flatmate.

Despite all of this looming on the horizon, the two women continued to love and live as the completion of Huda's studies approached. Simi fell into her role of administrative assistant in the government buildings without any trouble. Her job was rather simple, and that made it easier to balance alongside her degree. Her main tasks included inputting a list of names into the government database for the Talent Surveillance department. The aim of the department was to take note of the great minds all around the country based on their social media presence as well as academic records. Sometimes, in order to show initiative, Simi would look up the names and find obscure information to add that wasn't included in the spreadsheet about the talented person. If they were going to be approached at some point to be commended for their excellence, it would be nice to have extra elements that would make them feel seen.

The department seemed to appreciate this extra input from Simi, and within a few months of working there her role morphed into finding out even more information about these talented individuals. Simi had wanted to share the news of her progression at the Talent Surveillance department with Huda, but that would've been a security breach. Huda had been right about the security clearances. The department made a big show of letting Simi known that she was chosen to work with them out of hundreds of applications. Apparently, the technology used across governmental platforms to select staff, whether part-time or full-time, allowed for a fast but in-depth search to be done in order to assess a potential employee's propensity for danger. Simi continued to feel lucky and proud to have been selected.

But time was against them. Simi and Huda didn't want to admit that what was happening was a break-up, because that would've been too much for both of them to bear. Instead, upon Huda's graduation with first-class honours, they agreed that they would see each other every month once Huda found a job in London and could travel back up to Edinburgh. Simi promised to visit on the holidays while staying with her parents.

Yet quickly Huda was swept up in working for an activist organisation similar to RS once she arrived back in London. Within a matter of weeks, she was no longer living with her father and had instead moved into a flat of her own, supported by the organisation: Edge of Here. Simi tried her best to push down the lump in her throat as she listened to Huda excitedly talk on the phone about her new role, because she knew it meant the distance would grow between them beyond just physical miles.

'These people are amazing, Simi. They're activists, but they're, like, super advanced. They raise funding and use it to support technologies that challenge the notion of inevitable structural inequality.'

Simi had listened with longing as Huda described her new life, which seemed to be less and less connected to hers. This time she felt a pang of jealousy.

'It's hard to explain,' Huda had continued, 'and obviously

there are people involved in funding this stuff that I haven't met yet, but ultimately Edge of Here are working on software that would cause the idea of monetary currency to be obsolete. They always stress that various seemingly unrelated technologies would eventually work in synergy to create a world that *looks* like this one, but it's the edge of it. It is what we could be if we collectively tried hard enough.'

'It sounds like you're happy,' Simi had muttered.

'Yes. But just because I am happy doesn't mean I don't miss you. We are always connected, Simi. Just think of this year as us being in the same house but just in different rooms. I'm only in the other room, OK? And I'll see you soon.'

The wordsmith in Simi couldn't help but float with longing and desire for Huda, who always found a way to make her feel safe in their love. And yet, after a couple of visits to see each other, it was silently agreed that they would both focus on their own lives and hopefully pick up where they'd left off once Simi completed her degree.

After a while, Simi found her rhythm. Her new flatmate was a second year teaching student who spent most of her time out with friends. Simi liked this setup, because it meant she had the flat to herself most evenings. She would start off by getting any written work for university out of the way, because all that came so easily to her. Then she would spend the rest of the night looking up names assigned to her from the Talent Surveillance department, finding information about them that would enhance what was known by the government and show just how excellent they were. Simi was somewhat envious that these individuals were so brilliant the state wanted to track them inconspicuously, and to then pull strings to align these individuals with funding organisations that would allow them to continue their great work. Almost like governmental secret angels, Simi liked to think. In a way, she wanted to make Huda proud that she was doing good for the world – well, the UK government – in her own small way, too.

After a while, Simi was summoned by the head of department to be thanked personally for her 'outstanding capacity for in-depth surveillance'. Simi had been proud of her own initiative to create various anonymous social media accounts to follow some of the talented individuals and use their posts to populate more fields in their government profiles. When Simi finished her degree with one of the highest marks in the country she was happy, but what made her even more elated was the offer from the Talent Surveillance department to take on a full-time role with them in London.

'You're great at this, Simi, there's no doubt about it,' her boss told her. 'We, of course, wanted to support your focus on your education, otherwise we would've promoted you long ago. London is best suited to you since that is your hometown, but also a lot of chatter takes place there, and often the greatest minds we would like to keep track of tend to reside there. The perks are more than that of student employment. We will cover your accommodation and such, and your salary will reflect the importance of the work that you'll be doing. As such, your security clearance will increase somewhat, too.'

Simi would often play that conversation back in her head years later to see at which point she could've picked up on the signs that something wasn't quite right. That maybe things with her role hadn't been right from the beginning.

The enhanced security clearance changed everything.

The profiles that Simi had been putting together over time for the Talent Surveillance department extended further than she realised, and her eager desire to show her own excellence had led to more information being unearthed about the individuals than would've otherwise been found. Their files now included their hospital records and sub-profiles for their family members, as well as any phone tracking data that was mined from sites with low security measures.

Simi was flabbergasted. She now understood that what was presented to her as simply talent surveillance of the UK's brightest minds was something far more sinister. The people being surveilled were definitely incredible minds, but Simi realised that they were also affiliated in some way or another to activist organisations. Those organisations varied from animal rights to climate change to racial injustice, as well as LGBTQIA+ rights. The limited information that Simi previously had access to meant that she couldn't have fathomed just how much information the Talent Surveillance department was actually collating. What Simi had previously been exposed to was so carefully isolated that it was clear to her it had been intentional. She naively gathered information, believing that her work served a positive purpose.

The surveillance of each individual was triggered by their decision to use their excellence to impact social change in some way. What was peculiar to Simi was that in all the names she could see, none of the surveillance targeted right-wing 'brilliant minds', only those on the left.

Simi had sat in the office of her stunning, state-of-the-art apartment in Vauxhall, staring at the screen and feeling nauseous as the realisation descended on her further, and she began to understand just how much she had contributed to this covert operation. For someone with such great observational skills, Simi was disappointed in herself for not realising sooner what was happening. She felt ashamed that she was now deeply embedded in a system that would've enraged Huda, not made her proud.

Due to her enhanced clearance, what Simi could now see was the risk rating of each individual. The majority of profiles remained on low-risk. Any medium-risk profiles required a 'bumping', which was a new part of Simi's job description. Bumping required the surveillance operative, her new role, to orchestrate a situation where they would bump into the surveilled individual in person in an unassuming way and extract any information possible through a seemingly normal conversation. The department gathered enough information through street cameras and geolocations to narrow down the areas that they had the highest likelihood of bumping into the individual. Sometimes it took days and other times it took weeks to execute a bumping, but once it happened, it was imperative to gather as much information as possible and hopefully create enough rapport that the surveillance operative could meet with the surveilled again.

Since beginning the new role, Simi made sure to cut down on her contact with Huda. She could not shake the disappointment in herself at being so enmeshed in such a sinister system, but she was even more conflicted because she knew she could not leave if there was a chance that she could do something to help these amazing activists from the inside. It pained her that on the occasions when Huda did have some spare time and hinted at them meeting up, Simi, the master of words, would have to pretend like she didn't know what was being asked of her.

It had been her hope that once she moved to London they would pick up their relationship from where they left off, seeing as they both had their own apartments and wouldn't have to worry too much about their families. Huda had been enthusiastic about the idea, too, but was also deeply engrossed in the work she was doing with Edge of Here. Every other week there would be a viral video of Huda circulating the internet as she made her matter-of-fact points about the state of the world and the inequality encouraged by the government. Young people signed up for Edge of Here campaigns in their droves because of Huda. She was striking and full of conviction, and that spoke to the hearts of many. That, at least, kept the reason for the two of them not picking back up feeling mutual.

High-risk profiles were what worried Simi the most. These profiles were not readily available to view, and would only be visible if they needed to be 'actioned'. From what Simi had come to understand, the surveilled became high-risk if they were gaining too much power – whether financial or in social currency – to the point that they had the potential to under-mine the government.

Whenever Simi came across a video of Huda, she would instinctively look at the number of views the video had amassed. Sometimes Huda's reach would be in the hundreds of thousands, and it filled Simi's heart with dread that the attention could lead to Huda being surveilled by even more sinister departments than her own. She appeased herself with thoughts that maybe misogyny could work in Huda's favour – that she could be perceived as too pretty to be a threat, no matter how passionate she was. Maybe she was hanging out in a pile of somebody's medium-risk assignments and they were too enamoured to see her as any higher risk. Simi hoped that was the case. Although her clearance wasn't to the highest level, Simi was also aware that it was intentional that the department had agents like herself work in isolation and remain uninformed as to what other departments or agents were up to. That way nobody had too much power. So all she could do was speculate and stay alert regarding Huda's safety.

The high-risk profiles didn't get a bumping, because usually this would've happened already if they had been surveilled from an early stage. If they had suddenly appeared on the government's radar as high-risk, then higher departments than Simi's would get involved. Simi's security clearance didn't allow her to know what happened at that stage. All she knew was that the high-risk profiles Simi *could* see were the ones who had been surveilled for some time and would now be presented with the ultimatum.

The ultimatum would usually be presented by the surveillance operative who did the bumping, since the surveilled would recognise them and understand the extent to which they were being watched. Unlike an initial bumping, where the surveillance operative would aim to meet the surveilled in the natural mix of their lives so as not to raise suspicion, an ultimatum would usually take place near the surveilled's home. This would usually be enough to let them know that there was sufficient information available about them to track them all the way there – a tactic that worked best with activists who had families or children they cared about protecting.

The ultimatum was usually simple and short: 'It is clear to us that you believe in your cause. Is it worth your life?'

That was usually enough for the most ardent activist to quieten down. They had no way of tracing who this person – who was practically a stranger – was who had approached them in this way, and thus their fear was heightened. When people were fearful, they were easier to control, Simi had learnt.

When Huda's name finally showed up as high-risk, Simi's world crumbled. She had carried the heavy burden of expectation that one day this would be the case, and would often comfort herself by believing that at worst Huda would be astute enough to not divulge too much information about her work to the operative tasked with her surveillance during a bumping.

However, Simi saw that Huda's file was flagged as 'transferred', which would indicate that the operative previously assigned to her was no longer working in that role. Simi cautiously clicked on the background information to learn about the operative who had surveilled Huda.

The picture of the operative loaded on her screen and shock radiated throughout Simi's entire body. It was the man who had handed her the flyer at university. Hundreds of thoughts careened through Simi's mind. Instead of bumping Huda, this operative had bumped *her* all those years ago. And Simi had unwittingly provided Huda's email address. This was a method that was available to operatives but was rarely useful because loved ones weren't as close to each other as they sometimes imagined themselves to be. Hence, it was best to bump the surveilled to get the information necessary. In Huda and Simi's case, though, the operative had clearly identified that they were indeed close enough for him to get to Huda through Simi.

Simi remembered Huda opening her emails and clicking on the link the man had sent, only to decide that she wasn't interested in the role. From what Simi had since learnt about the methods they were trained to utilise in her new job, Huda was never *expected* to actually want the graduate role. She was just required to click the link, which would allow direct access to her computer and possibly her phone. Without realising it, Simi had helped the government to track Huda throughout the time they lived together at university, and possibly after.

At the discovery of all this, Simi felt guilt wrapping itself around her and squeezing her tightly, making it difficult to take in air. How was it possible to love someone so much, yet unwittingly be the means that they had been opened up to potential harm? As she pulled in gulps of air to calm herself down, Simi clicked on subfolders to see how much information was actually available about Huda – and there it was. A folder on *her*. Simisọlá Adebanjo.

Her folder was flagged as 'neutralised', which meant that the operative deemed Simi to not be a threat – presumably since she had been brought into the fold of helping the government instead. As much as Simi felt sick to read the in-depth information gathered about herself and Huda, she saw the advantage immediately in being labelled as neutralised. There was still time to do something. But it hurt to know that the operative had clearly taken the time to collate information from when Huda and Simi lived together, even emails and texts they'd sent each other, some trivial and some deeply sensual. There had been a shadow present in their relationship the whole time and neither of them had been wise to it.

Simi knew she had to warn Huda now, and although she hadn't seen her since moving to London, she knew where she lived from visiting while at university. It was only a matter of time before the department would realise the conflict of interest in Simi having access to Huda's file. A few hours if she was lucky . . .

When Huda answered the door, she was met with a panicked Simi standing in the rain.

'Simi, I wasn't . . .' Huda was confused and tried to usher Simi into her apartment.

From what Simi could view from the hallway, Huda was living comfortably. In their time apart, Huda had travelled and collected memories along the way while speaking up against injustice. On a low shelf in the hallway was a picture of the two of them, next to a bowl where Huda seemingly kept her keys. Just seeing this and knowing that it would be the first picture Huda must see every time she entered her home, or anybody entered her home for that matter, made tears spring from Simi's eyes.

'You have to go, Huda,' Simi told her urgently. 'You have to leave this place. They've been watching you for years and somehow I helped them without realising it, and I hope you know that I'm sorry. You were right – they don't just take students to work for the government. You have to be useful to them, and I've been useful in providing access to you but also helped them find information about other people. I had no idea. I hope you know I'm sorry. I don't know what is going to happen to me, but you need to leave. They've flagged you as high-risk and it's only a matter of time before someone shows up asking you to choose between your activism and your life. Maybe even this is a set up and I'm doing exactly that by telling you all this, but I can't take the chance that you might not take them seriously and persist with your work anyway. I wish I had never given your email over to that recruitment guy. That was your surveillance operative.' She finally drew a breath. All of the words had come tumbling out of Simi's mouth in a rush, but she hoped they had formed an order that Huda would understand. Huda, stood in her hallway in her bathrobe, with her jet-black hair framing her face like a halo.

Huda's eyes also filled with tears as understanding dawned on her face. 'No need to be sorry, Simi. I'm not shocked at being surveilled. It's wild that they'd been doing it before I even felt like I had any impact. You weren't to know. But I've made such progress with Edge of Here, I don't know how I am just meant to leave all of that? How am I meant to leave my family and you?'

Simi wasn't expecting to hear herself as a consideration, since they'd spent a year apart in a break-up they had never even discussed. Then her eyes sought the picture frame next to the keys, and she understood that the love between them wasn't affected by distance, or their aspirations.

Huda continued. 'Simi, you know I thought when you moved to London we would figure this stuff out with our families and just get on with living? I thought maybe you were busy settling into your new place for the first few days. But then your number stopped working, and I didn't understand. I didn't hate you or anything, though. I figured whatever it was, you clearly thought that was the best course of action. To me, we are always in the same house even if we are in different rooms. I told you that. That's why our pictures are all around this apartment. I may be doing all this amazing work with Edge of Here, but there isn't a day where I don't think about you.'

Simi could see the life that she, too, had dreamt of with Huda slipping away from her, all because of a stupid part-time job she had taken on at university believing that she was doing some good in the shadows. She knew that this would be the last time they would get to speak if they both had any chance of remaining alive.

'On the first day I arrived at the London office and all the security checks were done,' Simi began, her voice quiet, 'I was taken into this room with a massive electronic map on the screen. It was a map of the UK, and it was covered in dots. My new head of department watched me look at the screen in confusion and he said all those dots were the active activists they were aware of in the country. He said our role was to ensure that none ever gained enough power to challenge the integrity of the government. Any means necessary as long as our tactics never brought shame to the monarch. Huda, for two years in Edinburgh I was filling out all this information about random people and finding extra information because I was told that they were talented and worth watching and would get funding to continue being great. How naive was I? I feel like I can't leave now, though. Instead, I have to make sure that at least the people who pass across my desk aren't ever hurt. That's why you have to leave. Another country. Carry on your work with your organisation somewhere where these people don't have direct access to you. They know everything. Start again somewhere else.'

Neither of the women wanted to leave the other, yet they knew there was little choice in the matter.

'What time is it?' Simi asked.

'8.35 p.m. Why?' Huda responded.

'My phone has been off for about thirty minutes. I didn't want them to track me here. I have to go, so it doesn't look suspicious. I'm going to alert them in about an hour that I have your file and I shouldn't. Is that enough time for you to go?'

'I can't take anything or tell anyone?'

Simi gazed at Huda silently, because she knew that Huda knew the answer to her own question.

'I love you, Simi. You doing this for me lets me know that I will always love you.'

'I love you, too. And even if we never see each other again, I'll know that you're somewhere in this world so technically, you're just in the other room.'

Huda motioned a kiss without moving closer to Simi, and Simi did the same before turning away and running out of the door and into the night, ensuring that she avoided cameras in the same way she had done when she'd arrived at Huda's home.

When the internal investigation was conducted as to whether Simi had any hand in the sudden disappearance of Huda, they would conclude that she did not, because she was seen at the supermarket buying groceries for her dinner and had forgotten her phone in her apartment, which had unfortunately succumbed to a low battery and switched itself off. The only cause for confusion was the time between the metadata recording the receipt of Huda's profile on Simi's computer and the two-hour lag before Simi reported the conflict of interest. What worked in her favour was that Simi *did* report it, and couldn't be traced as having contacted Huda.

Maybe it was a matter of coincidence, but no more high-risk cases came Simi's way thereafter. Meanwhile, the internet was awash with speculation on what could've happened to Huda, with Edge of Here providing very little information as to her whereabouts.

After two years, a video of Huda appeared as if no time had passed at all. Huda was in what seemed to be a high tech bunker, telling the world of Edge of Here's latest innovation: Cities of the Future. These containers could be built on the most barren land, as the building materials could adapt to extreme cold or heat while the temperature inside the container was perfectly set for comfortable living conditions. solar-powered electricity and clean water was provided through a spectacular irrigation system. It was cost-effective and would essentially mean that everybody could have access to amenities currently denied to many. This technology worried many governments, because they would no longer be able to maintain the myth that budgets and elusive austerity measures were the reason for everyday people being unable to have decent accommodation and resources. Whoever was funding Edge of Here was clearly geared towards proving the world's governments redundant.

Despite rigorous searches, nobody could track down Huda's location, and so her supporters were free to look forward to her daily updates about world events and what the public could do about advocating for themselves.

Over the next ten years, Simi worked with the Talent Surveillance department undetected, and more and more people were added to the database as low- or medium-risks as a result of Huda and Edge of Here's meteoric rise. Simi assuaged her guilt by doing her utmost to watch over the activists who would come her way, using her bumping interactions to carefully and subtly advise them on how to remain no higher than medium-risk, yet never giving too much away as to why she would be sharing such information.

The years continued to pass, and Huda disappeared from the public eye altogether after taking on much more senior roles within Edge of Here. In her place, younger and equally passionate campaigners popped up and led the charge with educating and galvanising the masses. In Huda's final video, announcing her advancement within Edge of Here, she had closed her moving speech by saying, 'Throughout the decades, where some of you have watched my first young and wide-eyed videos as an activist student, all the way up to the videos you've seen of me in recent years, one thing has remained consistent – your unwavering belief in me. To the family and friends that I had to sacrifice contact with to do this very important work, I understand that it will be especially hard for you to not see videos of me anymore, but I need you to understand that I am still here, and I am doing the work I have always felt called to do. I miss you all every day, but I remind myself that we aren't ever really apart. We're in the same house, I am just in a different room. That applies to those we are separated from by physical distance, or for those who have passed on. Love doesn't stop because our bodies move further apart. If you love me the way so many of you claim to do in the comments, I implore you to live full lives and to let Edge of Here help you to realise your inherent worth in this society.'

People would often quote Huda's speech, and even though she missed her terribly, it pleased Simi to no end that Huda's love wasn't just hers, but the world's. Cities of the Future created by Edge of Here began popping up in various countries, prioritising those who were experiencing homelessness and poverty. As Edge of Here pioneered initiatives focused on liberation, at the other end of the spectrum data chips, which were initially voluntarily inserted in people's brains as Ally-chips, became repurposed and mandatory for all as a way of gathering data about every citizen by the government. With her years of knowledge as a surveillance operative, Simi knew how unethically the data sourced from the chips could be used, especially if the average person with a chip installed was as unassuming as she had been all those years ago at university.

Simi made it her mission to closely monitor how information about the surveilled was being used, so that she could inform those she had access to and try to keep them safe. Every activist was Huda for Simi.

Simi navigated the hostile intentions of the department as a means of protecting those championing unity. There was only so much she could do, however; Simi was only given a certain number of profiles to surveil at any one time, and she understood the work of the department to be far greater than the access she had.

And then finally, unable to enact change from the inside anymore, Simi had decided to leave her surveillance job and run for local council. Within four years, she had become lead councilwoman for her borough. There had been calls for her to run for mayor and the like, but Simi also understood the murkiness of her previous role and how that could come back to haunt her, possibly even opening up further questions about how exactly her former girlfriend, Huda, had managed to disappear from the surveillance of the government . . .

Simi later decided to adopt two children, Mariam and

Sumner, a girl and boy who had come into her care as babies. She had always wanted a family, and although she had made her sexuality clear over time, she'd found it challenging to fully commit to relationships when she knew that all of her heart still belonged to Huda.

She eventually told her children about Huda, and while they thought their mother somewhat mad in her devotion to this woman, who they only knew as someone in the framed picture from university by their mother's bedside, they respected and were intrigued by her unwavering love.

Over the years, Simi had other romantic relationships that varied in length. Some lasted months and some lasted years, but Huda's presence was one all of these lovers grew to respect, as if Simi were some kind of widow.

Nevertheless, her life had been full of love and duty, and she was proud of it. Her awards, ironically received from the government, commended her on her services to ethical practices regarding cerebral chips as well as their integration with the Cities of the Future designed by Edge of Here.

Simi worried about Huda at times, like when the scandal broke regarding Edge of Here and its links to UteruStar, thanks to the work of their president of technological innovations, Dr Tòmíwá Fọlọ́runshọ́. Public confidence in the organisation began to wane, but Edge of Here worked diligently to regain the trust from the public when they finally decided to enter into a massive legal battle with William Bunker, the billionaire philanthropist who had been found to be integral in many human rights violations via technology throughout the decades.

★ ★ ★

She had lived quite the lifetime, but now, in her old age, Simi lived in a container similar to the Cities of Future homes designed by Edge of Here decades earlier. Her container was by the sea and, although minimalist in nature, it had beautiful glass doors that opened out onto the beach. This day, the day that might be her last, had gone by in a haze as she'd contemplated the strange vision she'd had that morning as she woke.

As the sun began to set, Simi unlocked her bedroom doors, which led out to the sand. With the sweet and salty breeze from the sea blowing in through a window, Simi climbed into her bed as it emerged via the thought-signals she sent out using her chip, and lay comfortably as she prepared for the final stage of the winding down of her life. Looking up at the ceiling, Simi saw flickers of yellow light above her that glowed gently. As she watched the droplets of light closely, they began to merge and intensify in their brightness.

Huda flashed across Simi's mind. Her darling, her forever love. Somehow, Huda felt closer now, closer than the image she had placated herself with all these years, with the reminder: *I'm just in the other room* . . .

The droplets of light had now formed into a ball of yellow radiance, pulsating as if beckoning her. Simi sat up, feeling her silver locs kiss her back, but as she made to swing her legs off the bed, she noticed that she was floating. Beneath her was her own body, eyes closed with a peaceful smile. Simi smiled at herself. Ageing had been one of the best things about her human life. To have been able to watch a body and a face store the memories of life in the wrinkles and in the greys was a wonder to behold. Even when she hadn't remembered her self-appointed assignment as a celestial councilwoman, who entered into a human body in order to vouch for Soil-beings to be offered more leniency in how they completed their soul tasks, a part of her must've known that the physical body was something to honour but not to be defined by.

Simi was distracted from the thoughts about her beautiful human form by the sound of singing. The song sounded far off, but Simi couldn't help but to feel elated at hearing it. The song of home. Angel beings communicated through melody, but as a celestial councilwoman she had never thought to consider that where she came from the singing was in fact constant. An incredible harmonious soundtrack to the story of the lives of millions throughout eternity.

As Simi floated through the open bedroom doors and out of her simple beachside dwelling towards the sea, the ball of light she had seen in her vision stretched itself vertically, just where the water met the sand. *The doorway home . . .* The singing became even more audible and the doorway of light became so bright that it enveloped Simi entirely, blinding her.

When she could finally see again, Simi was back in the amphitheatre with the rest of the council looking upon her, and in the presence of the cascading pillar of water and light. Simi realised that for the rest of the council she had been gone but only a moment, when in fact she had lived an entire lifetime down on Earth.

'*And what say you, Councilwoman, based on your own incarnation as a Soil-being, do you still propose leniency for varying the interpretations of soul assignments?*' The question was asked in the language of crashing waves and wind chimes, but Simi understood.

'*Spirit, life on Earth should be simple, but it is not. The free will that is instrumental to the experience means that without having a memory of that which you have been tasked, completing those assignments can take lifetimes. Even with the timeless knowledge I have gained in this role, I was unable to complete tasks to the specificity of the Book of Souls. And yet I loved greatly and hurt deeply. I experienced being both the blade and the wound, and I experienced being both the problem and the solution. According to my assignment in the Book of Souls, it was intended that I go to Earth to gain immense power and change the world. Instead, I loved and supported another life that was able to gain immense power and change the world, and I did everything to keep her and others safe in whatever way I could. Thus, my assignment was fulfilled indirectly rather than directly. I was also an earthly councilwoman for a short time, and although it was not the prescribed assignment as defined in the Book of Souls, I still exercised power by advocating for those in my community.*

'*What I have learnt is that every Soil-being is a universe unto themselves. Of course, you have always known this and I thank you for the opportunity to understand this. Thus, it is my understanding that these assignments are not so much about how something is done, but rather what is learnt from doing it. With that being said, as the member of the council calling this case to order, I would like to present my decision . . .*'

Simi watched the rest of the council across the vast amphitheatre rise in anticipation of her verdict.

The being that had sparked the celestial debate also looked on in the form of an orb of water, still hovering in the middle of the amphitheatre, and began to tremble.

Simi continued, '*It is my wish as is deemed acceptable to Spirit and the council, that this being and others who interpret their assignments similarly are recognised as having completed all soul tasks. As it is the structure of our celestial realm, this completion entitles them to incarnate recreationally should they choose, or join the Committee of Watchers to help other Soil-beings on their inter-dimensional assignments.'*

The hundreds of thousands of celestial council members who had dissented to Simi's observations before her earthly quest now swished their robes high in agreement. They had watched an entity like themselves attempt life as a Soil-being and could now appreciate how creative one could be with their own destiny.

There was a pause in the swishing as the cascading pillar of water and light spoke again in its language of water and wind chimes. *'Then it will be so.'*

Simi watched the hovering orb of water cease its trembling and instead begin to swirl in elation. The council swished their robes even more in celebration that they too had moved closer to a higher level of understanding similar to that of the pillar of water and light who presided over all. The light beings' harmonious melody grew louder to mark the momentous occasion.

Simi looked towards the thousands of Soil-beings, who hovered in different elemental forms pertaining to their temperaments, waiting for their own verdicts. Somewhere in all these orbs, at some point in eternity, would be her own family from her earthly experience.

Somewhere in these orbs would be Huda, ready to reunite with her once more.

Acknowledgements

Mum
Culture did not hold you back from letting me be me. Thank you for reading so much when I was younger. Being able to sneak off with your books set all of this in motion.

Dad
Daddy mi, thank you for loving me in life and in death. Man like Michael. Big up yourself in the ancestral realm.

Daddy Ayo
Thank you for being there in your own cute way.

Sadiq
That Brandy tune with Ray J in the video will always be dedicated to you and our bond. Thank you for every moment I've laughed and cried. Accepting me well before anyone else ever did.

Dapo
You have been a karmic catalyst for my growth and understanding of unconditional love. I am forever proud to be your big sister.

Lami
Bestie!! I love you. You cheer me on even though you see 'behind the scenes'.

MJ
Even before I was the wave, you were always ready to surf. Thank you for believing in me.

Lew
My little bubba, thank you for bringing so much abundance with you when you arrived earth side. You chose me and asked the spirit guides to step my life up because you clearly weren't coming to earth to do broke. Love that for us.

Sallyanne Sweeney
Thank you for being on this journey with me. Even when I didn't have much for you to go off as an agent, your patience allowed me to grow and figure it out. A babe!

Dapo Adeola
Meeting at an event in Brixton really led to you being instrumental in this book existing. Introducing me to Sallyanne. Our long walks and chats. Everything brought us here. Thank you for being my friend.

Sareeta Domingo
I don't know what you saw in me, but I am glad you saw it. Without you, writing fiction would've been a dream much further away. Thank you for being an editor of dreams innah real life. Thank you so much!

ACKNOWLEDGEMENTS

Lola and John Byrne
Love you both so much. Thank you.

Rianna
My Baby Girl, thank you for being a real one.

Kevin Morosky
Thank you for helping me to gather my hundred pennies to make a pound in every aspect of my life. Virgo king.

Hodan
Our hot chocolates and lunches taught me safety in another woman's presence, that I wouldn't have learnt any other way. Love you sis.

Richie
It was touch and go for us for a moment there, but there was no way I wasn't going to thank you for being in my life when I was proper problematic. Now I am just Problematic Lite. Ha!

Oludare
Our timeline together goes beyond words for these pages. Love.

Magdalena
Mashia! Keanu's mum. We are mums together now and our travels continue. Love you girl.

Lizzie Egbase
You trusted me to read Tarot for you. You stepped in to help a friend's daughter when I asked. I trusted you to help me with 'The Ally-chip' and getting the terms right. You are a true Baby Girl.

Kọ́lá Túbọ̀sún
Thank you for bringing out the beauty of my characters in the honouring of their names.

My therapists
My journey with each of you shaped the woman I can proudly accept myself to be. Thank you for saving my life.

Leona Nichole Black
Without your YouTube videos when you began to explore Tarot, I don't think I would be here doing all of this. Thank you for staying.

Yakari Gabriel
My Aruba love! Your astrology readings for me sparked so much. 'Broom' is dedicated to you.

Daniellé Dash
I can't thank you enough for jumping in my DMs on Twitter to advise me to stop sharing my words for free. Ha!

Siana Bangura
You have championed every stage of my growth thus far and like an elephant (you see what I did there?) I will never forget.

Finally to my Baby Girls, Baby Boys and Baby Non-Binaries, your prayers via DMs and emails made all of this a reality. I am doing bits and bobs because of your love. I pray that the same love finds you thousand-fold. Two slaps on your chest.

To all my naysayers, this book is the equivalent of a straw. Enjoy.

Credits

Trapeze would like to thank everyone at Orion who worked on the publication of *Edge of Here*.

Agent
Sallyanne Sweeney

Editor
Sareeta Domingo

Copy-editor
Deborah Balogun

Proofreader
Laura Gerrard

Editorial Management
Susie Bertinshaw
Carina Bryan
Jane Hughes
Charlie Panayiotou
Lucy Bilton
Claire Boyle

Audio
Paul Stark
Jake Alderson
Georgina Cutler

Contracts
Dan Herron
Ellie Bowker
Alyx Hurst

Design
Nick Shah
Rachael Lancaster
Joanna Ridley
Helen Ewing

Picture Research
Nat Dawkins

Finance
Nick Gibson

Jasdip Nandra
Sue Baker
Tom Costello

Inventory
Jo Jacobs
Dan Stevens

Production
Sarah Cook
Rachel Walker

Marketing
Yadira Da Trindade
Lindsay Terrell

Publicity
Francesca Pearce

Sales
Jen Wilson
Victoria Laws
Esther Waters
Tolu Ayo-Ajala

Group Sales teams across Digital, Field, International and Non-Trade

Operations
Group Sales Operations team

Rights
Rebecca Folland
Tara Hiatt
Ben Fowler
Alice Cottrell
Ruth Blakemore
Ayesha Kinley
Marie Henckel